SANJUKTA AND THE BOX OF SOULS

First Published in the UK 2013 by Belvedere Publishing

Copyright © 2013 by Elizabeth Revill

All rights reserved. No part of this publication may be reproduced or transmitted, in any form or by any means, without permission of the publishers or author. Excepting brief quotes used in reviews.

First edition: 2013

Any reference to real names and places are purely fictional and are constructs of the author. Any offence the references produce is unintentional and in no way reflects the reality of any locations or people involved.

A copy of this work is available through the British Library.

ISBN: 978-1-909224-46-9

Belvedere Publishing
Mirador
Wearne Lane
Langport
Somerset
TA10 9HB

SANJUKTA AND THE BOX OF SOULS

BY

ELIZABETH REVILL

Author's Acknowledgements

Sanjukta and the Box of Souls/ Union started life as a screenplay, which was optioned by Lee Levinson in USA but the initial idea came from my son, Ben Fielder author of Land of the Awoken.

Ben was searching to find a super power never before seen on screen or featured in any book. We talked and Sanjukta's unique power was created. Ben had gone further and looked to Cherokee Legend for inspiration and was entranced by the story *'The Daughter of the Sun'*. He also had some amazing ideas for scenes but confessed, "Mum, I can't write this. I don't have time. Will you do it?" I jumped at the chance, having never written anything quite like this before and I fleshed out the plot, subsequent story and then the idea took a surprising twist. Originally, a male hero with a somewhat different approach and tale as Degataga and the Box of Souls, Lee Levinson suggested making the protagonist female. So Sanjukta was born. I also invited my U.S. co-writer Debbie Majinska to help me write the screenplay, which we completed and subsequently was optioned. Debbie would Americanise dialogue and injected some great ideas to the story but when it was completed I wasn't satisfied.

After talking with Debbie I said I would like to translate the story into a novel, which would require a lot more work and she was happy for me to do so. So my thanks to both Ben and Debbie for allowing me to run free with the idea and plot.

I must also thank my best friend Hayley Raistrick-Episkopos, who is always supportive and when her son Harry Featherstone heard about the storyline he became intrigued with the idea and provided me with numerous drawings of his impressions of monsters from my description of Utkena, the demon, which served to cheer me up and encourage my own imagination to run riot.

I must also thank my long-suffering husband, Andrew Spear who allows me to tap away on my computer at all hours and spoils me rotten.

Finally, I cannot forget my commissioning editor, Sarah Luddington, a multi-talented author in her own right, who has become a very special person in my life.

So I hope you enjoy this offering, which is vastly different from anything else I have written and trust you will continue to support me by reading my novels. The next one planned is more in my usual vein a stand alone historical, *The Black Rider*. Look out for it later in the year as I am currently embroiled in writing a film script for Discovery Films. Wish me luck and here's to the next!

Previous titles by Elizabeth Revill include a psychological thriller trilogy:

Killing me Softly,
Prayer for the Dying
God only Knows

And with my current and exceptionally great publisher, Belvedere:

Llewellyn Family Saga:
Whispers on the Wind
Shadows on the Moon
Rainbows In The Clouds

Stand Alone Novels:
Against the Tide
The Electra Conspiracy

Prologue

I don't remember being born. I don't expect anyone does, but I am told mine was a particularly traumatic birth. It was certainly out of the ordinary. So, in order for you all to understand my life, the extremely strange events that happened, my crusades, both personal and otherwise, and the origins of my power, we need to go right back to my beginning. You have to know the history of what happened to my mother and my family. It is what shaped me into the person I am today. And, extraordinary as it may seem it is down to my mother, Louella that I am who I am.

I will tell the complete story as it has been told to me until I reach the age that I am able to remember the events for myself and then you will all know the truth of how I came to be Sanjukta, Union.

Chapter One

Twenty-Two Years Ago

The late afternoon sun beat down relentlessly on the sandy roadside in Tennessee. There were very few puffball clouds in the azure sky. It was a dry summer and the usual lush green grass was looking parched and brown.

Forty-eight year old Chief Onacoma stood in front of an access gate to his land and village community and he frowned. He was a tall athletically built man of bronze complexion with startlingly clear mahogany eyes. His hands shaded his vision in the glaring sun as a speck on the approach road threw up dust clouds from the wheels of a vehicle. Closer inspection, and as the motor drew nearer, revealed a dark coloured Dodge pickup travelling at speed toward him.

Onacoma's wise eyes surveyed the scene and the approaching vehicle with growing distaste. A vein pulsed in his temple. His long dark hair flecked with grey showered his shoulders and he stood proudly in his blue denim jeans and fringed tan buckskin shirt. His brow was furrowed. Sadness had etched lines in his weathered complexion but he had a regal, majestic air about him. He looked every inch a leader, a chief.

The Dodge RAM's wheels spun in the arid dirt and sand, and sent a mass of earth and debris billowing up into the hot dry air. Emblazoned on the side of the black pickup truck in white letters was the logo: Land Shift - Director: Max Phipps and a company phone number. The truck squealed to a halt. Onacoma steeled himself and stood tall.

Two men, in their late thirties to early forties alighted from the vehicle wearing plaid shirts, denims and scuffed worn cowboy boots. One of them, Rick Mason spoke in low rough tones to his scrawny-legged boss, Hal Steadman warning him, "Don't make this hard now, Boss. Take it easy."

Steadman sneeringly replied in his thin reedy tones, "Huh! It'll soon be ours anyway."

The two men strode doggedly and confrontationally toward Onacoma who took a deep intake of breath and prepared for the verbal onslaught, which he knew would come. He stared hard at the men.

"We just want to carry out a few checks, so please step aside." Steadman's request was not polite but more of a direct order. When Onacoma didn't move, Steadman ignored him and rudely walked around him.

"This will never be your land. Money cannot buy history," Onacoma's voice was resonant and level. "We worked long and hard as a collective to buy this area for our, and our children's, children's lifetime. We will not be cheated or have its value eroded."

Steadman stopped, his shoulders rose and he squared up challengingly to Onacoma, and said sharply, "Listen here. I don't want no lectures or pretty speeches. So you can get off your soapbox. Just take a look around town…"

Onacoma was distracted by the sight of a beautiful bald eagle flying overhead, which screamed wildly. Onacoma's eyes fixed on the bird in total awe as he watched the majestic creature fly while Steadman continued to talk.

"Land Shift's buying this whole area and one mule headed Indian's not going to stop us. Get a life, Geronimo. Times are changing."

They were interrupted by the arrival of a silver Buick Roadmaster Estate Station Wagon. The men turned as the car pulled up and a heavily pregnant American white woman, Louella Burnstein, in her mid to late twenties stepped out and hurried toward them. She was just in time to hear Steadman's final words.

"You think you got trouble now? You don't know what trouble is. We'll own this place and everyone in it!"

Oncama replied with solid, quiet conviction and resolve, "Not everyone."

Louella's eyes blazed with fire, "Mr. Steadman, do I need to remind you that Land Shift doesn't own or hold any access rights to this land parcel, and you even being here could be perceived as harassment? I just have to make a call and get you removed, forcibly if necessary. I have Sheriff Weldon Reeves on speed dial." She pulled her cell phone from her pocket and flipped it open her finger poised.

"Lady, this ain't none of your business. Besides, what do you care?" scoffed Steadman.

"I don't like bullies! Never have and never will, especially Land Shift," Louella defiantly tossed her head of glorious chestnut shining locks and glared at them, looking from one to the other with her bright turquoise green eyes. She lovingly stroked her firm, but swollen belly that was almost full term; "I want my daughter to grow up free to roam the countryside like I did. To enjoy this land as we have been allowed, thanks to the chief here. Now, are you leaving or shall I call the authorities?"

Steadman and Mason shuffled their feet in annoyance and reluctantly backed down, when they saw Louella scrolling through her contacts for the Sheriff's number. They turned and left, driving off in a flurry of sand and dirt as the wheels spun as if reflecting their repressed anger. Onacoma and Louella watched them go. Onacoma placed his hand on Louella's shoulder and proudly announced, "White sister, you have the heart of a warrior."

"I fight for what I believe in, Chief. I've been keeping my eyes open and my ears to the ground, and when I saw those jackals leave town I followed. I somehow knew they were on their way here to cause trouble. But, we are going to need much more support, not just locally, but at state and possibly national level if we are going to save this land."

Onacoma nodded, "They are powerful. They have already bought much of the area using underhand means and bribery."

"Oh, I know how much money talks... but if we can gather enough people, and make enough of a protest, by attracting some high profile publicity then maybe, just maybe we can succeed. I for one will do my damnedest. I'm scheduling an interview with the Tennessee news consortium. It will go out to all the newspapers in the state from Nashville to Knoxville and beyond."

Onacoma nodded silently in agreement and looked up at the sky to watch the eagle that was still circling in the sky. It shrieked and dived before it soared back up and hovered high above Louella's head. Onacoma stared at the bird, mesmerised and sensed something magical about its appearance as if the eagle was trying to tell him something about this young woman.

Louella glanced up, "See! That's just what I'm talking about. These precious sights will be a thing of the past if Land Shift get what they want."

Louella retreated to her vehicle, "Be careful, Chief Onacoma. These men are unscrupulous. They will do anything to get their way even if it's against the law. Your little Indian community is in grave danger."

Onacoma was silent. His face was serious as he watched the feisty young woman drive away. He waited until her car was just a tiny dot in the distance and all that could be seen was a smoky trail pluming up behind her. He turned thoughtfully and strode back to his house with powerful steps, a steely determination in his stride.

Onacoma stepped up onto his wooden veranda and watched the sun dropping in the burnt umber sky. It was a beautiful sight. As the sun fled to another part of the world the fire that remained painted the heavens with a luxuriant orange and pink brush that no artist could ever faithfully capture. Nature's colours were far more vivid than could be imprinted on a canvas.

His lifelong friend, Inola, crossed the sand road from his own lodge and joined Onacoma as he looked out surveying his territory at dusk. They stood together in silence and a wolf howled in the distance, a low mournful wail at the emerging silver light of the moon. Soon other voices joined the wolf song. Their plaintive tune seemed to stir Onacoma and he shivered.

Inola turned to his friend, "You're thinking about the white lady… Louella. I can tell."

"Then, you can also tell that she is special."

"How?"

"A great power lies within her. She was brought to me for

a reason. Our ancestors have willed it. The signs are everywhere."

As he spoke a white feather fluttered through the air and landed at his feet. Inola looked on in wonder. Onacoma stooped and picked up the plume. He twirled it between his fingers.

"Why do you think she was brought to you?" asked Inola.

"Because I know she will need my help. In what way yet, I do not know but our lives are inextricably linked. I feel it and feel the power of the Great White Spirit. I will have to follow my heart, as she will hers. I know this will bring us together. There is more to this woman than what we see, much more."

"Well, my friend you have not been wrong before. I will leave you with your thoughts I have to take Saskia for her walk."

Onacoma grunted his acknowledgement, "And I have to prepare food for Ridge... and... yet... Oh, I don't know..." Onacoma stopped.

"What? What is it?"

"I don't know. There is something in the air. Something is coming, a storm... something catastrophic. We must be prepared."

Onacoma exchanged looks with Inola before he turned and went into his house. He noted Inola's puzzled expression, but could not explain further. He heard him tramp across the wooden porch and back to his own house as he called to his dog slumbering on the veranda. Onacoma looked out at the evening and glanced across to Inola's lodge where Saskia stretched and shook herself. She happily followed her master out onto the road to the woods and the nature trails, which Onacoma had tramped as a child. He drew away from the window, sighed sadly and closed the curtains.

Chasing away the feeling of doom, which had settled on his shoulders he began preparing the evening meal and took the eating utensils from the drawers and dishes from the cupboard. He set the pan on the stove and began to make a light batter for savoury pancakes and waited for his son to return home.

He did not have long to wait as twenty-eight year old Ridge, and Onacoma's son, breezed in from his work at a nearby ranch where they bred horses. Onacoma studied his son's face. He had an aura of happiness around him that was blighted by a guarded veil of secrecy present in his eyes.

"You have something to tell me my son?"

Ridge looked surprised, "No... yes."

"What is it? Come, you can tell me."

"I have been thinking for sometime now..."

"What? What is it that troubles you, my son?"

"I don't know how to say it. I don't want to hurt you father but I feel..."

"Yes?"

"That I need to get out and live my own life."

"It is true. All fledglings must leave the nest as must young cougars leave their mother and lair."

Ridge paused, "I need my own place and my own family."

"And you will. Once you meet the right Cherokee maiden..."

"Not necessarily Cherokee," Ridge said hesitantly.

"No, there are Chickasaw and Shawnee and many more to which our family would be pleased to become aligned."

Ridge hesitated and stopped, "Yes, maybe."

"Who else? You know the pride of our people lies in you and your line."

Ridge seemed uncomfortable and looked down, "As you say, Father. In the words of the Medicine Man I know the wolf will not lie with the lynx, nor the eagle with the owl."

Onacoma nodded, "It is right. And when you find the one as I found my Ayasha, you will know." Onacoma began to fry the batter and tossed in some succulent roasted chunks of meat and juicy peppers. "Will you see to our horses while this is cooking?"

Ridge smiled, "Of course," and he slipped outside to the corral to top up the herd's water and hay. Onacoma looked concerned and muttered aloud, "When you are ready, my son, I know you will speak. I must be patient."

Night had fallen on the small Indian community. The

cicadas chirruped crazily in the night heat calling for love. The inky sky was clear of cloud and filled with a myriad of tiny stars. The moon was full and shone its pearly sheen across the rooftops of the wooden houses and bathed the surrounding woodland in a ghostly glow. A solitary owl hooted plaintively in the wood. The night appeared serene.

The thunder of rumbling wheels and the grumbling whine of engines belonging to approaching pickups disturbed the harmonious night. The thrumming crickets were abruptly lulled into silence as six trucks burst through the forest into the small hamlet of wooden houses. Roughneck men and thugs whooped and shouted as they sent shotgun blasts skyward and catapulted sleeping birds into the night sky.

The trucks drove frenziedly and circled the little village in a deadly dance of death. The drunken ruffians aimed at anything they could see and shot out windows shattering the glass, which made them laugh raucously. They tossed empty liquor bottles and homemade bombs onto the verandas and porches setting the wooden framed houses ablaze. Flames leapt up greedily devouring the dry and seasoned wood with crackling glee.

The Indian occupants of the houses dashed out and looked on in horror as they witnessed the senseless and relentless attack. They tried desperately to extinguish the growing fire and fetched water in an attempt to drown the flames.

Onacoma ran out from his house and onto the sand road hardly believing the mayhem before his eyes. Inola, too, came out but remained on his own porch and dodged the bullets that whistled past his ear.

Ridge emerged from the shack after his father and looked aghast at the wanton destruction before him. An older grizzly looking ruffian jubilantly waved a rifle, as he stood on the footplate of a truck. He closed one blood shot eye, levelled his gun at Ridge and took aim. His shot rang out and the bullet flew through the searing heat and fatally pierced Ridge's chest, and he fell back and crumpled to the wooden floor. The men in the trucks jeered and laughed. They hurled obscenities and licked their lips jibing at Onacoma calling out, "Hey chief, white woman's meat. How do you like this, then?" They brandished their weapons in the air and shook them as might primitive man threatening an enemy tribe.

The renegades laughed dementedly letting off more shots before speeding back they way they had come leaving chaos and their bewildered victims in intense distress. Their sub-human triumphant cries could be heard as they drove back through the wood and out to the road.

Onacoma watched the departing trucks in cold anger before turning. He was horrified and shocked to see his son collapsed on the decking and Inola kneeling at Ridge's side with Saskia who barked and whimpered. Onacoma, his heart thumping, raced to reach Ridge. He placed a finger on Ridge's neck pulse. There was nothing. Blood seeped through the young man's clothes and there was no movement in his chest.

He desperately attempted resuscitation and pumped hard on Ridge's chest. He adjusted his son's head to clear the airways and tried to breathe life back into his son's still warm body. His agony was engraved on his face as he struggled to stir the lifeless body.

Inola watched in sadness, and eventually caught his friend by the arm. "It's too late. Nothing can be done. You must let him go."

Onacoma shook Inola's hand off, "I must try." He continued to make an effort and bring his son back. He grunted with the exertion and sweat beaded on his brow. He worked feverishly like that for many more minutes and eventually let out a sob as he finally realised that Ridge's life was no more. Then he removed his jacket and placed his son's head on it as a pillow and stroked his hair. He began to rock back and fore in a silent rhythm of internal sorrow.

Inola lifted his face to his old friend and gazed into Onacoma's despairing eyes. Tears streamed down Inola's face. He spoke in low tones and swore, "They won't get away with this." He called out above the sound of sizzling wood and burning, "We all know who was at the back of this... this violent rampage." He turned to his friend, "It's a tragedy Ridge was a remarkable young man."

"He was just talking of starting out on his own," said Onacoma in muted tones.

"I mean it, Chief. They won't get away with it," asserted Inola.

The sound of a wolf howling mournfully was carried on the night air as if it, too, knew of the grief that had befallen the Indian community.

Onacoma's reply was icy and deliberate, "No they won't." He looked up to the starry heavens and was filled with such sadness that his body began to judder with silent sobs. He cradled his son in his arms smothering himself in the arterial blood that had pulsed from Ridge's heart.

Inola tried to prise his friend from his son's body, "Come, Onacoma. Come. We must get help and the law."

Onacoma raised his wise face now ravaged with pain and forced out his words choked with emotion. "They have taken everything. My wife driven into an early grave with worry over our land and future, and now, my only son, my beloved son, so cruelly murdered. All I have left is my home and they are not going to take that from me, too. I will fight. Fight for what is rightfully mine. Make the call, Inola. But such is the white man's heart that I believe the white man will do nothing."

Inola rose and took out his cell phone and dialled 9-1-1. He quietly reported what had happened and flipped his phone shut. "An ambulance is on its way. The sheriff will be out first thing."

"Not now?" said the Chief with incredulity.

Inola shook his head; "He said something about clearing up trouble in Marwood, first."

Onacoma frowned, through his rising tears and passion, "We are unimportant. This proves the white man doesn't care. They merely pay lip service to our needs. We are on our own." He sighed, struggling to contain his emotions, "Why do they want this land so bad?"

Inola shrugged, "Greed?"

Onacoma shook his head, "No it's more than that. Something else is at the root of this evil. And now this battle is personal." Onacoma dropped his head in desolation and

Saskia licked his hand as Inola took the chief into his arms and allowed him to sob.

In a subterranean cellar under an elegant town house in the dead of night a strange meeting was taking place. Max Phipps owner and director of Land Shift spoke in hushed tones to someone or more correctly something that lurked in the gloom and shadows.

Max seemed in awe of this creature known as Utkena whose massive horned head threw weird almost puppetry pictures onto the dripping walls. Part reptile with a scaled body, and serpentine tail, it stood on two cloven hoofed feet. This monster towered above Max who was himself over six feet. It had huge hands that were better fitted to wreck and kill than to save. Its eyes with its baleful orange glow seemed filled with hatred.

The smell underground was rank and earthy. Moss and algae grew freely down the brick channel that led to a dank, dark, musty cavern. From the cavern led numerous tunnels penetrating deep underground. Fungi grew in profusion and scavenging insects scuttled into dingy recesses in the rock. Large cockroaches waving their filthy antennae roamed the dirt floor trying to escape from the dim light to lurk anonymously in the shadowy gloom.

Max Phipps was a tall but thickset man in his mid to late forties. His eyes had a feral light that almost matched the malevolent flickering wickedness emanating from the monster's own reptilian eyes. Max insisted, "I must get that land. Its resources are too numerous to mention. There's more than enough oil underneath that village to drown the whole state."

Utkena's rasping tone added accusingly, "And it is there that you will have the means to gain access to the Box of Souls. Isn't that the real reason why you have summoned me?"

Max sidestepped the statement but then admitted, "First the oil and then the box. The liquid gold will give me the money to buy silence and more importantly, loyalty."

Utkena shook his huge horned head and warned, "Don't

underestimate them. Not all humans are foolish… and nor am I."

Max interpreted the creature's hostile tone and hastily assured him, "I won't. I won't. In return I intend to bring you what you desire."

As if to punctuate his warning the fearsome, demonic being opened his huge mouth and roared. The terrifying noise was so loud that the ground and passage walls shook. The cement and sand between the bricks was disturbed and some of the coarse grains tumbled down to the rock floor. Max closed his eyes and ears to the ugly sound. He waited until Utkena had lumbered away through the labyrinth of tunnels. Each huge thudding step the creature took shook the very foundations of the house.

Alone once more, Max climbed the wooden steps from the dungeon cavern into his basement and then up into his house. He moved into his study where his answer phone light was blinking and bleeping. He hit the play button. Steadman's voice rang out.

"Boss. We did as you said but the Indian won't go for it. We've tried everything. This chief and his friend won't budge. He turned us down flat. There's a hard-core group of Indians in the centre of the land that refuse to move. Everyone else has sold except for them. The others seem to be guided by those two stubborn mules. So, we paid some rednecks to go and rough the occupants of the village up a bit. Thing is they got a little carried away one of them shot the chief's son. It's bound to lead to trouble."

Max picked up the phone and hit the call back button. He marched impatiently around the room waiting for Steadman to answer. His face was filled with cold anger.

"Steadman," came the man's thin reedy tones.

Max steeled himself and launched into a tirade against the man and the stupidity of their actions. "You stupid, stupid man. What the hell were you thinking?"

"But, Sir. We thought if we roughed them up a little they might see sense. We would make them listen."

"That's not how it works. The bully tactics are for the city not this band of Indians we have to find the right key."

"But, it's worked with some…"

"But not all. What the hell do I pay you for?"

"But we thought…"

"I pay you to act not think. I do the thinking for this organisation. Now I'll have the local sheriff on my back…"

"No, Sir. I think we fixed that. We just need to keep our heads down for a while."

"You two couldn't fix a puncture. Next time, listen. Do as I ask… not what you think. Is that clear?"

He finished in his acid tones with, "Just remember, anything is for sale at the right price. Anything. You just need to find the right angle."

"But, Boss… I truly believe we need to lay off for a while."

Max shouted, "It was stupid killing the Indian!"

Steadman countered, "This is about more than the oil, isn't it?"

Max refused to answer. He bristled as he could feel the discomfort of his henchmen on the other end of the line.

"Boss, you need to think carefully as I think things are going to get a lot worse."

Max slammed down the phone and left the office his face suffused with his growing rage.

Steadman stared distastefully at the phone as it was slammed down. His partner in crime, Mason probed, "What is it? What's going on?"

"I don't know, but he sure gets tetchy when I mention that this vendetta is about more than oil."

"But the oil is important, isn't it? It'll make us rich. He's promised us all a share."

"Maybe. He's been acting odd ever since his wife died and he met with that spiritual witch doctor guy."

Mason nodded, "I remember. He does miss her though."

"Yeah. Do you know they meet every couple of days. In my book it ain't healthy. He even thinks he can talk to her through this creep."

"Maybe he can. I've heard of stranger things than that my grandma used…"

Steadman brusquely cut him off, "Don't you start." He paused and considered this suggestion for a moment and then dismissed it. "Nah! He's not a nutcase. Known him too many years. Got to be the oil... Do you think?" The doubt had crept into his tone again.

Mason shrugged, "Who's to know? As long as I get what I'm promised, I don't really care."

The following day the Indian community was unusually busy as men tried to restore their houses and repair the damage caused by the thugs and their wanton violence from the previous night. Charred timbers lay in the road ready for clearing and the smell of burning still lingered in the air.

The local sheriff, Weldon Reeves, a big bellied man in his fifties, stood in the street with his young deputy, Harvey May. They were in deep discussion with Chief Onacoma and trying to placate him as tempers began to rise.

"My people know who's responsible as I am sure you do," said Onacoma accusingly.

"But, we ain't got no proof," countered Sheriff Reeves.

"Yeah, you know how it is, don't ya?" he used an affable tone as if they were comrades. " ... Guys are just out for a little fun... they have a few drinks and get carried away," said Harvey in support.

"Shooting up Indians is fun?" growled Onacoma, unimpressed. "My son is dead."

"And I'm sure sorry about that," said the Sheriff. "You can be sure we'll look into it."

"When?"

Inola crossed to join them. Harvey nodded to him in acknowledgement. Inola's face was grim.

"If this was reservation land you'd be forced to do something about it," he attacked. "The law wouldn't allow for men to usurp treaties or condone cold blooded murder."

"Oh, we'll be looking into it for sure," said Sheriff Reeves.

"But nothing will be done," said Inola.

Harvey had the grace to look to the ground shame faced.

"There is no point in talking to you," said Onacoma. "We

will find out the truth one way or another."

"Now don't you go taking the law into your own hands," warned the Sheriff.

"And what am I supposed to do? Stand by and let them get away with this?"

"Leave it to the law. Chief, I don't like this anymore than you. But we have to do this legally."

"I will give you time, then I will act myself," said Onacoma.

Inola put his hand on the Chief's shoulder, which he shook off and he strode back to his house.

"It's a bad business," said the sheriff.

"Then do your job," growled Inola and went after his friend.

Sheriff Weldon removed his hat and smacked his thighs, "God damn. How am I going to deal with this and keep my job?"

"We must look as if we're doing something, Sir," said Harvey.

"I know that. Let's get back to town and pull in the Land Shift crew for questioning."

"We won't find nothing. Give it time it'll all blow over."

The stealthy cloak of the black velvet night had fallen. Max Phipps was in his study, at the foot of the stairs off the hallway, poring over an ancient map with a tall Indian Shaman. The study door was open and crouching on the stairs, hidden in the shadows, watching his father and listening to the conversation was Max's fourteen-year-old son, Cornelius. He was an unhealthily thin and bony teenager prone to biting his nails and was now engaged in a frenzied nibbling as his face scrunched into a mask of disbelief and panic. Every now and then he would jot down notes on a small pad of what was being discussed before returning to his manic nibbling.

The Shaman, who spoke in resonant and measured tones, pointed at a place on the map, "There. There is where you will find the pathway to the Box of Souls."

Max set his jaw in a determined line and said with

resolve, "As I thought, Chief Onacoma's property. Are you absolutely sure?"

The shaman nodded, "All clues lead there."

Max snorted, "Huh! That's if it exists!"

"It exists." His voice took on the sonorous boom of prophecy, "Seven days to the West to Usunhiyi, The Darkening Land. Where the sourwood tree crosses the circle of elders. The tunnel leads to Tsusginai, The Ghost Country."

"But, how do you know?" An element of doubt had crept into Max's voice.

The shaman's response was definitive, "I know."

Cornelius strained his ears to hear the rest of the conversation, a curious expression manifesting on his features.

Max grunted, "Even if it isn't, I will still have the oil. That will make me even richer."

The Shaman warned, "Remember your pact with Utkena. If you anger him or don't follow through on your promise, many will die. Is that a price worth paying?"

Max glowered, "If it brings my wife back… then, I don't give a damn. She was taken from me too soon."

Cornelius shivered. He had listened to every word. He scrawled down the name Utkena and bit into his last remaining nail. Deciding that he had heard enough he crept back to his room intending to make sense of what he had just heard, and at some time he was going to sneak a peek at that map.

Chapter Two

Protests

Sheriff Reeves stood in Land Shift's office facing a middle-aged secretary, Moira Barnes, "Look I know it ain't got ought to do with you. But these employees of Land Shift have been fingered and I need to speak with them. This has to be cleared up now."

"I'm sorry, Sheriff. These men are working over at Marwood," she consulted a work schedule. They won't be back in the office until tomorrow dinnertime and from there they start work on the Indian property."

"Let me see that." Weldon Reeves grabbed the roster. "Does this detail the whereabouts of the men over the last few days?"

"See for yourself."

Weldon scanned the work schedules and spotted the names of the workers he wanted to question. "Says here they were on a job out of state, in which case they have alibis. Is there a number I can call to check they were there, Moira?"

She crossed to the filing cabinet and pulled out a file. She removed a sheet and photocopied it. "Here, you can take this. They'll be able to verify or not if they were there."

Sheriff Reeves grunted his thanks and left. He got back in his car where his deputy Harvey May waited anxious to hear what had transpired, "Well?"

"Seems the chief suspects have an alibi. We'll check it out but if it holds up we'll need to go further afield."

"I heard they weren't there. They kept a low profile and hired the guns in. One of the drunks at Jake's Saloon was shooting his mouth off earlier."

"Who's that?"

"Marvin Burr."

"What did he say?"

"Seems someone gave him the job of rounding up all the Indian haters he could find. One old guy was busting his chops about staking out the Chief's son. Said he disapproved of mixed race relationships."

"Yeah?"

"That's all he'd say. He just keeled over, drunk as a skunk. I couldn't get no more out of him and took him to gaol to sleep it off."

"Then perhaps I'd better be there when he wakes up."

"Surely, this will all go away. If we can't find no proof…"

"But we must be seen to be doing something. I'm due for re-election end of the year. Can't risk losing my job and pension." He glanced across at Harvey, "Come on, let's get out of here. You can write a report."

Harvey groaned, "That's my least favourite bit of the job."

"But, it's got to be done."

The smell of burning wood was still in the air and had drifted across to the boundary entrance. No one took any notice assuming someone was having a bonfire somewhere on the property.

Louella had gathered together a lively but small collection of people who were persuaded to block the entrance to the access gate in protest against Land Shift's bullying tactics. Even though the bulk of the land was now in the company's legal possession.

The machine drivers were standing about scratching their heads in frustration and muttering obscenities under their breath. The swing shovels, dump trucks and bulldozers stood idle.

Louella's sympathetic protesters, some of them Native American Indians, chanted loudly, "What do we want? Land Shift out! When do we want it? Now!" The chorus of voices repeated the mantra over and over again.

A young woman, Sarah Jeynes, from the local village with distinctive flame red hair waved a banner demanding the return of the land. Shopkeeper, middle aged Ned Baines shook his fist at the workers while another villager, Dave Parker led the chant vociferously.

Any attempt to start the machines was blocked as a mother and her young child stood defiantly in the path of the bulldozers. Others sat on the huge wooden gates. Louella was pleased. She placed herself in the centre of the group orchestrating the protest.

Louella shaded her eyes as a dust cloud was seen in the distance and a pickup truck approached at speed. The vehicle pulled up short behind the waiting machinery and Steadman and Mason stepped out and considered the scene before them.

Steadman swore softly and muttered, "Aw man!" He removed his phone from his pocket and he dialled a number. He didn't have long to wait for an answer and responded, "About fifteen protesters. That Louella woman, a few villagers and some Indians." He listened closely as he paced in his dusty scuffed cowboy boots. "But… I can have them removed…" He listened some more before speaking again, "Okay, understood."

Steadman flipped his phone shut and Mason stared at him curiously as Steadman tramped past the protesters to the workers and spoke to them quietly underneath all the shouting and chanting. The workers listened and then silently walked off site, moved to their cars and drove away. The protesters seeing this as some sort of victory cheered and clapped loudly. They engaged with each other in a congratulatory style and whooped in triumphant glee at the workers' departure.

One person didn't join in – Louella. She looked suspiciously at Steadman, who glanced back before returning to his truck. He called out, "Guess you didn't hear, did you lady?" Louella stared at him and he mimed shooting a gun at her and mouthed, "One of your Indian band died last night. He was shot." No one else seemed to hear. The others were caught up in the moment of euphoria that triumph brings. Steadman paused, then nodded at Mason who climbed aboard and the two henchmen left.

Louella looked stunned. The crowd of protesters went

wild. But Louella didn't smile or share their jubilance. She studied the remaining trucks and machines whose work had been interrupted and she was worried. Sarah and Ned did a high five and Dave jumped like a child in sheer joy.

"Come on, Louella, smile. It's a victory. Look they've gone," Dave pointed out.

"Maybe." Louella was noncommittal.

"We've stopped them today. That's got to be worth something."

Louella forced a smile and thanked her supporters. "Good job! Hope I can call on you again?"

"Sure thing, Louella. We'll stick around just in case they're being sneaky. Okay, folks?" said Dave."

The rest of the group nodded their heads in assent.

"Did any of you hear about any trouble last night? A shooting?" asked Louella.

One of the Indians nodded, "I heard a bunch of guys came driving by and shot up the homes, one person was killed."

"Who? Who was shot?" A note of alarm had entered her voice, "Was it the chief?"

"No, not the chief."

"Who then?" Louella realised that she was starting to sound a little hysterical. The others stopped and stared at her.

"I don't know. I didn't hear the name."

"Oh... It just shows how we must keep at this protest." She struggled to compose herself and control her emotions running so close to the surface. "These bastards will stop at nothing. We have to succeed. If it had been the chief then that would finalise things for them." The group appeared to accept this and they chatted amongst themselves as they watched the sun slip rapidly down in the sky to the horizon.

As the stars came out they agreed that no one was coming back to harass them now. "I think it's safe to assume they are not coming back," said Dave.

"Yes," agreed Ned, "It's the first success for us. We could finally be on a winning streak."

"Come on, Louella, Ned is right," agreed Karen. She looked at her watch. "Anyhow, I'm off. Let me know when you want me again."

Louella nodded and tried to force a smile.

They chorused their goodbyes to her before dispersing and getting into their own vehicles to drive home.

Louella smiled brightly but the smile didn't quite reach her eyes. She watched them go and muttered under her breath. "Just what are you up to Max Phipps? What part of your game strategy is this? And who the hell have you killed?"

Dave Parker drove into town, a big smile on his face. Night had now fallen. He intended to purchase a little something to take home. He stopped at the liquor store and picked up some bourbon then proceeded to the supermarket to buy some candy and chocolates for his wife, Beth and daughter, Amy.

Dave was feeling good. He grabbed a bunch of flowers, too; and a giant pizza for them all and he began to whistle as he jogged back to his car and headed out for his village. As he hit the village street something didn't feel right. He passed a pickup truck filled with armed men driving out of the small hamlet. They were strangers and mean looking.

Dave turned into his road and approached his house. He was shocked to see his wife and daughter crouched on the front veranda. His wife was weeping and his daughter, Amy, was sobbing hysterically. They were leaning over something. Dave hurriedly parked his car and forgetting his purchases he leapt out and ran to them, "Beth, what is it?"

He looked down to see the body of their beloved family pet, a gentle golden Labrador. She had been shot. "What, how?" Dave tried to make sense of it and called out above the noise of the crying. Beth cradled the faithful dog and spoke angrily, "This protest. This damned protest. Land Shift is too big to fight. We can't win. They have sent us a warning."

Dave's face was filled with anguish. Suddenly, they heard a loud explosion. Beth looked at her husband, "Someone else… someone else has been hurt."

Dave's mouth was set in a grim line and he jumped back into his car. Black smoke could be seen billowing up a few streets away. He drove to the source of the sound. People were gathering in the road watching in horror where a car had been set ablaze.

Sarah Jeynes came running out of her house and stopped. She stared numbly at her car disintegrating in flames before her eyes. "Who? Who would do this?"

A neighbour spoke up, "Land Shift. They're warning anyone who had anything to do with the protest."

Sarah began to cry, "I can't afford to buy another vehicle…" The neighbour put his arm around her to comfort her when she saw Dave approaching.

"I'm sorry, Sarah. I don't know what to say."

"It's not your fault. I joined the protest of my own free will."

"Yes, but I told you about it and what it meant. I feel responsible."

Sarah sniffed. "Please, don't blame yourself. Yes, it's tough for me. But I'll get by. I have my home and my life."

Dave shuffled his feet miserably, "They killed Caleb."

"What? Oh no. Your beautiful dog. I am so sorry." Sarah opened her arms to Dave and he embraced her and they poured out their sorrow together.

"It's the end of the line for me, Dave. I don't know about you but I can't risk my home and family. Next time it might not be a pet or a car, it could be your daughter or my son."

Dave nodded grimly, "I know and much as I agree with Louella I can't risk anything else happening. But I will go and see her and tell her face-to-face. She deserves that much."

Word soon spread like an out of control forest fire throughout the surrounding small villages and towns. The Indian community was frightened and those that supported the protest against Land Shift were now running scared. That afternoon Dave went in search of Louella and knocked on her door. Louella answered, her eyes were red from weeping.

"You've heard?"

Louella nodded.

"They killed the Chief's son."

Louella bit back a sob, "I know."

"You have to give it up. They will be after you, too. They won't care about your unborn child."

"For that reason I have to continue. For my baby." She rubbed her swollen tummy that was almost full term.

"Louella. Give it up. You will be alone in this, now. Please."

"No, Dave. I have always fought for what I believe in. I will not give up or I will lose respect for myself, nor do I want my daughter to grow up intimidated by bullies like Land Shift."

Dave smiled apologetically, "I'm sorry, Louella. You are on your own."

Louella gave a crooked smile, "I know. Please pass my sympathies out to all those who have been threatened."

Dave nodded.

"I'm going to see Ned and then I will call and see the chief. I need to speak with him. There is something he needs to know," said Louella and her voice cracked with emotion.

Dave gave Louella a hug. "Take care. And watch your back. These thugs mean business."

Louella attempted a smile and walked to her car. She gave Dave a cheery wave before getting in and driving away. Her face was a mask of sorrow and tears continued to flow freely down her cheeks.

She soon reached the township where she had gathered some support for her campaign and made her way to Ned's antique shop and parked up. Louella eased herself out of her seat and tapped her tummy remonstrating, "Now hold on, poppet. Quit kicking a moment. I've got to walk." She smiled with pleasure at feeling her baby move inside her.

Louella crossed to the wooden boardwalk and was horrified to see a deluge of broken glass that had been swept up outside 'Ned's Antiques'. She pushed the door minus its glass window and entered leaving the shop bell clamouring behind her alerting Ned to her presence.

Louella stopped and viewed the scene before her in horror. Ned was trying to clean up an appalling mess. His shop had been trashed from top to bottom, china and glass smashed, wooden furniture overturned and splintered, and valuable first edition books torn to shreds. Even the shelves and display cabinets had been tumbled and ripped apart. Louella did not know what to say. There was a pause as she surveyed the devastation in front of her.

She finally found her voice, "Ned, are you all right?"

Ned looked up, and leaned on his broom, his eyes filled with sorrow, "I'm okay. It's just stuff. I've got insurance. Others got worse."

Louella's eyes sparkled with fire, "I know. We can't let them get away with it."

"Get away with what? The police told me this was kids. If you ask me they're being paid off. The law round here can't be trusted anymore." Ned shrugged despairingly. "If the cops aren't going to do anything, what can we do?"

"We need to show them we're not scared."

"But, we are scared, Louella! The only person who isn't, is you." A note of futility entered his voice, "We don't want to see them take that land anymore than you do, but some fights can't be won."

Louella pursed her lips and said grimly, "But, we can win this, Ned."

"Can we? I can't fight anymore. I'm too old for this. And you should think about your baby."

"I am, Ned. I am. Don't give up. Please." Louella looked pleadingly at him.

"Sorry, Louella." Ned shook his head regretfully and lowered his eyes.

Louella stared at Ned and sighed. "I understand. You're not the only one." Louella's eyes filled with tears. There was an embarrassed silence between them. "I guess Land Shift got what they wanted."

Ned said nothing but looked up miserably, his expression a mixture of sadness and shame. He whispered again, "I really can't do this anymore. I'm sorry."

"It's okay. I don't expect you to." Louella embraced her friend, who hung onto her and buried his face in her shoulder with a sob. She released him and spoke softly, "Goodbye, sweet friend."

Louella left Ned and his destroyed store and made her way back to her car unaware that she was being watched. She walked back along the boardwalk and crossed the street. Hostile eyes watched her.

Louella started her motor and drove off. Her observers fired up their engine, pulled out and followed. Louella drove on blissfully unaware of her tail that kept at a discrete distance.

The setting sun melted into the horizon and as the dusky pink sky began to darken. Sombre clouds gathered in the distance. A storm was on the way. It would clear the mugginess of the humid air, she thought. Louella drove on and soon she reached the open road leading to the protest site and Chief Onacoma's property. It was important that the Chief knew the truth and she couldn't leave it any longer.

The rumbling of thunder in the distance accompanied Louella's growing misgivings and the baby stirring inside her. During the journey Louella had plenty of time to think. She thought about her unborn daughter who would grow up fatherless and a piteous cry escaped from her lips. There was nothing she could do but steeling her resolve she determined to fight on and would let the Chief know as much.

Thousands of stars filled the night sky and the gibbous moon taunted the wolves in the surrounding hills, which howled their lament, first singly, and then, in a mournful chorus that reflected Louella's mood that was becoming more desolate with each passing minute. Louella felt that she had never been so alone, but she needed to rid herself of this encroaching despair. She knew she had to be strong.

The crash of the once distant thunder was nearer now, and it appeared to be travelling toward her. The road out of town was long and stretched ahead of her. She was beginning to feel a little stronger in herself, she thought, when she was startled out of her reverie by the roar of another engine, a blare of a horn and a car raced up behind her dangerously and overtook her leaving her way fogged with a thick choking mass of dust. Louella swerved as the car raced past and sped up the road toward the intersection.

Louella stopped in a flurry of dirt, narrowly missing a

ditch and she muttered something under her breath. She watched the dust cloud rip up the road and vanish over the rise before she began moving on again. As she drove on in the black strap of night, the comfort of the dark enveloped her. It seemed to fill her with a renewed energy and she pushed on past the intersection that lead to the Interstate highway, taking the smaller road that twisted off to the right to the foothills and the Indian land.

In the distance she could see the shape of the machines and trucks silhouetted at the top of the small incline against the velvet sky. Buckets on swing shovels were lifted up as if in salutation to the moon. The thunder rumbled nearer.

The branches of trees spiked out at the gate as if there was an eerie malevolence waiting. Louella drew closer and her headlights lit up the idle machinery, which clothed in their bright yellow colours no longer looked menacing. She exited her car and slammed the door.

A feeling of foreboding ran through her and she shivered, in spite of the warmth, as she walked toward the access gate squeezing past the trucks and machines that lay in wait. Louella stood by the entrance, alone with her thoughts once more, as she strove to undo the hasp. Behind her there was a loud clang, like metal on metal and the scrape of a door. Louella turned.

She shouted, "Hello!" Her voice momentarily stilled the crickets' thrum. There was another softer noise like the chink of keys. Louella yelled again, "Who's there? Chief? Inola? Anyone?"

Having heard no reply Louella moved toward the truck where she thought she had heard the sound. She moved to the front of it and stared about her and called again. "Hello?" As she looked out front viewing the approaching storm and the dust road ahead the truck suddenly rolled forward knocking her to the ground. She had no time to crawl out of the way when the lorry lurched once more running over her and crushing her shoulder. Louella screamed out in agony.

Louella tried to move but couldn't; the pain was too intense. From her position under the truck she saw a pair of scrawny legs in jeans and familiar, dusty, scuffed cowboy boots. They jumped down from the truck that had floored her and walked off. She heard a car start and drive off with a squeal of tyres.

Louella cried out in anguish. She was in extreme pain but still somehow had found incredible strength, from somewhere; she hauled herself out from under the truck. However, the effort was so great that she almost fainted, but the fighting spirit of a mother striving to protect her unborn child spurred her on and she forced herself to remain conscious. "Help! Please, anyone? Arrgh!" Her cry echoed on the wind and the sound drifted to Chief Onacoma who was sitting on his porch listening to the wolf song that had stopped abruptly.

He stood up and listened hard. His eyes narrowed as he, too, saw the rolling storm clouds drawing closer.

Louella struggled to call out again, which ended in a gurgle as her waters broke and she felt the need to push.

Onacoma stepped off his porch and walked on the track toward the access gate with urgency in his stride. As he approached it, Louella's sobs were becoming louder. She had gone into labour and was struggling to breathe.

Onacoma undid the gate and searched for the source of the sound. He saw Louella lying in front of the truck and ran to her. Her face was tearstained and her clothes dusty. She had lifted her skirt above her knees and squealed with the action of bearing down.

"Don't move," Onacoma answered with grave concern in his voice.

Louella's relief was apparent and although in agony she greeted him. "Onacoma, Chief, please. My baby. Please!"

Onacoma removed his jacket and covered her to keep her warm. He knew what to do and began to guide her through the delivery process telling her calmly when to breathe and when to push. He reassured her, "Don't be afraid. We will do this together."

The baby was coming quickly and with each contraction Louella screamed. She bellowed with the pain of childbirth combined with the excruciating shoulder injury.

Onacoma could feel the power of the emerging child,

"This girl has amazing strength," he said in admiration. "Her head, it's crowning."

Louella grunted loudly with the exertion and Onacoma continued to soothe her with his voice, "She will have your passion… your fight… and something else… Come on, Louella, one final push and the shoulders will be through. Push!"

Louella gave one last screaming shriek and the baby slipped out red faced and her head bloodied with a mess of membranes. Onacoma took the baby and presented her to Louella. The tiny infant screwed up her face and let out a lusty cry as Onacoma took his hunting knife from its sheath at his waist and severed and tied the umbilical cord.

Louella was now totally drained and as she felt her life slipping away she pleaded with Onacoma, her voice becoming fainter with each word. "Thank you. I was on my way to see you. There's something you must know. You have to know…"

"Hush. Do not talk. Rest now and I will get help."

"No!" Louella mustered some power from somewhere, "Please, I want you to take care of her. I have no one and…" Her face twisted in an agonised grimace and she struggled to continue, "She's… she's…" Louella's body convulsed as the placenta was expelled. She shuddered and slowly dropped her head. Her eyes closed and her voice faded to a whisper, "She's…" Louella had breathed her last.

Onacoma raised his eyes heavenward in turmoil and made a solid vow as he looked again on Louella's lovely face, now pain free, and helplessly watched the lionhearted young woman die. He raised the baby that was me, up to the sky and pronounced, "I will raise you as my own as your mother wanted and I name you, Sanjukta! You will never have to stand alone, you will never lack the support you need when tested. I make this my promise to you and your mother in spirit."

A flash of lightning streaked through the sky renting it asunder and as a tiny infant, I'm told, I filled my lungs and cried out in harmony with the booming thunder of the arriving storm.

Chapter Three

Rituals and Childhood

I had heard many times from my grandfather what happened next. He said it was a travesty, a travesty of justice that my mother's death was deemed an accident. Sheriff Reeves claimed that my mother had gone out to sabotage the machines preparing to dig up the Indian land and that one of the vehicles had not been secured properly. It had simply slipped out of gear and because of the incline it had rolled and hit her. He insisted that no one else was involved and anyway all the suspects, at which the chief had pointed a finger had sound alibis. The inquest ruled that it was death by misadventure, an accidental death. The law dictated that no further investigation was necessary just as they had with his son, Ridge. He knew he could not rely on the white man's help. These killings would just be forgotten and brushed away.

He had made a solid promise to my mother. It was one he intended to keep so that when the authorities had wanted to remove me from his care. He fought them and won. In this instance Louella's friends rallied round supporting Onacoma's claim that this was what Louella would have wanted. I was in effect the Chief's daughter although in reality I was more like a granddaughter.

Child services didn't want to become embroiled in a legal wrangle and objections were quashed and forgotten. In a bigger township or city this would not have been so easy, but as my mother had no family the chief was legally allowed to adopt me and bring me up as his own.

He never tired of telling me about his first ritual in enrolling me into the Cherokee nation. He recounted it so well that although I don't physically remember it, heck I was only a little baby, I can see the events clearly in my head as he described them and as I shall tell you.

Onacoma was in his official regalia wearing full Indian dress and feathers. He knelt on a rug in front of a cheerful fire burning brightly in the grate at his house. The baby girl, Sanjukta, me, was lying in front of him kicking my little legs and gurgling happily. He shook a rattle over me to ward off evil spirits and the light from the fire played on my face and in the room casting shadows everywhere. Apparently at that point, I giggled.

Sacred white sage burned filling the air with its distinctive aroma. It filtered into every corner cleansing the house and filling it with sanctity and healing love. He waved a smoking bunch of it over me to purify me. The smoke must have tickled my nose and I sneezed. This was a good sign.

Onacoma began to chant in mystical Cherokee tones. He took a miniature horn with a clasped lid and opened it. He tossed the powder contents over me before carefully unwrapping a buckskin roll containing paints, in which he dipped his fingers daubing coloured stripes on my cheeks.

The fire appeared to have a life of its own and responded in intensity with the flames burning brighter as Onacoma's chants became louder and it flared whenever he threw these flour like grains into its heart.

The percussive music of drum and rattle reached outside to the road where Onacoma's friend Inola stood, with Saskia at his side. He told him he was watching the night sky where a shooting star suddenly streaked across the heavens. He heard Onacoma's ritualistic chanting and listened, an inscrutable smile on his face, and when he turned to face Onacoma's house and the fire was now so bright it filled the window and made it look as if the place was ablaze. It was an incredible sight and one he never forgot.

At that point Saskia howled and answering wolf song was returned from the hills.

Back inside, Onacoma lifted his arms and prayed to his ancestors calling on them to bless me. It seemed that I took a huge gulp of air and a white heavenly light surrounded me. Onacoma smiled happy that his prayers were being answered and as I breathed in, the white light entered me and flooded through my little body. I stopped kicking and a serenity of perfect peace encompassed me. Onacoma nodded his head sagely; this was good. I had been singled out to be special.

This was the history of how I had got my name and dictated who I would be.

I have no recollection of any of this but my first memory was at the age of two and this I do remember, when I was toddling in the yard outside and determinedly heading for the corral where the horses were kept. I loved the horses. Most of them were untamed but I had a fascination for them and loved to go and see them. I had one favourite a beautiful Palomino mare with a blonde shaggy mane. Also, chickens ran freely on the homestead and scratched in the earth. They had a long, narrow feeding container filled with corn, and big tubs of water, situated close to the barn. That day I toddled toward the chicken feed. For some reason they were scuttling away with alarm from their tray, clucking and fussing. Burrowing into the trough to eat was a very large rat. I remember its long scaly tail and curiously I sat down with a bump to study the creature, which feeling threatened turned on me and leapt in the air toward my face. Saskia appeared at my side and caught the creature and began shaking it violently between her jaws. She tossed it up in the air and it scampered into the corral where the mare whinnied and reared up beating the rodent with its feet, crushing it's skull. It kicked the creature out and the chickens pecked at it and attacked it. It was only when I was older that I learnt the significance of this.

SIX YEARS LATER

The problems with Land Shift and the battle for our land seemed to come to an abrupt halt with the sudden death of Max Phipps. Their bullyboy tactics had paid off and many Indians had sold their homesteads and encompassing land but there were a few that had held out who remained and the intimidation stopped. It wasn't clear how he died. Rumours were that his heart had stopped. Others speculated on something more sinister. With his passing the focus of Land Shift turned to the Metropolis and the reins of the company were taken over by Max's son, Cornelius Phipps. I knew very little of what went on, as I was shielded from all the anxiety and problems with the company by Onacoma and my Uncle Inola.

Twenty-two year old Cornelius had now taken the pressure off the stalwart few Cherokee that had remained. Although, Onacoma felt the threat was never far away he needed to focus on raising me, his little girl, who had no one except for him. He told me that it was this, which eased his pain for the loss of his son, for whom no justice had yet been found. Onacoma had spoken of Ridge to me at times and he sounded a wonderful man. When he talked of him I could sense his pride and his sadness at such a tragic and unnecessary loss.

My formative years were happy with Onacoma whom I regarded as a father or as I called him 'Grandfather'. Indeed, I had no one else. He and Inola were my family. Between them they filled my days with joy. Although, I had been told that I was special there were no obvious signs of it until one savage night when I was eight years old.

Thunder crashed in the wild night sky, which was lit up with jagged streaks of lightning. The wind was howling and rain lashed against my window, which woke me with a start to the sound of the wrath of nature and I got out of bed and opened my door to see Onacoma throwing on his coat.

"What's happening?" I asked.

"The horses. Do you hear them? They are very frightened. I must take them from the corral and into the barn to dry stabling."

"I will help," I grabbed my boots and a jacket and followed Onacoma to the horse pen.

We ran through the soaking, driving rain, which was pelting down. The wind had whipped up to a fury and lightning floodlit the raging sky that was boiling with clouds. Our few horses cantered around in their enclosure whinnying in fright. Onacoma captured my favourite mare whose eyes were rolling in terror. He managed to calm her sufficiently to put on a head collar and he began to lead her to the safety of the barn.

The horse, who I called Jazzy because of her prancing gait reared up in distress and whinnied piteously, spooking the remaining horses and her young foal. Thankfully, I caught the baby palomino that was trying to hide amongst the rest of the nervous and jumpy steeds and succeeded in encouraging the little colt to follow the frightened mother. I just managed to close the corral gate and hurried after Onacoma to the shelter of the barn. By this time I was drenched. I had never seen such a violent storm and if I am honest it terrified me.

Onacoma swung open the creaky barn door, which squealed in complaint and he fought to get the agitated animal inside. Jazzy was skittish and didn't want to move but Onacoma tugged at the rein and she eventually allowed herself to be led into the dry stable at the back and Onacoma settled her with some hay.

There was a splintering crack as a lightning bolt flashed down from the aggressive storm and struck a beam on the roof truss. The crash it made was deafening and the beam began to crack and smoulder. I didn't realise the seriousness of this and continued to try and lead the foal.

The little colt was stubborn and hard to move. I tried to do as I had seen others do, I whispered in the little one's ear to coax it and smoothed its velvet muzzle as I waited and watched Onacoma.

He checked the mare's water and closed the stable door before on moving through the barn to help me with the foal. The wind was roaring through the barn in demented fury and the big wooden door banged noisily back and fore on its hinges smacking the side of the shed. No wonder the baby was scared. I was frightened, too.

The fissure in the splintered beam spread rapidly as would a crack in melting ice and it began to smoke as the seasoned wood ignited and burned out its joints. Too late Onacoma glanced up and saw the smoking beam. He tried to reach me and safety. He strode toward me but stupidly I was rooted to the spot looking on fearfully. I could see what was happening in the roof and yet I couldn't move or speak.

Before he could get to me the beam thundered down

knocking Onacoma to the dirt floor and trapping him underneath its deadly weight.

The terror I felt at seeing him pinioned in this way will live with me forever and I screamed, "Nooooo! Help me, please!" But my cry was lost in the devil wind and the angry, oppressive night sky. I remember dropping the foal's rein, which Inola picked up. He had arrived to help with the horses.

I ran to Onacoma's side and fought to lift the heavy crushing beam from off him. I knew I had to move this deadly weight or he would die, but my small hands were impotent against the burdensome weight. Tears streamed down my cheeks, almost blinding me as I grunted with exertion and effort. It all seemed futile, what could I do? I was just a child.

My tiny hands were about to lose their grip when another pair of hands grasped the wood. Inola, I thought, but then another set of hands joined mine on the beam. I was choking with emotion when to my surprise, another... and then another... and another pair of hands joined me in my struggle until six pairs of hands had united with me in the task and we battled to lift the load from Onacoma's chest, together. It was a sublime moment and one I shall never forget.

I looked back gratefully at my six helpers, fellow Indians, silhouetted in the doorway against the turbulent rain filled sky and then at Onacoma who seemed too still. I called his name but there was no response. He had slipped into unconsciousness.

Activity was frenetic as the community formed a human chain to transport buckets of water to put out the spreading flames and I tried to calm the horses, while we waited for the Emergency Services that Inola had already called.

Soon sirens were heard approaching as an ambulance with paramedics arrived along with a fire truck and fire fighters that finally eliminated the flames. Onacoma was quickly examined, given oxygen and whisked away by paramedics to the local hospital. By this time the storm had abated and passed over to the next county. All this was just a blur to me. I stood there numbly in bewilderment and shock. My 'grandfather' was gone.

Saskia, Inola's dog, trotted across and gave me a consoling lick, and unable to help myself I buried my face in the dog's fur and wept. Inola placed his hand comfortingly on my shoulder, and tried to reassure me. "He will be fine. Don't worry. Onacoma is strong."

"Please, Uncle Inola take me there. I want to see him."

Inola looked at my pleading face and relented, "Come." He gestured to his pickup and I climbed aboard with Saskia and we set off for the local hospital.

The journey was uneventful and the way clear. We soon arrived at the small town's Accident and Emergency Centre, in Marwood. Inola parked his truck and ordered his dog, "Watch and guard, Saskia." The dog sat up straight and cocked her head, fully alert. I scrambled out of the pickup and slammed the door almost running to the entrance. I glanced back at Inola, who just smiled, and called after me, "Hey! Sanjukta, wait up!"

We entered Mercy Hospital together and walked up to the admissions and information desk where a plump Hispanic woman greeted us, "Yes?"

Inola spoke, "You have an emergency casualty brought in earlier…?"

She appraised our appearance and clothes, "Ah yes, Chief Onacoma. He is in Intensive Care."

"Can I see him?" I pleaded.

"Are you a relative?" questioned the receptionist.

"Yes."

"I have strict instructions only to allow one visitor at a time and only family members."

Inola nodded, "I am a friend, she is family."

The receptionist acknowledged and said, "Third floor. The elevators are straight down the hall.

Inola walked with me to the lifts and pressed the call button. "I will come up with you. You can see him alone. I will wait outside."

The elevator door opened with a ping and we entered it. I had never before been in a hospital, nor in an elevator. It was all very new to me. We said nothing as we travelled to the third floor until we stepped out.

"I will wait here for you. Go, go and see him," said Inola.

I nodded and entered the ICU and spoke to the nurse on duty, who ushered me into a room with an order, "No more than twenty minutes we don't want to tire him out."

When I entered and saw Onacoma lying propped up on a mountain of pillows with his eyes closed, my heart almost stopped. His pallor was grey and his chest was swathed in bandages. A profusion of wires, like tangled spaghetti, were attached to machines that monitored his heart rate and other vital functions. I felt my eyes widen in dismay and I bit my lip in an attempt to stop myself from crying out. I took a deep breath to calm myself before drawing up a chair and sitting at his side. I rested my head on the crisp fresh bed and sighed despondently. He must have heard me as his eyes fluttered open.

"Sanjukta…" he whispered hoarsely. I looked up at him, a thousand emotions running through me. He continued, "There is something you must know…"

"Don't speak. Save your energy. You must get well," I insisted, the worry of what might happen to him was clear for him to see in my face.

Onacoma struggled to talk, "You have to know…"

My heart filled with love for him, and I pressed on, my fear obviously apparent. I really believed he was going to die. "No… you will get well. You can't die. You…" I desperately tried to stop myself from crying but it was an impossible task and choked with emotion the tears began to flow down my cheeks.

Onacoma's voice became stronger as he stilled my words, "Peace! I will be well. I will not leave you." At his words I know I became calmer. "The ancestors will it. But you… you must know the truth about yourself."

His words struck a chord with me for although I knew a little I knew there was a lot more. I looked up curiously and with my interest growing I listened to what he had to say.

"Your mother had the heart of a lion as have you," he wheezed. "But you have more, much, much more. Sacred powers have been bestowed on you. Do you ever wonder at your name?" he asked.

"Sanjukta?"

"It means "Union". The Great White Spirit has blessed you. That is why in the barn many hands came to help. It is what saved my life."

"Yes, Inola called an ambulance, which came quickly."

"What happened in the barn was just the beginning. You will always find that strength and comforting support. It will surround you in times of trouble and unite all those of a good heart behind you. This gift to you is for your mother who dared to stand alone and died for her bravery."

"I wish I had known her."

"Sanjukta, your mother lives in you and I no longer have a son, for that reason I will teach you as I would a boy warrior. You will be a match for any man or woman."

The relief I felt that my beloved grandfather was not going to die filled me with joy and his promise delighted me. I yearned to know more and begged him finally to tell me all. I remember my feelings as he related the story of Land Shift's greed and my mother, Louella's protest. He began to cough a little with the effort and the pain etched on his face became more apparent, which is when the nurse entered.

"Time's up I am afraid," she said looking at her watch. "You can see him again tomorrow."

Reluctantly I left the room and returned to Inola and I told him all that had been said. Inola took my hand and we made our way back to the truck.

"We will stop by again tomorrow, Sanjukta. He will get well for you. By the sound of it he has much to teach you."

I visited my grandfather each day and was gratified to see his colour gradually return. With every passing day I saw him grow stronger and it helped me to chase away the horror of that night as I watched him get well.

I chattered inanely about inconsequential nonsense each time I saw him. I couldn't wait for him to be better and come home for although Inola looked after me well, I missed Onacoma. We had a very special bond like a real father and daughter; after all he had brought me into this world.

Eventually, he was released from the hospital and life continued as normal, school lessons, chores and learning about the horses. The young palomino foal, Jazzy's young colt was promised to me. He vowed to me that on my tenth birthday my training would begin. I couldn't wait.

Inola's words were true. My grandfather had much for me to learn. I was already attending school and doing well at my lessons in spite of the teasing I endured for being brought up as an Indian. I didn't mind. I was proud, proud to be part of the Cherokee nation. I had the same dark colouring as my 'grandfather' even though my mother had been white. I was keen to learn the old ways and the history of our people.

Onacoma had many wise words that were guides by which to live our lives. He told me of the great Chief Dan George who was chief of the Tsleil-Waututh Nation in neighbouring Canada. This chief had embraced much of the white man's world by becoming an actor but he had never forgotten his roots. He spoke sometimes in sheer poetry and had said this gem that I have never forgotten,

'May the stars carry your sadness away,

May the flowers fill your heart with beauty,

May hope forever wipe away your tears,

 And above all may silence make you strong.'

I loved sitting around the campfire and listening to the many wonderful stories and legends as told by the Medicine Man. We would sit enraptured at his tales of bravery and in honour of our warriors.

At weekends I would go out into the vast forests and mountains with Onacoma and learn how to track. We started off at the muddy banks of a river.

"All animals need water. They need to drink and here where the ground is soft is the best place to see the prints of our animal cousins. Look!"

In the silt and dirt were many marks. I learnt how to recognise the small cloven hoof of the deer and the larger hooves of the elk. The paw prints of possums and raccoons, coyotes even the sidewinder trail of a rattlesnake.

He showed me how to track an animal, what signs to look

for with broken twigs and flattened grass or bits of fur stuck on brambles. I was becoming very observant and used this knowledge for enjoyment to secretly observe animals at play.

I particularly remember going out at dusk and following the trail of a coyote that my grandfather indicated had young. We tracked the animal to its home and waited. My excitement at seeing the mother emerge from her den with four little ones in tow and my enormous delight in watching the youngsters, called pups, play and tumble in the grass was too much for me and I exclaimed in pleasure, alarming the mother who called to her babies and they disappeared swiftly back into their den. I had frightened the creatures away. From that I learned how to be still, quiet and attentive.

I recall how Onacoma laughed when he told me to examine the droppings of various animals to see if it was fresh even from birds. Owl pellets revealed fur and bones from small rodents. I began to understand the animal hunters and their prey. Those that were being hunted, their eyes were at the side of their heads for better vision and awareness; those that preyed on them their eyes looked straight ahead to focus on that they wished to kill and feed. There was a hierarchy in the food chain. I was taught not to interfere with nature. All this was leading to my first big test.

"You now have the knowledge to find the big cats and recognise the spoor of the mountain lion, and how they establish their territory. Your task is to find the lair of one such creature. I will follow and watch."

I started down by the water and searched amongst the mess of muddy prints for a big cat. It wasn't easy to trace the path with other animals criss-crossing the tracks. I eventually found one to follow and my hunch was confirmed with the strong smell of urine that assaulted my senses showing where the feline had marked its territory.

The trail wound through dense undergrowth and forest and all the while I was on my guard and I knew my grandfather followed me at a respectful distance. I hoped he would be impressed with my progress and what I had learnt.

I soon reached a rocky outcrop that was the steppingstone leading to the mountain. I could see and smell that the cat had scented here. Bits of fur stuck to a jagged point of the rock where the big cat had rubbed itself. And scat, a small pile of round ended droppings, had been carefully laid on a little heap of leaves and twigs gathered by the creature and left as a marker to its territory.

I looked back at Onacoma knowing I was getting nearer my quarry and that the cat was not far away. He looked up to the top of the mountain where a ledge protruded. I followed his gaze and saw a beautiful sight. A female mountain lion had emerged and was standing surveying her land. She had caught the whiff of an intruder and she rasped a low warning growl telling me to keep my distance and stay away.

I glanced back at my grandfather and he gestured for me to come back. I scrambled back across the rocks and trail to where he stood. He nodded proudly and put his arm around me. "Well done, Sanjukta. You have done well. I am pleased, well pleased."

"What's next?" I was so anxious to continue with these studies.

"Next, I teach you how to heal. You must learn about nature, what the flowers and herbs have to offer."

I couldn't wait. Grandfather showed me how to use herbs for infusions and poultices, what would make me sick, what would soothe: Comfrey, valerian, all healing chamomile; even the humble buttercup had its uses.

I had a chance to put this wisdom into practice and made a poultice for one of our young horse's injured fetlock. The same palomino foal that I had strived to help the night of that fateful storm and I was privileged to own had caught his leg on barbed wire and the wound was in danger of becoming infected.

I treated the horse, which I had named Dancer, and changed its dressing daily using the best herbs I could forage and to my utmost happiness, when the final poultice was removed, the horse's fetlock was clear and free of injury. I rejoiced as did Onacoma who pronounced, "I am satisfied. You have proved you understand the old ways."

As the months went by my training was to become more difficult as survival techniques were the next programme of activities for me. I had to learn how to survive in the wild and select the wood to make a bow.

Grandfather took me into the forest and made me look at the variety of trees and asked me, "Look at the abundance of nature around you. We only ever take what we need and no more. Feel the different woods and tell me, which you think would make the best bow?"

I touched the trees. I felt the bark and flexed the branches. "Hm, this is tough." I found the flexibility of the willow, which sprouted like a fountain and drooped by the river bank, the sturdiness of the oak, which grew freely in the forest, the heart of the osage; a wood that was favoured for whittling, and frowned, "Maybe the Osage… I am not sure."

"Ah! Then use hickory. It is a good tough resilient wood that is very forgiving."

"I will do as you say, but why not the osage?"

"Osage makes great bows, but you have to remove the sap wood and work the heart wood down to one growth ring, working it properly around the knots while doing it. It is hard work."

"I'm not afraid of that."

"No. But, osage is not a beginner's wood, and some pieces will make even a seasoned bowyer swear." Onacoma laughed, "With hickory all you have to do is cut the tree, split it, paint both ends with Elmer's glue to prevent checking, and peel the bark off while it's still green. Then let it dry."

"All I have to do?" I sighed. "You make it sound so easy."

"Where you peeled the bark off will be the back of your bow with no wood removal at all. All wood will be removed from the sides and the belly during the tillering process."

"So hickory is the best wood for me?"

"Other hardwoods like persimmon, hop horn bean, oak, and dogwood can be used in the same manner as hickory, but hickory is the most forgiving of small errors or mistakes."

"Then hickory, it is."

Grandfather was with me every step of the process and I was proud to make my first bow and couldn't wait to try it out. He set up a target of sorts and instructed me, tying a strip of buckskin on my bow arm as a guard. I learned how to shoot, how to pull back and keep the bow steady with my nose to the string and closing one eye to aim; and releasing my three fingers quickly from the string. I was surprisingly good and he was pleased.

Many of the Indian children were dubious about the way I was being taught a warrior's skills but when I began to prove myself it silenced the critics and I began to feel like an Amazonian that I had read about in school history books. I was determined to be as good as any boy, girl, woman or man.

Every day after school, Onacoma would instruct me in the art of self-defence and unarmed combat. I learned how to use my opponent's weight to my advantage and could sweep an attacker to the ground by sidestepping and flipping them. After I had felled my grandfather three times in this way, he announced, "You are ready."

I'll never forget that first trial. It was night. The sky was lit with a million stars and a hunting moon. A bonfire blazed brightly as I faced Abir. We were both fourteen and had painted our faces with ochre and another red clay dye. One hand was strapped behind my back as I faced Abir in combat. Working against someone nearer my own size and weight came easily and I soon floored my rival to applause from those watching. Abir and I clasped each other in friendship. He was without resentment and we were to become good friends. Other young Indian maidens in their teens laughed shyly at my encounter. They tittered over the fact that a girl could beat a boy and patted me on the back. My confidence was growing and word spread that the chief's granddaughter was a force to be reckoned with.

Onacoma loved teaching me the old ways and ancient traditions as he had taught his son, Ridge. Sometimes he would pour his heart out to me, regaling me with stories of his warrior son and he exclaimed, "No parent should ever be expected to bury a child. But the ancestors must have willed it and that is why you were brought to me, you are a gift from the Great White Spirit." Grandfather was now sixty-two and his hair was almost completely grey but his eyes were as sharp as a hawk and he was still nimble on his feet.

Most trying was achieving success in another important skill; to follow or pursue someone or something without being seen. I got frustrated in learning how to be invisible. Onacoma was so shrewd he would spot my efforts at trying to surprise him and catch him unawares. I worked harder at this more than anything else and soon my penultimate test was upon us.

It was a fine sunny day with not a cloud to be seen and we went out into the prairie, a treeless grassy plain with no ground cover. Onacoma waited in the centre of this grassland and I had to reach him and surprise him without being spotted. My movement was stealthy and I only moved when the wind blew that rippled the grass like water. My clothing toned with the colours of nature and I chose to move when Onacoma was staring in another direction. I used the swish of the grass being blown and the sounds of animals and birds to mask my movement. Onacoma scanned and searched for me with his eyes until I succeeded in creeping up and tapping him on the shoulder. Grandfather was satisfied and I was jubilant.

But, my final test was definitely the worst I had ever faced. We had been taught to respect all life and only take what we needed to survive. But in order to become a full warrior I had to face a rattlesnake in a pit. In olden days I would have been expected to catch the rattler, kill it and take its rattle, but this time I had to capture the snake and place it in a bag to be released into the safety of the rocks later.

The snake merely wanted to slink away and hide. I knew they only attacked when being confronted. Drums played and the percussion pipes and rattles joined with the voices in song as the smoke drifted up from the fire.

It was time. On the given signal I jumped into the pit and the snake had nowhere to go. I was nervous and sweating. Fear churned inside me like the rising bubbling froth on raging white water. One thing I had been taught from the start was to respect nature in all its forms. I didn't want to hurt the snake, but I didn't want the snake to harm me. It lunged at my legs and I jumped over it caught it behind the head and held it aloft. The snake twisted and spiralled in my hand. It was angry and eager to escape.

The cheering around me filled my ears and someone tossed down the canvas bag and I was able to pick it up still holding the thrashing reptile. My palms were becoming slippery as I struggled to hold onto the frightened creature. Using my teeth I tugged at the string and opened the top of the bag. Then, it was as if a magical calm had spread through the snake and it lay still allowing me to place it in the bag and tie the top.

My final test was complete and I had passed.

Chapter Four

Growing up

Abir and I had become firm friends after our test. We spent much of our free time together and out of school we would roam the land and the woods around our homes. One weekend we were running through the forest and laughing together when we fell into a clearing and began play fighting. Abir pleaded with me, "Come, Sanjukta, teach me that move. I have my initiation tests soon and I need to prove that I am ready to be a warrior."

I taught Abir as Onacoma had taught me; how to use an opponent's strength against them when attacked from the front. I showed him how to judge their movement, sidestep and cover, while letting them travel past and then sweep them to the floor. We practised and practised. He soon got the hang of it and I felt certain he would be able to defeat anyone, now, regardless of size.

While we went through various routines and movements, another of our school friends, Chitto, who was also fourteen, arrived into the same clearing with a younger Indian boy and two female friends. They stopped to watch us. Reluctant to let them see the secret defensive moves we ceased our play.

Chitto boasted to the girls, "Come, let Abir practise. He will need all the skill at his disposal if he is drawn to face me in the pit next week."

The banter between the boys continued when I suddenly became aware of some rustling in the undergrowth on the other side of the clearing. As soon as I saw what was making the noise, I stopped them. "Ssh!"

I put my fingers to my lips and Abir seeing my concerned expression questioned, "What is it?"

I moved my hand very slowly and pointed to a small brown bear snuffling amongst the ferns and bracken and whispered, "Where there is baby, mother will be close by.

It's not safe." I gestured to Chitto and his friends who were standing close to the baby and with their backs to the bear and said quietly, "Walk slowly toward us. Don't run and do it quietly."

Chitto, his friend and the girls began to move toward Abir and me as the baby bear scampered into the clearing. There was a huge roar and the mother bear came crashing through the undergrowth and followed on her hind legs. Stupidly the girls screamed and ran behind the boys, I ordered them to hush.

"Be quiet! We don't want to alarm her…"

They all gathered behind me and faced the terrifying sight of the lumbering mother bear standing more than seven foot tall. She roared and we could see her fearsome yellowing teeth. I held up my hands and held her gaze, and spoke soothingly to her. She stopped advancing and something connected between her eyes and mine. It was as if time stood still. We all waited in some kind of limbo. I could feel my blood rushing through my ears and in my head yet somehow I knew it would be all right. The others told me afterward that they hardly dared to breathe.

She dropped onto all fours, nudged her cub back into the forest and waddled calmly away. I heaved a sigh of relief. The others seemed totally lost for words. Finally, Abir spoke, "I have never seen anything like that. You are truly remarkable."

I couldn't explain what had happened I just had this weird feeling that the animal understood me and knew we meant them no harm. I didn't question it but was thankful that we were all safe. I feel I earned some respect on that day and I didn't feel alone.

Not so, when I was sixteen and I had to make my way home by myself one evening after school. I had a strange feeling of foreboding as I walked along the virtually deserted dusty town road after baseball practice at school.

I kicked a stone as I passed a battered blue pickup truck parked outside a bar. In the back were two wolf hybrid dogs. They followed me with their eyes as I dribbled the stone in the dirt. I stopped and looked at them. They didn't move.

They were so beautiful. I don't think I had ever seen them before. I had a real thing for wolves. I truly believed that they were a much-maligned creature. I had been taught to respect them and my grandfather had told me that we humans could learn much from wolves about family life. I carried on up the road and an uneasy feeling ran through my bones and I shivered.

Across the street two teens, who must have been nearly seventeen, and youths that I had seen in school and who I knew to be bullies began jeering and taunting me. I walked on and tried to ignore them when one, I had heard called Jed, picked up a stone and chucked it at me. I jumped out of the way and he laughed cruelly.

"Well, if it isn't the white girl trying to be an Indian brave," he sneered.

His equally thuggish friend, Seth, started mocking me, too. He raised his hand with his palm flat facing me in the semblance of an Indian greeting, "Yeah. How!" He exaggerated his accent and laughed.

Jed crossed the street and swaggered toward me and I felt my heart sink. "Hey, Indian, I'm talking to you."

I stopped and faced him, "I don't want any trouble."

Jed turned to his friend and scoffed, "Hear that, Seth? She don't want no trouble."

Seth bent over and began hollering with his hand over his mouth whooping like an Indian from a movie doing a war dance. He started jigging around me. Jed silenced him and moved menacingly toward me. I felt uncomfortable, frightened and very alone.

Jed came almost level with me. I could smell his chewing gum breath as he spoke, "I sure would like to see what parts of her are Indian and what parts are white. Wouldn't you, Seth?"

"Seems like we need to get her clothes off for that, don't you think?" Seth said leering at me.

Jed started to bear down on me and sleazily continued, "Come on, Girly. Let Jed taste you." He lewdly ran his tongue across his lips as if he was licking or lapping something.

I felt more than uncomfortable. I started to panic as Jed started to grab at my clothes. My training was forgotten in the moment and I smacked his hand away, trying to look much braver than I felt. Jed just laughed. I swallowed hard as Seth stood alongside Jed and they faced me head on. They began to paw at my body and clothes. I debated whether I should kick Jed in the crotch when to my surprise and almost immediately one of the dogs jumped down from the pickup and settled at my side snarling, curling its lips and baring its teeth.

Seth stepped back and picked up a stone, which he threw at the dog. The canine didn't flinch. Then, the other dog jumped down and stood on the other side of me growling and with hackles raised.

This unnerved Seth even more and allowed me to regain my equilibrium. He took a step back and muttered, "What is this?"

Undeterred Jed moved threateningly toward me getting right in my space but, as he did so, both dogs moved forward and stepped protectively in front of me snarling frighteningly. Reluctantly Jed and Seth backed off raising their hands in submission.

"Hey, it's cool. Didn't mean nothing. It was just a bit of fun. A joke that's all."

The bullies backed off and the animals stayed right by my side until the youths had moved on and were out of sight. I bent down and ruffled both dogs' fur still astonished at what had happened.

Just then a guy, I knew, strolled out of the bar and was amazed to see his dogs with me in the street. I was fondling their ears when the rancher, Trip, approached, "Well, I'll be damned," he drawled. "Hey, Sanjukta! I ain't never seen my dogs allow anyone to do that. Not ever."

I stood up, "They came to my rescue, Trip. They have been great. They saved me from some bully boys."

Trip didn't ask any questions but ordered the animals back to his truck and they jumped straight back in, but in the amber glow of their eyes that still watched me, I could see and feel their trust and their good hearts.

"Well, that's good, Sanjukta." Trip smiled and gave me a wink, "You take care now and say 'Hi' to the chief for me."

"I will," I answered before continuing to walk out of town. I walked on and soon came to the brush-land that surrounded the enclosed land of my village. Here again I was alone. I felt alone and the uneasy feelings returned. It was soon clear why I had such misgivings as Seth and Jed knew the route I would take home and had been lying in wait to ambush me.

I passed a small thicket and both lads jumped out and blocked my path, but this time I was prepared. I would not be caught unawares again and instinctively I knew what to do. I had, had time to think and my training with Onacoma would be put to a real test.

Jed challenged me, "Hey, Squaw … Let's see how brave you are without your dogs."

"Yeah," sneered Seth. "We're going to see just what you are made of…"

"Underneath those clothes," finished Jed.

Both youths drew nearer and Jed pulled out a hunting knife. It was as if I went straight into test mode and I automatically stood tall and unflinching. As they rushed me I neatly sidestepped and swept Jed off his feet. He fell face forward into the dirt. Seth roared and tried to grapple with me but with all that Onacoma had taught me it was easy. I flipped Seth over and he fell onto his back.

Jed spat out a mouthful of earth and dived at my legs. I jumped, avoided his attack and kicked him back down before turning swiftly to evade Seth. I landed a sharp blow to his solar plexus, which winded him and sent the bully sprawling.

Both teens crawled away. Jed wiped his mouth. I didn't know whether they would come at me again when my attention was caught by a bald eagle circling and screaming above me. Quickly, I focused my attention back on the young men ready for the next attack, which fortunately didn't come. It seemed that the two bullies had had enough and nursing their wounded pride they retreated muttering obscenities under their breath. I stood still and watched them go, and although alone I felt proud at what I had achieved.

The eagle flew down and landed on a bush and fixed its eyes on me. I had never been so close to such a beautiful bird. I somehow knew that if Seth or Jed returned that this magnificent bird would protect me. It was as if we had communicated with unspoken words and thoughts. Our eyes locked and I could feel the creature's powerful spirit and hear its rapid heart beat. As that connection was made the eagle opened its beak and let out a cry before flapping its mighty wings and soaring off majestically into the azure sky.

My remaining school years passed relatively uneventfully until after our final exams Abir and I together with some friends decided to camp out in the woods and celebrate our excellent results. We had built a roaring campfire, which blazed brightly in the thick black of night. Sparks and ash flew up with the plumes of smoke and we relaxed after our party. I wasn't ready for my sleeping bag and bed yet, and although the others had retired I sat against a large boulder and sharpened a stick to a fine point whilst I enjoyed stargazing in the night sky.

It was easy to pick out the constellations with no light pollution and such a clear sky. I reminded myself of all the names, Orion the hunter, Ursa Major the great bear and Ursa Minor the little bear. I searched for the chained lady, Andromeda and revelled in my memories of studying the heavens with my grandfather who had taught me the common names as well as our Indian ones.

Abir joined me and sat opposite on another rock. There was no need for words. We were all talked out and just enjoyed the stillness and beauty of the night. In the distance coyotes and wolves yammered and howled and the cicadas made music in the grass. I continued to whittle away at my stick until the end was good and sharp. It had come to a razor fine point. I looked up and to my horror saw something approaching Abir's head. There was no time for warning and I quickly hurled the stick. Abir froze and looked in fright at the deadly missile, which whistled over his head and struck its target.

A large snake dropped at Abir's feet. The dart had gone

clean through its head and Abir stared at it with astonishment. "My God! A cottonmouth! You saved my life."

I was beginning to get used to amazing things happening around me. I wondered if it would continue once I had left the area. Was it something magical about the territory and only occurred when I was close to my roots? Perhaps. Maybe, it would be different once I reached college and the big city.

I was soon to find out.

It was a day of mixed blessings and emotions for me when I stood with my suitcase and a small bag, and waited for the Greyhound bus that would take me across country to the big city. I stood in line with my surrogate father or as I called him, Grandfather, who had come to see me off.

I could see the pride in his eyes and hear it in his voice as he bade me farewell. "You have done well, Sanjukta. Now go to college and make our nation proud."

I had no words. Onacoma had been my family since the beginning. He had equipped me well for life and much, much more, and I loved him dearly. Now I was embarking on another adventure to study law. I fully intended to champion the causes of our people and on my hit list was Land Shift.

But, who knew how my life would change and who I would meet?

The line moved up and the driver took my case to stow in the luggage compartment under the bus. I hugged my grandfather and held onto him tightly and barely managed to whisper, "I promise I will do my best, for you and my mother."

My legs were wobbly as I clambered aboard and moved down the gangway. I had never been away from home before. I found a seat by the window and I placed my small bag on the rack above my head. My fingertips touched the glass and Onacoma stood back and nodded sagely. He raised his hand in a wave as the bus pulled away.

I was on my own.

Chapter Five

University Days

The first few days at university were a whirlwind of filling in forms, registering for activities, settling into my rooms on Campus and attending lectures. There just seemed so much to do, so much to learn and so many notes to write. For the time being I was keeping myself to myself. I wasn't ready yet for too many social occasions. Freshers' week and stories of hazing alarmed me. I kept a low profile. I wondered how Abir was faring away from home. He had gone off to do a course in journalism and I was uncertain when our paths would cross again.

Life in the big city was very different from what I had been used to. I missed the open spaces, the countryside and nature and more importantly my Indian family. I found it difficult initially to make new friends and spent every day after lectures on the running track. The freedom it gave me to run filled my heart with joy. I could forget myself as I ran and being alone with my thoughts helped me unravel some of the trickier problems I had come up against in class. I intended to study hard and get the best law degree I possibly could.

One afternoon I was feeling particularly homesick and as I changed and put on my running shoes I wished that for once I had a running partner, someone I could relate to and talk to. There was no one in the ladies changing room so I sighed and focused my mind and went out onto the track and began to jog. I had done three circuits and was beginning to feel good when I sprinted around the curve past the entrance to the changing rooms.

I was surprised when another student ran out and caught up with me. He began to chat, "Hi. I've seen you around. You're in my Law and my Econ class. I'm Dante, Dante Burgham." I glanced over to him as he kept pace with me stride for stride around the track. I recognised him from lectures. He was about the same age as me, tall, broad shouldered and quite handsome, I thought. That notion made me colour up so I faced front again and concentrated on my running.

Dante kept pace with me and spoke again, "I hope you don't mind but, I admire your dedication... your need to run. I've seen you on the track before. Do you mind if I join you and run with you?"

I shook my head, it seemed as if someone had been listening to me, "No problem. In fact I didn't want to run alone today," I admitted.

"That's good, because I felt like joining you. Well, actually, we all did!" Dante gestured behind him with a flick of his head and I glanced back. To my amazement about thirty students were pounding the track behind me. They smiled and acknowledged me and before I knew it they had all surged forward and were shaking my hand and introducing themselves. It was as if a light had been switched on in my head and I fully understood. In fact, Dante's next flippant comment nearly had me laugh aloud. "Anyone with this much of a following should be called Union."

I grinned with enlightenment, moved up a gear and sprinted ahead. To my joy everyone followed me. I was living up to my name. Dante and I completed another three circuits and desperate for a drink of water I stopped at the entrance and drank from the water fountain. Dante joined me and we flopped down in the seats overlooking the track and watched the others completing another lap as we caught our breath.

Dante made me, I don't know, how can I describe it? He made me feel feminine. This in itself was a new experience for me and I found myself smiling shyly at his chatter, laughing at his jokes and freely answering his questions. He soon had the best part of my life story and I his. I hoped I was reading the situation correctly and that he, too, could feel the rapport growing between us.

His life had been so very different from mine.

"Me? I'm a city boy, born and raised. I love the good

things in life. But don't get me wrong, I love the countryside too."

"But you know nothing about it?"

"No, but you can teach me, when we get an opportunity."

"Do you have any brothers or sisters?"

"No. I'm the only one. Mom lost two. In some ways that makes me sad but then it meant I always had the best of everything. No arguments, no fighting. I had their undivided attention. It suited me fine."

"That's a bit like me. I'm the only one. The Chief's only son died, well he was horribly murdered."

"Gosh, I'm sorry. That must have been awful."

"It was for the Chief, but not for me as I never knew him, but I would have liked to."

"You lived the whole Native American Indian thing?"

"Uh huh. I learned all the skills of a young warrior even though I was female. I'll tell you about it some day."

"I can't believe it. You're not kidding?" I shook my head, "Wow! Brought up by Indians? That's cool."

"My mother died shortly after giving birth to me. Chief Onacoma has been a father to me."

"And you intended to go to Law School to help your people?"

"Anyway that I can."

"It was always expected of me. My father has a big law firm, very successful. I will go into the family business."

"So no worries about employment for you?"

"No. Although I do sometimes wonder if that means I'll miss out. You know, experimenting with different jobs, travelling. But then again I love the law." Dante stopped, pensive for just a moment as he considered his future and his dreams. "I suppose I'm luckier than I thought, talking to you has made me realise that."

"What?"

"Well, my father's dreams are in fact my dreams. So, I'm on the right course."

"Then we both know where we're going... And you may be interested... my name... Sanjukta. It means union. So, you were right!"

Dante laughed, "Union it is! And from now on your nickname will be Union."

FOUR YEARS LATER

Dante and I had become inseparable. We socialised together and studied together, sitting together in lectures. He was a popular student and his friendship with me had opened many doors. There was always an undercurrent of something special between us but he didn't push it and I didn't encourage it and our friendship flourished going from strength to strength. Neither of us needed the complication of a relationship. Anyway, I was a novice in these stakes. I had never had a boyfriend. Onacoma had not taught me anything in that department. It had been down to my friend Tayanita at home in the village to help me through puberty and into womanhood.

The same could not be said about Dante. Women loved him but Dante never seemed serious about anyone. He was too focused on his studies as he said to me, "Plenty of time for that when I'm qualified." He went on a few dates but invariably the romance was short lived and he would prefer spending time with me than playing the field, as he called it.

So, I continued to enjoy his companionship but sometimes, just sometimes I would allow my mind to wander, to wonder what it would be like to be kissed by those soft lips, to have him embrace me in more than a friendly hug. I also knew that the mixing of our two cultures might be a step too far. But, I left those romantic thoughts born from idle curiosity and banished them to remain in my dreams. Although as time went on I was irrepressibly drawn to him more and more. Sometimes I would catch him looking at me a certain way. Then I would look again and he would be laughing innocently at something I or someone else had said and I wondered if I imagined it.

Dante never directly invited me to meet his parents but I had been privileged to attend a couple of functions, which were hosted by them, so I knew who they were and what they looked like but that is as far as it went.

There was the Law Society Gala Dinner held at the Waldorf Astoria Banquet Hall. I was invited to accompany him by default. I was uncomfortable in a borrowed dress from a fellow student who was supposed to attend but she was struck down with some horrible bug, which prevented her from attending and at Dante's suggestion she asked me to go in her place.

The dress was like nothing I had ever worn before. To say I felt like Cinderella was an understatement. I normally lived in jeans or comfortable slacks. I would describe myself as a jeans and sweater lady. This was a very elegant, sequined gown that fitted and clung to every part of my body. I brushed my hair and braided it in a single plait that fell on one side of my face. What I didn't have was a pair of shoes to suit. I could hardly wear sneakers or flat pumps. I needed something better and something I could walk in without tottering over. The fashion for killer heels was just not me.

Another sympathetic student, Martha, with the same size feet, lent me a pair of kitten heels. They fitted and I practised walking in them and although I was unsteady in them to begin with I gradually became used to them. I pranced up and down my room and eyed myself critically in the mirror. I didn't look like me at all and that made me nervous. I glanced at my watch, "Yikes!" Dante would be here any minute. I threw on a jacket and left my room carrying a shoulder bag that went with nothing I was wearing. Too late I didn't have anything else.

I stepped out into the corridor and bumped straight into Martha, "Surely, you're not wearing that?" she exclaimed.

"What?"

"You can't wear that coat. It's like something off a Reservation or from a Thrift Shop! Nor can you use that purse. It's totally wrong. Come with me."

"But I'll be late, Dante is meeting me in the foyer," I glanced at my watch again, "Now!"

"Dante can wait. Come." She grabbed me by the hand and pulled me into her room. "Here." She dragged out an embroidered pashmina, a short velvet black cape, which covered my shoulders and a faux fur wrap. "Try one of these."

I took off my fringed jacket, she was right; it didn't go and I tried the alternatives while she rummaged in her wardrobe for an evening bag.

"Leave your purse with me and use this." She had found a black sequined one that went perfectly. "Here pop your lipstick, mascara and money in this. I'll look after yours until tomorrow." She looked me up and down, "The velvet cape. That's the one."

Martha titivated my make-up as I wasn't wearing any. She gave me a diamante pendant with matching earrings and declared, "That's it. Perfection. Now go and have a great time."

Muttering my thanks I left her room and proceeded to the stairs and foyer where Dante was waiting. He looked so handsome and was holding an orchid corsage for me. Suddenly, I felt very shy. He gave a low whistle, "Union, you look… wow… you're beautiful, more than that, you're stunning."

I didn't know what to say. I felt like Julia Roberts in that film 'Pretty Woman' with Richard Gere. He pinned the flower to my dress and took my hand and led me to the waiting cab outside. The touch of his hand in mine set my stomach fluttering. There was an awkward silence between us as if he was seeing me with new eyes. I tried to make light of it, "I didn't know that you scrubbed up so well," I laughed.

He relaxed, "You know me, always prepared to make an effort."

Now the awkwardness was over we felt more at ease. I couldn't tell him that he excited me like no one else ever had and I didn't want to spoil the perfect friendship we had. I told myself sternly that I needed to get a grip.

We arrived at the Banqueting Hall, my cape was ticketed and whisked away to a cloakroom and we were seated at a table with a number of Dante's father's employees at the Law Firm.

His father and mother were on the top table as VIP guests of the President of the Law Society and I saw his father incline his head in acknowledgement at his son and he smiled politely at me.

The evening passed in a blur. I had never seen so many glasses and pieces of cutlery laid on a table. I watched everyone else very carefully and did as they did. This was a new experience and I was grateful to one of the wives of a young lawyer who guided me with her eyes as what to do. She made an unobtrusive play of what to pick up when and I was able to copy her without anyone noticing that I didn't know what was what.

When the sumptuous dinner was over, tables were moved to the side and the band struck up for the dancing. I was embarrassed. I had never been to a dance like this and I didn't know how. Dante pulled me up amidst my protests and whispered in my ear, "I'll lead. Just follow me." He brushed aside all my excuses and steered me to the floor.

We began to dance. My heart was thumping so hard I was sure he could feel it vibrate from me into his chest. I was so glad the music drowned out the thud of my heart. My insides were in turmoil and I was wary of doing something wrong.

He tried to help me move around the floor but I knew I wasn't very light-footed. I had just started to get the hang of the dance when the music stopped. He looked at me and his eyes seem to bore right through me, "There that wasn't so bad, was it?" he asked and he began to incline his head to mine when an attractive woman tapped me on the shoulder.

"Do you mind if I cut in?" she smiled expectantly at me.

"No of course not." I stepped out of Dante's arms and returned to my seat and watched as the woman began to charm Dante as they glided around the floor. The horrible writhing I felt in my stomach was worse than anything I had ever experienced and seeing Dante holding someone else hurt me so much I made up my mind that if the situation ever arose again I would walk away. I would take friendship over romance and keep my sanity. It was not in my nature to be jealous but this must have been was what I was feeling and I didn't like it.

I was rescued from this train of thought by one of the

junior partners in the firm who asked me to dance. He didn't expect me to follow him around the floor but danced loosely and freely in an abandoned style that was easier for me to match. Dante caught my eye as he moved around the dance floor and mouthed at me, "Sorry," and gave me a wink. I shrugged and smiled as if it was of no consequence and tried to enjoy the young man's company as we jigged around the floor.

Dante excused himself from the adoring young woman and traversed the floor to my side, and this time he cut in saying affably, "Sorry, do you mind if I have my date back?"

The young man nodded agreeably and sat down as a slow ballad began and Dante took me firmly in his arms and hugged me to him. My breath seemed crushed out of my body and I didn't know how to react. I looked up at him and saw his eyes burning into mine with a look that I had not seen before. I quickly averted my gaze and excused myself mumbling something about needing to return home to study. "Sorry, Dante. It's late and I still have an essay to write."

"I'll take you home."

"No, It's fine. Stay here and enjoy the rest of the party. I'll see you tomorrow."

I thought I detected a flicker of hurt in his eyes but it vanished and he relinquished his hold on me, "Okay, Union. Catch you later." His tone was slightly abrupt and I fled to the cloakroom to retrieve my borrowed cape and left the building to look for a cab.

I eventually found one and remonstrated with myself for leaving so abruptly and with such a lame excuse. Dante probably thought that I had no interest in him and I wondered how it would affect our friendship.

I needn't have worried. The following day it was as if the evening had never happened. Dante and I were back on track as friends and nothing more, but a part of me wished that I had taken the risk and explored what our relationship would have had to offer, but now it was too late. So, I buried my feelings and misgivings in a light-hearted show of banter and frivolity. It was the best way for me to deal with it. I was clearly mistaken in what I thought I had seen reflected in Dante's eyes.

One afternoon, about three months later, we were studying together in the library and Dante was trying to convince me to do an internship. "You need to do an internship, Union. It will make such a difference to your CV. Look, I know you haven't met my dad, seen him a couple of times, albeit briefly. I just know he'll be happy to interview you. Go on. Please let me speak to him. It will be fun. We could work together."

His father, Troy Burgham, as I already knew, ran his own law firm and Dante was going to work there once he'd completed all his exams. However, I didn't want to take advantage of Dante's kindness and said as much, "I don't expect any special favours, Dante. You can't pull strings just because we're friends. It's not right."

Impulsively he took my hand and looked deep into my eyes, which totally unnerved me. "I know that. Believe me, you'll be a great asset to him. And I'm not saying that because you are my friend."

"I just…" I found myself floundering. His intensity disturbed me and stirred up all my feelings from the night of the dinner dance. Fleetingly I saw something reflected in his eyes to be replaced by a fierce look of determination.

"No arguing. I'll talk to my dad. It'll be great, you'll see… we'll be a team."

Dante's upbeat manner and enthusiasm was infectious and I found myself burying my misgivings and the feelings, which stirred inside me and I grinned back.

"Okay, but only if you're sure?"

"Of course, I'm sure. Is there a 'd' in the name of every weekday?"

I laughed in response. "What do I have to do?"

"You will have to listen to me and obey my every whim, Union. Are you okay with that?"

We were soon giggling like schoolchildren, talking too loudly and making plans. The Librarian looked up at the unaccustomed noise and frowned warningly at me. Then

Dante said something I found particularly funny and I burst into laughter again. Soon, the prim librarian was on her way over to us to tell us off for making too much noise. Dante picked up his books, grabbed my hand and we fled. I tried not to notice the tingle that raced up my arm. I shook the feeling off. We were friends, no more, and I wasn't going to ruin that.

We hurried out of the library and sat on the steps outside laughing. Dante announced, "No time like the present." He flipped open his phone and rang his father. "Hi, Troy Burgham, please…. Dad? Yes, it's me… Remember what we discussed at supper last night? Yes… about the internship on offer… I have the perfect candidate. Yes, she's in my class and way above me in marks…" To hear what he said about me made me blush. He gave a positively glowing report on my personality, my academic record and results. Finally, he glanced across at me and winked, "Sure, Dad. I'll tell her. She'll be rapt." He flipped his cell shut. "Done!"

"What? Tell me…"

"You have an interview, Thursday at four. Take your portfolio, dress professionally and just be yourself. You will make a great impression. He's going to love you. Wait and see."

"Yikes! That just gives me two days to prepare."

"Relax. You'll be great."

"I need to go shopping. First impressions count, right?"

Dante laughed, "You go, girl. I'll catch you later at the track."

I fled. I needed to buy something smart and never having had a mother or strong female influence in my life. I wasn't confident that I could pull it off.

I didn't have any close female friends and had never spent girly time with anyone. Looking back I had nearly always had male friends, Abir, Chitto, and Dante. Although, there was Tayanita until her family moved to Florida. I could have done with someone to accompany me, but told myself I had just better get on with it and there was no time like the present.

I jumped up and left my books with Dante and headed for

the mall, alone. The place was overwhelming, so many stores, so many styles. The choices were varied and amazing but I was no nearer making a decision after trundling around two major stores when I headed into JC Penney and made for the women's department. I looked at a rail of smart classic suits and picked up one with simple revere lapels in a muddy green and held it against me in the mirror.

An assistant crossed to me and studied my reflection critically in the mirror. "Interview?" I nodded. "If you don't mind me saying, the colour doesn't do you justice and green is unlucky. Try this." She selected a blue-black skirt suit. "You look like a six to eight. Take both." She pulled out two sizes and handed them to me. "Team it with a red shirt, shoes and purse and you'll look the part." She looked at my hair, "You have glorious hair. You should get it cut and styled. Oh, still keep it long but just give it some shape. You will be able to put it up for work and wear it loose, long and casually when you go out."

"Thanks," I peered at her name lapel, "Roxy. You've been a great help."

"Tell you what, the changing rooms are over there. I'll source a shirt and bring it through."

I had to smile to myself. It seemed that the 'magic' if that's what you could call it worked whenever I needed it.

Roxy went out of her way to help me and by the time she had finished I had a changing room full of discarded items but an outfit that was perfect. I knew where I would come next time I needed something special. I had one thing left to do and that was have my hair styled. I was going to take Roxy's advice and do just as she had said. "Roxy? Can you suggest anywhere, for my hair? I'm just sort of used to trimming the ends myself."

"Sure. There's a great salon here in the mall. Called 'A Cut Above'. Ask for Hayley. She's a star she'll do your hair and entertain you at the same time. In fact you can't mistake her. She's one of a kind."

"What do you mean?"

"You'll find out. Trust me. In fact I'll give her a ring for you." Roxy led me to the information board outside the shop,

"See. You are here. And there's the salon. Okay?"

"Thanks, Roxy. You have really helped me."

"My pleasure. I really enjoyed it. Don't forget to stop by next time you're this way. We must do it again. It was fun." She smiled as I walked away and gave me a quick wave when I turned back to look before she retreated back inside the store to her department.

Somehow I got the impression that she had never helped anyone like this before and I somehow knew she would do it again for someone else. I hurried on through the mall and found the way to 'A Cut Above' and went in.

A Receptionist sat on the desk filing her nails, looking bored and chewing gum. She perked up as I entered, "Hello, welcome to 'A Cut Above'. Do you have an appointment?"

"Sorry, no. Do I need one?"

"You're okay, we take walk-ins, too, when we're not busy. You the lady Roxy rang about?"

"Roxy? From JC Penney's?"

The Receptionist nodded, "That's the one. She rang and said she was sending someone to us."

"Yes, well, she did recommend you."

"Take a seat. Hayley will be with you in a moment. There are some magazines over there." She indicated a rack overflowing with fashion mags.

I grabbed one, sat down, and mindlessly flicked through the pages. I looked around at the up market salon with stylists busy with their clientele. I spotted Hayley straight away with her flowing blonde hair cascading in ringlets around her face. She was incredibly pretty with a terrific smile and infectious laugh. She spotted me staring and grinned, "Won't be long. I'll be with you shortly." She continued to chat to the young woman whose hair she was trimming. When she had finished she took a mirror to show her client the back of her head. The woman nodded appreciatively. She went to the desk to pay and returned with a big tip for Hayley and gave her a hug.

"Thank you so much. You really have helped me. Thanks." With that she left the shop.

Hayley turned to me and smiled again, "Come and sit here. Now what would you like done?"

I sat in the stylist chair, "I'm not sure. I want to keep the length but maybe have it styled so I can wear it up or down and for it to look more professional instead of just a shower around my shoulders."

"That's easy. You have lovely hair. I will take some of the weight out of it and shape it so it frames your face at the front. In fact, I think I'll dry cut and then wash and blow-dry it for you. Is that okay?"

"Sounds good to me."

She began to trim my hair; "You've had a very eventful life for one so young. Hmm, let me see. I can see the card of Strength above your head together with the Queen of Wands. You are a woman of exceptional powers. I can see that both your mother and father are dead. You were brought up by your... grandfather... a most unusual upbringing, if I am correct."

I gasped in astonishment, "How do you..."

"How do I know? I know a lot of things. I also know you will face many challenges and tragedy. But, there is a young man. He is not to be trifled with... he is a good friend and the best relationships are formed through initial friendship. His name begins with... D yes, definitely D."

I was aghast, "You're talking about my best friend."

"But he wants more than that... and so do you. You both need to admit it."

I was stunned and couldn't speak.

Hayley pursed her lips, "I'm picking up a wonderful female energy around you. It has to be your mother. You never knew her, did you?"

I was now quite choked with emotion but I managed to whisper, "No."

"You will. She will visit you in your dreams and I believe you will have a very meaningful encounter... She loves you very much. I get the initial, L... Lou... Louise... no ... Lulu... Louella."

I was staggered that she seemed to know so much about me.

She went on, "You have the gift. It's not fully developed yet, but you will soon hear, see and know many things. I promise you. Trust your gut instincts. They won't betray you. Inevitably, you'll be right. You... You have many other gifts in your arsenal of spirituality. Some are quite unique." She began to laugh, "It's going to be so useful in court. I see you working for the law, no... with the law... in court. You are going to be a very high profile lady, believe me.... Tell me, who is... she frowned as she tried to pronounce a name... Urt? Ut... something Ken...I'm not sure... this is like nothing I have experienced before. Be careful especially when travelling on a train." Then she stopped; "That's enough of that. Let's chat about something more pleasant. You're having your hair done for a special occasion. Tell me all about it."

We spent the next few minutes discussing my upcoming interview. She was such a positive lady, encased in and giving out a bubble of light and love. I couldn't help but like her and warm to her. I could see exactly what Roxy had meant.

When she finally finished doing my hair I was feeling brightly optimistic and my hair looked better than it ever had. She gave me her card, "If ever you want an in depth reading, give me a call." I thanked her, paid her and gave her a tip. "Don't worry, you'll sail through your interview, you'll see."

I felt really good as I left the salon and determined that I would see her again and I would recommend her to all my friends, this woman had a very special talent. She had lifted my spirits and replenished hope in my heart.

Thursday swiftly approached and I found my way through the city to Troy Burgham's Law Office. It was a busy practice but I made up my mind not to get phased by all the smart suited lawyers and paralegals. I noticed that the majority were men. There were female secretaries and one female paralegal. I prayed it wasn't an omen. And yet Hayley had predicted all would go well but I was still nervous. I waited sedately, or so I hoped, and bang on the dot of four Troy's secretary ushered me in, "Mr. Burgham will see you now."

"Ah yes, Sanjukta, Dante's friend." We shook hands. "Do sit down. Do you have your CV and college reports?"

I passed him my portfolio and he placed it on one side. He asked me about myself, my schooling and upbringing and what I liked to do outside of my studies.

I felt more relaxed now we were in ordinary conversation, which he obviously did to make me feel at ease, and I continued to answer his queries politely. I didn't want to appear gushing or over confident.

The interview progressed well. He paused for a while as he studied my file and then asked some searching questions to test my knowledge of the Law. I managed to come through that unscathed and after half an hour he shuffled a sheaf of papers before rising and facing me across his desk and offering me his hand, again. I stood uncertainly unsure what to expect and shook Mr. Burgham's hand.

"Dante has good judgement. I have heard many good things about you, Sanjukta, right from the start and not just from Dante. I have spoken to some of your college professors who are equally supportive and enthusiastic about your capabilities and potential."

I smiled and nodded shyly, "Thank you."

"I'm pleased to have you as an intern. We need a good woman in the practice."

I was ecstatic. I could hardly contain my joy and fought to remain composed. "Thanks, Mr. Burgham. You won't regret it. I promise."

He nodded and smiled. I turned to leave when the intercom buzzed and interrupted us. His secretary's voice reverberated around the office.

"Mr. Burgham. The D.A.'s on the line. He wants to run through the evidence on Cornelius Phipps."

The mention of that name stopped me in my tracks. Max Phipps had stolen land and coerced my people to sell what was rightfully theirs and I believed caused the death of my mother. Land Shift's boss' death had been more than welcome, as the threats had then subsided, but I had heard recently from Onacoma that Max Phipps' son, was following in his father's footsteps and making trouble for the remaining residents. It was just too much of a coincidence that I should hear this name, now. I hesitated to leave and Dante's father noticed this. He spoke quickly to his secretary.

"Give me five. Tell him I'll call him back." He studied my expression, "Was there something else?"

I had to speak, "I'm not sure. Is this Cornelius Phipps related to Max Phipps the director of Land Shift?"

"Why, yes. Max died a few years ago and his son Cornelius took over the business." He paused, and scrutinised my face once more. I couldn't help but show my distaste at the family name of Phipps. "Come," he beckoned me across, "Sit down, Sanjukta. Tell me what you know."

So, I talked. I explained all that I knew of Land Shift's shady dealings and Mr. Burgham made notes.

"So it seems, to coin a phrase, like father like son. Phipps junior has been making life difficult in the suburbs and slums. Forcing people out of their homes and not maintaining the properties."

"A slum landlord?"

"More than that. He's a rogue landlord of the worst kind. He seeks out run down tenement buildings and buys apartments in there for a song and forces the residents, who refuse to sell, out by any means possible. He is not averse to using underhand means to get people out and then sells the entire property to a major development company and earns himself a small fortune."

"Like his father did with much of our land to get at the oil?"

"From all you've told me, yes. We have an ongoing case with the residents in one tenement that has seen everyone leave except for three families. An old granny, Mrs. Ableman, who is set in her ways and doesn't want to move; a young family, the Whitlocks, who haven't found anywhere else within their budget, yet; and an elderly man by the name of Curzon, who is standing his ground. He's a stubborn man, old school, and won't be worn down by bullies."

Feeling emboldened by what I had learned I asked, "My sort of man! ... Where is the tenement in question?"

"Now, Sanjukta, don't go doing anything stupid."

"I just want to see for myself. I have a history with this family. Please."

"Downtown below Freemont Street, the block that crosses West on Ninety-eighth Street. Melrose Court." Mr. Burgham looked genuinely surprised, "I don't know why I told you that." His mouth clamped shut as if he determined to say no more.

"Thanks."

He suddenly reasserted and composed himself, "I'll see you Monday at nine o'clock sharp."

Just then a starling flew onto the window ledge and pecked at the glass almost as some sort of confirmation of the crazy thoughts I was thinking. It was either that or it was nature taking a hand to warn me of some impending tragedy. I had to say my goodbyes.

I smiled and left. I don't know why but I had an idea; an idea that would seriously test me; and I seemed to have a hunch. What was it that Hayley had said? I had a gift and I should trust my instincts. I suspected that Max Phipp's old henchmen, Steadman and Mason who were in their late fifties and early sixties by now were probably involved and up to no good. I didn't know how right I was. It seemed my ancestors really had blessed me with more than one gift.

Across town right at the time I was travelling to the run down building the two bullyboys were in a leaking cellar tinkering with an old worn out boiler. I don't know where the thought had come from, but I wasn't going to ignore it and I knew I had to get there quickly to avert a tragedy. Hayley seemed to have unlocked something in me and just as she had predicted I heard their voices in my head..

"That should do it."

"How many left to sell?"

"Three apartments. The old granny, Ableman, she'll die of the cold. The Whitlocks, I think there are six of them, a young family who haven't found anywhere else yet and that stubborn old mule, Curzon. We'll wear him down."

"So, it's set to blow in…"

"...Thirty minutes. There won't be nothing left of this baby. No hot water, no heat... nothing."

This experience was something new to me, but their self-congratulatory tones made my flesh crawl. I could almost see them patting each other on the back. I had to hurry. It was getting dark.

By the time I had left the underground. More voices were crowding in my head. I could only assume they belonged to the tenants in the building. It was my feeling they were having some sort of meeting.

I heard an elderly lady's voice...

"Well, I ain't shifting. He can do his damnedest."

The crackling tones of an old man joined her, "I'm with you. He can't force us out, just because he wants to sell to some developer at an extortionate price. We've got rights."

I guessed it was Granny Ableman and Mr. Curzon, I could hear. I hurried on down the dusty city street studying the names and numbers on the apartment blocks. The voices were getting louder now.

A young man spoke, "We got no place to go, Joe. We have to stay no matter what."

A young woman began crying and I could feel her desperation and fear. I knew I was getting closer.

Suddenly, there was an almighty explosion, which rocked a building up ahead. Smoke poured from the basement of an apartment block where a crowd was quickly gathering. I heard a young child cry.

"Where's Brad?"

"I... I don't know."

"He said he'd be up after his homework was done."

"Oh, no. What if...?"

That's when I started to sprint to the scene. It was difficult in my new red high-heeled shoes so I pulled them off and raced to the block.

"Call 9-1-1," I shouted before dashing inside Melrose Court. I pulled my scarf up around my face and ran through the choking smoke billowing up from the basement. I reached the stairs and discovered a small boy about ten years of age unconscious in the stairwell. He was covered in debris from the blast. I cleared as much of the mess from him as possible and tried to make him comfortable, taking off my jacket and placing it under his head.

Footsteps clattered down the stairway as a family arrived on the scene. I later learned that their name was Whitlock. The mother of the boy, Jan, put her hand to her mouth in horror, "Brad!" She then turned and stared angrily at me, "Who are you? Leave him alone."

I wanted to reassure them, "Please, don't worry. I want to help. I am a friend."

As I spoke a chorus of voices were heard behind me where the crowd from the street had followed me inside. "We all are!"

I became choked up with emotion as these people, all strangers, began to shake hands with me, and with each other, and introduced themselves. We stayed in the cramped stairwell and foyer. It was amazing. Everyone was murmuring in agreement, "Something needs to be done."

I opened my purse and removed a small phial of peppermint oil that I always carried with me, and I gently dabbed some on the boy's temples and to my relief he began to stir.

A portly man of about fifty stepped forward, "I'll check the basement." He ran carefully down the stairs followed by a younger man who had got a fire extinguisher.

A middle-aged woman with her hair tied back in a bun crouched on the stairs beside me, "I'm a nurse. Let me help." She knelt down and began to examine Brad.

Yet another bystander spoke up, as he looked around at the damage, "What a mess. We'll get it back into shape though."

There was a consensus of agreement. People busied themselves by getting various tools and brushes as they started to clear away the mess.

The tubby man returned from the basement, "The boiler blew. Looks like sabotage. I'm an electrician… I'll do what I can."

The younger man with him set down the fire extinguisher and announced, "I'm a plumber."

"We can fix this. I'll get my kit," said the electrician.

"Hey, I know where we can get a scrap boiler," replied the plumber.

They both left as the approaching sirens could be heard drawing closer. I stood up and replaced my shoes as the police and paramedics forced their way through the crowds. My eyes filled with tears. I knew these people were sincere and I slipped away smiling in understanding at the power of the unity of these people against their oppressors. I knew that when I returned, and I would return, there would be a difference.

I turned up a number of days later and walked toward the tenement building when to my surprise I saw Cornelius Phipps, standing outside the apartment block nibbling his nails. I recognised him from his photograph on file and stories I had seen in the press. I dawdled past the building to see that the frontage had been freshly painted and I sneaked a quick peek inside the hall. Above the door was a new sign, which read: 'Welcome'. Not wishing to attract attention to myself I walked on by and heard Cornelius swearing under his breath, "What the…"

I crossed to the other side of the road, stood in a doorway and observed. Cornelius took out his cell phone and dialled a number. He paced while waiting for an answer and angrily growled into the receiver, "I thought you'd fixed this… It's not all right… The damn place has had a makeover…"

His words, with his voice raised carried to me on the breeze and I fought to stifle a chuckle before making my way back to the Metro. In the words of the Nina Simone song I was feeling good.

Chapter Six

Being kept up to date

I arrived back at my own apartment and although I should have been whacked, I felt energised and I just couldn't settle. The phone rang. I answered quickly expecting Dante to be on the end of the line. To my surprise it was Inola.

"Sanjukta, Union, I thought you needed to know we have a meeting; an important meeting coming up. Your father will be in the chair…"

"Yes?" I was puzzled, "What's going on?"

"Land Shift are up to their old tricks. I know you are busy and this is all last minute. It has been arranged in rather a hurry…" He paused, choosing his words carefully, "It would be wonderful if you could be there, to support us. Onacoma didn't want me to bother you but I know it would make an enormous difference to him, please."

"When is it?"

"The day after tomorrow. Will you come?"

I didn't need to think, "I'll be there. I'll call when I get a flight."

"I will arrange to have a car waiting for you."

I replaced the receiver and packed a small bag, and phoned the airline. "Hello? Can you tell me the first available flight to Memphis, please?"

The Delta stewardess answered, "Let me check… Both flights today are full… tomorrow I only have stand-by…"

"What about the next day?"

"Ah yes, I have a morning flight gets you into Memphis at ten minutes past twelve midday."

"I'll take it." I finished the booking, paid by card and rang Inola. "Uncle?"

"Union."

"I couldn't get a flight until the day of the meeting. I get into Memphis at twelve ten. It means I'll miss the start."

"That is unimportant, you will be there. I will have a car waiting. It will take you a few hours to get here. The meeting is at the Town Hall."

We talked for a while longer but at least the delay meant I could get up to date with all my studies and I would be there in time to offer my support to Onacoma and learn what new, dastardly tricks Land Shift were employing. It would all be fodder for building a bigger case against Cornelius Phipps.

I called Troy with my schedule and explained why I needed time off and cleared my absence with the firm. "So you see. I need to be there for my grandfather and I hope I will gather some more evidence against Land Shift and Cornelius Phipps."

"I understand. Have a safe trip and I'll see you when you get back next week. I'll pass you across to Dante," said Troy.

I was surprised, I didn't realise that Dante was in Troy's office.

"Union. Hurry back and keep safe. I'll be thinking of you," said Dante and I wasn't sure if I imagined it but there was an undertone of something in his voice. I hoped I interpreted it correctly and said, "Me, too. I'll look forward to seeing you soon."

I ended the call and gathered my notes on Land Shift to take with me. I could study them on the flight. But now, right now I needed to think and centre myself. A meditation was in order.

I selected some gentle pipe music and Indian chants, which accompanied nature sounds of waterfalls, birds and the gentle wind. I lit some incense, sat cross-legged surrounded by candles and crystals and drifted away to another world.

I was at the top of a great mountain with my friend the wolf at my side and I surveyed the wonderful valley before me, and the green lush vegetation that stretched before me. I felt utterly at peace. I was in a mystical place and could hear someone calling me and my name... 'Union... Union'. Suddenly I became aware that the sound was not in my meditative state but for real and someone was knocking the door and calling my name.

"Just a minute." I roused myself to full consciousness and

although I had been interrupted I felt refreshed, tranquil and at peace. I peeped through the spy hole and saw Dante outside my door. I felt a rush of heat as my face coloured up with embarrassment.

I opened the door to admit him, "Dante?"

He came in and stopped as he saw the candles and heard the music, "Sorry, I didn't realise. I didn't mean to disturb you."

"It's okay." I said shyly. "I just needed to calm myself before the trip."

"This all looks a little crazy. Perhaps sometime you will tell me all about it and how this meditation stuff works."

I picked up my files and shoved them in my briefcase. I was feeling self-conscious. Dante caught my hand, and with his free hand he tilted my chin to look directly into his eyes, "I just wanted to say to you that…"

My doorbell rang and I escaped from his soul searching gaze and opened the door. It was someone from the maintenance section of the building, "Sorry, Miss. Just warning everyone that the power will be off tomorrow for four hours between eleven and three."

"Oh?"

"We're working on the electrics. There's a fault in the heating and we are overhauling the circuits on the premises. We hope we won't have to disturb you but we may need to check your apartment during the course of the work. It's just a preliminary warning."

"Thank you," I muttered.

"Would it be all right if I came in and just checked your fuse box?"

"Please." I opened the door wider and stepped to one side to admit him. He was carrying a bag of tools.

He knew exactly where to go and fiddled around with the box over my airing cupboard. Dante shuffled impatiently but the mood between us was broken and the undercurrent of feeling that trembled through us was dissipated and lost.

We stood by and watched while the electrician checked the wiring and fuses. He turned to us, "Seems like all is well. Just be aware that it will all be off tomorrow."

The man turned to go and I spoke up. "Sorry, Dante. I have a few things to do before my trip. I'll call you when I get back.

I don't know if it was my imagination or not but Dante looked disappointed. This was something I couldn't deal with right now no matter how much I wanted it. Dante left with the workman and I leaned against the door with a sigh of relief, I put the chain on and retreated to my bedroom.

I flopped on the bed and stared at the ceiling. What was going on with me? Why were my emotions playing games with my heart? I had to focus and I had to concentrate on what I needed to do and put all thoughts of romance out of my head.

The wait at the airport was tedious as was getting through security. Fortunately, the plane was on time and I sent a text to Inola to confirm this. The flight was uneventful and four hours passed relatively quickly; I didn't have anyone sitting next to me and so the boredom was alleviated by reading a historical novel, "Against the Tide" and I became immersed in eighteenth century Britain in Swansea, Wales in a cutthroat world of riding officers, smugglers, romance and swashbuckling daring do.

True to his word, Inola had arranged for someone to meet me. We travelled the two hundred and fifty miles from Memphis and chatted inconsequentially about the situation at home until we reached the dusty road that ran through the town to City Hall where the meeting was in progress and drawing to a close. My grandfather, Chief Onacoma sighed sadly as his eyes roved the room filled with fellow Indians, interested town folk and representatives from Land Shift including the thugs, Steadman and Mason. I slipped silently into the back of the hall and listened.

"It has been a hard and bitter battle for all of us. I understand why so many have been forced to succumb and sell their hard earned land." Onacoma paused and scanned the faces before him. Everyone remained silent and still. There was no shuffling of feet or coughing such was the seriousness of the topic.

"Land Shift has threatened and forcibly bought over half the land we worked so hard to buy as a collective many years ago. They lie in wait patiently waiting for the final share to come their way, but they will not succeed. Even in the event of my death my land will pass to Sanjukta and she knows never to betray the will of the Great Spirit and our ancestors."

I was glad I was there to hear these words and acknowledged my grandfather with a smile. His face lit up when he finally spied me at the back of the room.

The bulk of the audience applauded emotionally and Onacoma nodded sagely. "I will consult with the Great Spirit as our ancestors did before us. Then I will know the right path to take."

There was a hubbub of noise as people commented on Onacoma's address and the Land Shift men scraped back their chairs and left.

Onacoma stepped down and he was immediately congratulated by many. He politely excused himself and made his way toward me. "Sanjukta! I am glad you came."

We embraced and my grandfather held on tightly to me. The warmth of the exchange made me swallow hard and I could feel Onacoma's love envelop me.

When he finally released me I managed to whisper, "I have a few days. Inola told me the meeting was important."

"Ah, Sanjukta, my Union, you have no idea what this means to me… that you took the trouble to come. I have been preparing with fasting and I will go to the Sweat Lodge and commune with the spirits of our ancestors. Cherokee law dictates that only men can take part in this ritual but now that you are here. I will ask permission from the elders that this rule may be broken just this once. Come."

I understood that this was a huge honour that was being attempted to bestow on me and I was anxious for the permissions to be given, but I was uncertain whether it would be granted or not. I followed him hurriedly out of the hall where he was stopped a few times by people with questions or giving him words of encouragement.

We eventually got outside and walked to Onacoma's Station Wagon. I placed my bags in the back and sat in the front passenger seat. "You look tired. You sleep. I will wake you when we reach Cherokee." I didn't argue. I was exhausted and rejoiced in the thought of closing my eyes and resting awhile.

Onacoma started the car and drove it was a two-hour journey through the hauntingly beautiful Smokey Mountains and into Cherokee. We passed the Museum of the Cherokee Indian and the huge totem that stood outside. He drove up the hill to the Oconaluftee Indian Village, mainly a tourist attraction now but it is where he would find the elders and Chief Degataga, a kindred spirit as his name meant 'he who brings people together', my male equivalent and he was a relative of Onacoma.

We walked through the village to a decorated tepee set back against the cliff and entered. The elders sat in a circle and he was invited to sit in the sacred circle. I was expected to sit outside of them by the exiting tent flap.

"Onacoma." The old chief cordially greeted my grandfather.

"Degataga," my grandfather respectfully responded.

Communal words travelled around the circle, at least that is how I would describe it. He was asked to share in smoking the peace pipe, which all of the participating elders joined in. One younger man pounded out a rhythmical beat on a small drum as the ceremonial pipe was passed around. I watched silently. It was not my place as a woman to speak at such occasions.

Once the initial traditional greetings were over Degataga asked,

"Onacoma, my brother, why do you come to us? What is your wish?"

Onacoma took a deep breath and announced, "I am here today to seek wisdom from my brothers in spirit and to ask the permission of the elders for Sanjukta to accompany me to my Sweat Lodge."

There was a slight murmur of disapproval from the wise men seated there. I could see that this was not going to be easy.

Degataga heard the dissension in the group and spoke,

"This privilege is for the male members of our tribe and the male line of any Indian tribe, and only for men."

Onacoma grunted in acknowledgement and prepared to press his argument, "This is a special case. You are all aware that Sanjukta has defied the tradition of our forefathers and already trained as a warrior. She became the best, beating all men in her field."

"Word of this did reach us. We know of her exceptional abilities."

"She has also been blessed with special powers from The Great White Spirit," continued Onacoma. I felt the colour flush to my cheeks.

"This is true but we cannot overturn tradition for one person, or how do we answer to other women if they request the same?" said Degataga.

"You forget, I would have initiated my son Ridge into our sacred tradition but that right was cruelly taken from me. Sanjukta is my child and heritage now. I have no other son and no other child. I beg that she be allowed this rite of enlightenment as she is as good as any man and deserves the right to be allowed to experience this. It is necessary as a final bonding between parent and child as decreed by our ancestors. It will consolidate all she has learned."

"You ask too much, Onacoma." Degataga paused, "We cannot continue this discussion with Sanjukta present. She must leave." Degataga was firm, stern and insistent.

Onacoma nodded to me, "Sanjukta, go. Take the car and return for me in one hour."

I didn't argue but I rose feeling a mixture of apprehension and annoyance. I was sorry that my Indian upbringing and its subsequent prejudices clashed so violently with the liberal views of the modern world where women were deemed to be the equals of men, and yet here within my family the old hierarchy and customs still prevailed.

However, I swallowed my words. I nodded politely and left. I took the car and travelled back to Cherokee and entered the museum. In the entrance foyer I was greeted by a hologram of a Cherokee Chief in full regalia, by a bright fire, chanting a welcome in our ancient language, which he followed with an English translation and I began to make my way around this impressive place.

I became lost in time as I relived childhood stories passed down through the generations but it was when I came to the section on our great past and the horrific tragedy, which befell us now known as 'The Trail of Tears' that I became incredibly emotional. It was bizarre. I was choked up and tears streamed down my face, so much so that one of the attendants approached me to ask if I was okay. I had to sit and tried to compose myself.

We talked a while and when he heard my name he insisted on taking me to the gift shop and gave me a miniature medicine bag pouch to wear around my neck and a runic talisman.

"Please let me pay for these."

He shook his head, "No, this is my gift to you. I have heard of you. You are fighting for our people in the city and your fame has spread. I also feel you will be facing grave dangers and these will help to protect you. Take them with my blessing."

I thanked him and glanced at my watch and saw the time had fast disappeared. I needed to get back to Onacoma. I said my goodbyes and motored back to the village to discover my fate. Had Onacoma been successful or not?

I parked the car and began to walk through the village toward the tepee, where I saw Onacoma emerge and he strode toward me. I couldn't read his expression and he said nothing when he greeted me, "Sanjukta, let us return. We have much to do."

"Well?" I asked in frustration.

"I will tell all on the way," and he smiled inscrutably.

Apparently, it was a long and gruelling argument. The elders felt that the experience was a totally male domain but with clever arguments from Onacoma the decision eventually swung in his favour.

I must admit, I did wonder about this and why Onacoma was so determined that I should experience this magical ritual that I had heard led to hallucinations. I thought fractionally that maybe he went against the elders for reasons of his own but I was not certain, and then again with my special gift they could well have voted in my favour. I felt that I would never be told the full story and I did wonder if my extraordinary power had somehow managed to unite the elders in their decision.

As we journeyed home I felt a strange exciting feeling of bubbling expectation. I was embarking into unknown territory.

We set off with the light of the moon to guide us. It was full and bright shining its magical, ethereal light, which bathed the land in its ghostly sheen. The moon had risen to its full height. There was partial cloud cover and the wolves in the hills howled their particular lament at the blessed light.

We climbed steadily without words. I had scaled these hills many times before and felt very at home on this terrain. We were aiming for a sacred spot where a canvas tepee sat at the mouth of a cave that went deep into the hillside. The signs of the protection to this hallowed site littered our path. Posts with ribbons and masks punctuated the path and outside the tent a group of bones lay in a holy symbol, as an amulet of protection, next to the laced entrance to the tepee.

Onacoma entered reverently and I followed. I gazed around the Sweat Lodge and marvelled at the paintings daubed on the inside of the tent. Animal skins adhered to the canvas walls and lay on the floor. I spotted the rattles of snakes, and horns belonging to the great buffalo.

He set out a flask of liquid and drank from it before passing it to me. It was milky in texture and colour with a bitter taste that sent my head spinning. We both took another draught and he set the container at my feet. No words were spoken. I somehow knew we would not need words.

The Chief laid a fire and lit it and the smoke spiralled up and out through the opening at the top of the tepee. I watched as my grandfather dressed in his regimental traditional Indian robes, his full-feathered headdress and daubed his face with paint. He took his medicine pouch and laid out various magical accoutrements and shook a powder onto the fire.

Flames leapt and danced into the air and sparks flew up and out into the night sky. He began to chant.

I sat still and meditated to the mystical music of rhythm and percussion. As Onacoma sang he beat on a drum and shook a rattle. It was mesmerising. Time passed and my grandfather continued stoically calling on the spirits to reveal to him the path to take and what he needed to know. By now the moon had risen higher in the night sky casting its silvery shimmering glow onto the mountains and us. I don't know how many hours had passed.

Onacoma fell silent and appeared to drift into another consciousness. I watched. The moonlight filtered through the laced entrance to the tent and played on his face, concentrated in meditation. It was becoming unbearably hot inside and I loosened my buckskin jacket and tied up my hair.

A lone owl hooted eerily in the night as if prophesying some melancholic revelation. The sound of the bird ripped through my soul. My senses were dramatically heightened and I was acutely aware of everything around me. I could even 'feel' the air. Textures, tastes, sounds and aromas tantalised me further. I swear as I touched my jacket it felt real and alive. I knew this had to be something to do with the potion I had drunk.

I studied Onacoma's weather browned face. His skin was like tanned leather with his strength of character etched in every line. His long grey hair fell loosely onto his shoulders no longer scraped back into his usual practical ponytail.

At the second owl hoot his eyes blinked open. His pupils had grown large. He focused on the flaming fire and pointed with his talking stick and I was compelled to do the same. I felt feverishly hot and nauseous. Whatever I had drunk in combination with the heat of the fire had caused an acceleration of all my senses.

He tossed on another bunch of kindling and a bundle of white sage. The air became laced with an aromatic infusion that was uplifting and cleansing. The scent was wondrous. I was indescribably drawn to the fire and like my grandfather I studied the flames, which had begun to change and I was amazed to see pictures form in the sticks and wood as they burned.

I watched in fascination as I viewed a buffalo herd thundering along a grassy plain chased by several Indians who raised their hunting bows and arrows and whooped like coyotes in the night. One of the powerful, impressive beasts was singled out from the herd. It had a pronounced limp and was dragging its leg. The hunters homed in for the kill. Its huge majesty tumbled and fell to the earth in a cloud of dust as it bellowed in its death throes.

One Indian in his sixties, Waya Adisi, Running Wolf, staked his claim to the beast and jubilantly waved his bow in the air in triumph. At this action, Onacoma sighed with a mixture of sadness and elation. I was riveted to the unfolding pictures and the chief's words. Although, whether he spoke them or whether I heard them in my mind I could not testify.

"Father!" The word was loud and clear in my mind. This was his father.

The flames flickered and the picture was lost to be replaced by another. Waya Adisi stood wearing the buffalo head and fur and on one side of him was the chief's dead son, Ridge and on the other was my mother, Louella. They looked happy and at peace. No one had to tell me. I somehow knew that this was my departed mother and Onacoma's murdered son. Something important was to be revealed to us.

I felt the wetness of salt tears as they streamed down my cheeks. I gazed on my mother's lovely face and could see many similarities between her and me; the shape of her eyes, the fullness of her lips and the way she held her head. And overwhelmingly I felt, no… knew they were truly contented.

Waya Adisi stepped out from the flames and like the hologram from the museum I had seen earlier or from a scientific experiment he began to talk to Onacoma.

"My son, you make me and the Great Spirit proud. But I am here because you must know the full truth of Sanjukta's birth."

I leaned forward closely not wanting to miss a single word. I watched as Ridge and Louella walked forward and took each other's hands. They gazed deeply into each other's eyes, as Onacoma and I looked on, amazed.

"True love beat in two hearts. Prejudice drove that love underground. Prejudice from our race of which I am not proud, and prejudice from the white man. But, their love was so strong they defied tradition and culture and bonded together. From that joining came a seed… Sanjukta, Union."

Onacoma whispered in awe, "She's my real granddaughter?"

"Your granddaughter, your flesh and blood and the future of our people. Watch carefully and I will reveal secrets for your eyes alone."

The flames danced and roared. I saw myself as a Cherokee bride in soft, white fringed buckskin, wearing multi-coloured woven beads giving my hand to a man in warrior robes. But I could not see his face. He had his back to us. The smoke obscured my view and the images flickered in the firelight like an old movie. Whether Onacoma, or my biological grandfather, as I now knew him to be, had seen his identity I was not to know, but I didn't think he had. I felt it showed that I had a future and a future, which included the Cherokee nation.

The aroma from the sage was filling my lungs and I was beginning to feel heady and faint. I peered through the lacing of the tent to grab a lungful of the crisp night air. The moon shone down with its silver beams when a cloud shrouded its countenance and eclipsed its light. A solo wolf howled its lament at the waning brightness. I pulled my head back inside. The glow from the burning fire barely dented the dark inside the tepee. Further visions were revealed in the fire, which made little sense to me. I saw shadows and small people, serpents coiling ready to strike and the shape of some massive creature. Most frightening of all was a pair of red demonic eyes that glowed evilly in the embers of the fire.

My grandfather began his ritualistic chant again and I sat in awe, wondering at all I had seen and felt. Many hours had now passed and the night was not yet over. I knew the dreams that invaded my sleep would be vivid and prophetic. My limbs became heavy and my eyes willed themselves shut and I drifted into a meditative state where enlightenment waited.

Back in the city, unknown to me, the machinations of my people's archenemy, Cornelius Phipps and a demon once banished to the bowels of the earth by the Cherokee nation were about to commune. I will relate what happened as best I can as it was told to me, much later, by Cornelius.

*****

Cornelius stood in a dripping, damp cellar and peered into the gloom of a rank tunnel that stretched ahead for miles. A rumbling groan echoed through the subterranean passage.

Holding a flashlight, Cornelius steeled himself and strode toward the sound. In the distance a huge, horned head cast a malevolent shadow on the rocky walls, which was slimy with moss and dank vegetation. The monster appeared to be half man and half beast and was flanked by serpents writhing at its feet. The monster bellowed. Cornelius stopped and wiped his hand across his sweating brow. He bit his nails and remembered.

Like a film reel, images played back, reflected on the walls of the tunnel with a private and personal picture show engineered by black magic just for him.

His face drained of colour as he thought back to the tragedy that had brought him here. He recalled and saw his wife, the love of his life, Suzanne, as she banged around in the kitchen and shouted at him, slurring her words.

"You don't understand. You have work. I have nothing!"

"Suzanne, please, baby, let's talk rationally about this."

"You're not listening. Baby, indeed!" she screeched. "I've lost my son, my only child."

"Jon was my son, too. We can work this out."

"Can you bring him back?"

Cornelius twisted his face away in pain from the memory. Suzanne picked up a tumbler of whisky from the counter and swigged it back then poured herself another from the almost empty bottle.

"Drinking won't help."

"It numbs me. Then I don't have to think anymore."

Cornelius, in the memory, turned away in misery and exited the kitchen. He slammed the front door.

He heard his car start and drive away. Glued to the stuttering pictures he watched as Suzanne sobbed. She smashed the glass into the sink, cutting her hand, and she grabbed the bottle and guzzled the remainder.

She caught sight of herself in the mirror and saw what she had become. Her hair was unkempt, her eyes puffy and red from weeping and she slumped slowly to the floor with a pitiful wail.

Suddenly, she took a deep breath and attempted to pull herself together.

Cornelius watched in horror, unable to tear his eyes away from the sepia images flickering before him and horribly fascinated by what he saw.

Suzanne scrambled up and placed the now empty bottle on the table. She inhaled even more deeply as if she was sucking all the life and oxygen out of the air. Decisively, she grabbed her keys from the counter top and exited.

Suzanne emerged from the house and ran dizzily weaving her way to the car in the driveway. She wrenched open the door and got in, started the motor and drove off, much too fast. The wheels spun violently sending a shower of stones into the air. The tyres screamed as she left her parking spot.

Suzanne sped down the freeway crying. Her car swerved as she tried to stay in her lane. Other drivers honked their horns as she weaved crazily between them.

Cornelius attempted to avert his eyes from what was unfolding but was unable to do so. He was inexorably drawn to the impending disaster about to happen.

Suzanne turned off the highway onto a smaller, deserted road. She revved up the motor and raced off down a narrow track then deliberately crashed head on into a towering brick wall. The car's engine exploded into flames.

Suzanne lay slumped. The steering wheel impaled her chest. Blood trickled from her temple as the flames spread over the hood toward the rest of the car.

Cornelius choked back a sob but he was condemned to continue watching.

The scene changed to an upscale bar late at night and he saw himself looking worn and desperate trying to drink himself to oblivion. He nibbled agitatedly at his nails. A youngish man approached and spoke to him quietly. Cornelius slammed his fist on the bar in rage and yelled, "I don't care how bad things are. I want my money and I want it now… or you're evicted!"

The man left in abject despair.

The middle-aged bartender wiped glasses at the end of the bar and turned to a customer seated in front of him who had witnessed the episode. He spoke confidentially, shaking his head. "I've never seen such a change in a man. You used to be able to reason with him."

The picture stuttered once more and Cornelius was forced to relive more of his terrible trauma.

The day was grey and miserable, with cloud and sky seamlessly inseparable. The gloomy ceiling allowed no sunlight to permeate through the murk and matched the mood of those gathered at a graveside and a gentle breeze ruffled the branches of the solid yew trees surrounding the church.

The minister completed the final words of the burial service and he nodded forlornly and sympathetically at the lean faced man whose eyes were downcast and whose shoulders continued to droop in despair. The small group moved off as more rain began to fall. They each murmured their commiserations to Cornelius Phipps who remained staring at the newly erected headstone. The rain mingled with his tears that streamed down his face. His drenched fair hair stuck to his face and he flicked his head shaking off droplets of water like a dog.

The minister placed a gentle hand on Cornelius' shoulder before moving off after the bedraggled few who were now walking back down the cemetery path with their umbrellas raised and out to the churchyard's car park.

Thirty-six year old Cornelius was expensively dressed in a black, bespoke suit and highly polished lace-up shoes. He remained still; his eyes fixed on the newly engraved tombstone possible because of the concrete raft he had arranged to have laid.

The engraving read, 'Here lies Private Jonathan A. Phipps aged 18 years, who gave his life that others might be free.' Below this inscription was another, 'Beloved wife and mother Suzanne M. Phipps aged 36 years,' and the respective dates.

His hand found its way to his mouth and he nibbled frantically on one nail.

Two gravediggers waited by the church watching the lone figure standing guard like a sentinel and waited for him to move away so that they could carry on with their job and bury the coffin. They talked quietly and enjoyed a quiet cigarette while they waited.

Cornelius didn't move, even when another funeral party, with heads bowed, processed sedately by, led by the former minister. The group began to enter the impressive sandstone church.

Suddenly, Cornelius lifted his head and his sorrowful face contorted with anger and in a coldly, emphatic tone he swore, "Somehow, some way, I will bring you back." Cornelius raised his arms together with the level of his voice rising he shrieked into the wind that had risen unnaturally and was whirling around the shrubbery and trees, "Utkena! I call on you!"

A deep rumbling roar erupted from the bowels of the earth so violently that the ground around the grave vibrated. The other funeral party stopped and looked in puzzlement at the fractional trembling of the earth and the two gravediggers steadied themselves against the church walls as if they were experiencing a minor earthquake.

Cornelius sucked in a deep breath, steeled his face and strode purposefully away from the grave and out from the cemetery. The vision ended.

Back in the tunnel Cornelius tried to compose himself after being visibly shaken by these vivid memories. Hardened and determined once more he moved on through the passageway and Utkena stepped out from the shadows to face him. "You come again to seek me out, as did your father. Why?"

"I need your help."

Utkena rasped, "Why should I trust you?"

"Because we need each other." Cornelius braved the monster and looked directly into his amber eyes, with their horizontal wedge shaped pupils that glowed with a malevolent, demonic flame.

"Your father tried to bind me to his will. He ended up dead."

"He didn't have my determination," countered Cornelius.

"His heart became stone. Cross me and your death will be worse."

"I'm already dead."

"What do you want?" rasped Utkena.

"The power of the Box of Souls," said Cornelius decisively.

"Your father tried…"

"And failed. I won't fail."

"And in return?"

"I will do your will whenever you call. You will have your revenge on man."

"On all men and the Cherokee Nation," insisted Utkena.

"Then so be it," Cornelius said emphatically. A vein pulsed in his jaw as he raised his hand to his mouth and began to nibble his already badly chewed nails.

Chapter Seven

Reputation

The time had come to leave my grandfather. We said a tearful goodbye at the access gate, but I knew that the bond between us was stronger than ever. Onacoma took me by the shoulders, "Sanjukta, my granddaughter you will bring honour to our nation this I know. You have a testing time ahead of you; this, too, is written in your destiny. Go my child with my blessing."

I embraced my grandfather once more. There was no need for words. Anyway, I was too emotional to speak. The car that had collected me to bring me here was waiting to take me to the airport. I sat in the back and looked out through the back window through the billowing dust and watched, as my grandfather became just a speck in the distance. When I could see him no more I turned back and settled in the seat and stared out of the window and watched the countryside race past. Small townships hurtled by until hours later we hit the edge of the city with its smoke and concrete towers. Traffic was snarled on all sides and I was able to observe the faces of the lost and lonely as they wandered the city streets. Some appeared aimless, defeated and sad while others were purposefully stepping out with pride to their place of work.

I enjoyed watching people, imagining their worlds and it struck me that every person I saw had their own life, family and friends and it was sort of humbling and a confirmation about the huge rise in our population; for each person I saw had connections and their connections had connections and on and on ad infinitum. I sighed. In truth that thought filled me with a kind of melancholia. Maybe it was leaving my grandfather after our experience together, maybe it was because I had an ominous feeling of foreboding about some impending disaster and yet, I was also filled with an optimism for my future. I was filled with so many contradictions but in my heart I was happy to be returning to work.

I caught a late flight and returned to the metropolis. I took a cab back to my apartment, unpacked and settled down for the evening. I wasn't feeling very hungry and made do with some buttered crisp-breads, cheese and salad. I had time to look through the notes I had made on cases pending before bathing and retiring for the night. I caught the late news. There was nothing there to capture my attention.

The following morning I showered and prepared for work. I just managed a slice of toast with some English marmalade and coffee. I called the office ahead of me to let them know I was on my way.

Since my time in the Sweat Lodge I was seeing everything with new eyes and I was eager to work. Subsequently, I was now fortunate enough to be fast gaining a reputation in the courtroom and had second chaired a couple of low profile cases and done well. It seemed the right of justice was on my side and I was able to help select juries that reflected this. Jury selection was becoming my forte and I was brought in to do this for a number of attorneys. My endeavours were gaining press attention and newspaper headlines heralded my success.

Native American Indian lawyer selects winning juries for Troy Burgham's law firm, resulting in major boost for the practice.

I felt fully confident as I sat at my desk in the swish law office of Burgham, Lehman and Frankle. A half full paper coffee cup stood at the side of me as I studied the case file of Cornelius Phipps, Max Phipps, and their company Land Shift. I turned the last page and scan read it before closing it and staring thoughtfully ahead. I had much on my mind. Not least the history of this family and this firm that was inextricably linked with my own heritage. I picked up my coffee. There was a light tap on my door.

My best friend, Dante popped his head in through the door. I even saw him anew. He had grown taller, or so it seemed to me, and with all his physical training and running I was struck by his athletically built frame and delighted in his ever-engaging smile and manner. His hair was smartly cut and a coppery brown; maybe it was before and I just hadn't noticed. I was soon snapped out of my state of idle and pleasant contemplation.

"I've just heard that Cornelius Phipps is opening the Veterans' Bazaar."

I drained my coffee, scrunched the cup and tossed it in the waste paper basket decisively and rose. "Then I'd better go. Coming?"

Dante grinned a perfect smile, "What? And miss the son of the arch villain who swindled your people's land away? I wouldn't miss it."

I grabbed my reporter's pad and pen and stuffed it in my bag, swung it over my shoulder and grabbed my coat.

"Union, you look the epitome of an investigative journalist let alone a lawyer!" grinned Dante.

"I try," I giggled and we left laughing together.

We hailed a cab and soon arrived at the city park. The centre lawn and square by the bandstand and Board of Honour, for those who had fallen in battle, was awash with colour. Gaily-coloured stalls and marquees adorned the grass area with a variety of arts and crafts, charity stalls and food booths. There were scoop and save spice tubs emitting exotic aromas, which pulled people across to them and tantalised them enough to buy; wooden children's toys from yesteryear, hand made clothes and jewellery, freshly made preserves, chutneys and marmalades, cookies and cakes. Charity stands with homemade lemonade, and vendors selling a variety of hot food and drinks were scattered around. Cheese and bread stalls completed the mouth-watering picture and it was all in aid of the excellent cause for service men's families.

Two women stood by with a bucket for donations and sold raffle tickets for goods displayed at the side of the bandstand.

A musical group waited patiently whilst the guest speaker opening the fete delivered the final words of his speech. I stood with Dante and listened with the assembled crowd to Cornelius Phipps who was at the microphone.

"So, I know firsthand what it's like to lose a son in a war. It's not the only time my life has been touched by tragedy." He continued ambiguously, "And although we don't have the means to bring our fallen soldiers back… yet, I hope you will do all you can to support our veterans and spend some money. Dig deep into your pockets; it's all in a very good cause and enjoy the rest of the day. I now declare this bazaar open."

There was an enthusiastic and appreciative burst of applause before people disbanded to visit the assorted stalls to see what was on offer. The bazaar became a flurry of activity as it got going. The band assembled on the stage and started their sound check before bursting into song giving the event a carnival feel. The music did much to lift people's spirits and encourage the visitors to spend money.

Dante indicated Cornelius Phipps who was now engaged in conversation with the Mayor of the city. "Seems squeaky clean now," he observed. "I've been hearing a lot about his charity work while you've been away. He's been in the press and heralded as a real philanthropist."

I remained noncommittally thoughtful, "Yes, but something's not right."

"Are you referring to the sins of the father resting with the son?"

I replied almost perfunctorily, "Something like that. Still, he gave a good speech."

"Yes, should prise the money from their wallets and purses."

I finished scribbling a final note and replaced my reporter's pad and turned quickly crashing into a young man walking past. "I'm sorry." I suddenly gasped in recognition and pleasure, "I don't believe it! Abir! What are you doing here?"

"Well, well, my little sister…"

"Is this your brother?" asked Dante in surprise.

"No, not brother…" I hesitated.

"Brother in spirit. We grew up together," explained Abir. "What I could tell you about this woman…"

"Abir is a very dear friend. And Dante… Dante is my

very best friend." The two shook hands in acknowledgement.

"Then I'm in good company. She saved my ass on many an occasion. She's one hell of a woman. We have many memories." Abir smiled shyly at me. "I can't believe it's you."

I laughed, "Come on, let's take this to the coffee shop. We have much to catch up on. Dante? Are you coming?"

"If I'm not intruding." A certain amount of reserve had entered his voice.

"Are you kidding? My two favourite men in all the world, except for the Chief, of course."

"Of course," said Abir. "And Dante, I'd love to get to know you, too."

I tucked my arm in Dante's and the other in Abir's and we stepped away from the green.

We quickly left the park and headed for the local Starbucks and ordered coffee. We sat at a table by the window and reminisced about old times. Abir chattered on continually. I could feel Dante's eyes on us, looking first at me and then at Abir. I had a peculiar wriggling worm of excitement twisting inside me. I knew it was something to do with my Sweat Lodge experience. I also knew I was looking at Dante in a different way. I tried to shrug it off and almost missed what Abir said next.

"So, I couldn't wait to leave, get out and see the world. I got myself a job on the local paper but I'm aiming for something bigger."

"Are you never going back?" I asked with a hint of regret.

"Never. The old ways are doomed. I can do as well as any white man. But enough about me. What about you?"

I dodged his question and pointed out, "Yes, you can do as well as any white man and make our nation proud."

"Why would I want that? Don't tell me you're rooted in the past."

"I'm proud of who I am."

"Well, I'm not," he said honestly. "I'm embarrassed."

It was then that Dante stepped in and tried to lighten the situation, "So tell me, how did this beautiful lady save your life?"

Abir regaled him with stories of our youth. It was my turn to blush and Dante listened in rapt amazement. He couldn't believe the stories about the female bear and cottonmouth.

This meeting set the seeds for a solid friendship between the three of us. We grew from strength to strength and met up regularly. Even Abir began to call me Union.

A year went by relatively uneventfully; both Dante and I passed our final law exams and I did my driving test. More importantly, I rose through the ranks at the firm to be able to take on even more of a variety of cases in second chair in court. I was hoping that Troy would take me on full time now he had the results of my final exam, which I had passed with honours. Dante was encouraging and led me to believe that I might achieve my desire.

I was working away on research for an upcoming property fraud trial when Troy Burgham knocked on my small office door, "Sanjukta? Can I have a quick word?"

I put down my notes and he came in. extending his hand, which I took and rose from my seat to face him.

"I think you are aware that we are very pleased with your progress here. You have impressed not only my fellow directors and colleagues, but more importantly you have impressed me; and, I am pleased to say we would like to make your position more permanent."

To say I was absolutely ecstatic was an understatement. But, there was a question burning inside me. Through this year I had been shielded from the progression of the case against Cornelius Phipps because of my vested interest, and although there was a thick pile of documentation on him, he seemed to be avoiding controversy and had miraculously been kept out of court. He only seemed to be gaining good publicity with all his charity work and appeals rather than exposés on his shadier dealings. Before I had a chance to speak, Troy continued thoughtfully, "I know you have been keen to be involved in the case against Cornelius Phipps…"

I was instantly alert; my eagerness must have shone from my eyes. "I'd like that," I beamed.

"How would you like to second chair the prosecution of

his New York Holdings Company?"

I was thrilled. My facial expression said it all.

"I'll take that as a yes, then," affirmed Troy. I could hardly contain my excitement. I wanted to whoop with joy but just about managed to hold it all in.

I was now a permanent member of Troy's legal team.

Abir, too, was doing well. He was now rising up the ranks at the paper and had moved on from covering small events like fetes and just been given an assignment reporting on a mega music event.

Dante and Abir tried to persuade me to go with them to attend this rock concert scheduled in the park. "Come on, Union. It will be great."

"I know. But I can't."

"No such word as can't," said Dante glibly.

"No! You must come. There are four bands. The best is last, and one of your favourites… Please," pleaded Abir. "Pretty please."

"You both know I would love to come but honestly, I just have too much to do. Really. I am making the opening arguments for the prosecution first thing tomorrow I need to be on form."

"You'll be fine. You work too hard," said Abir. "All work and no play as the saying goes."

"I have to work hard to be on top of my game."

"Well, why not come just for an hour? See the first group and then go. Compromise," said Dante.

"You're not making this easy for me," I laughed.

"Good. Come with us," pressed Abir.

"I can't, really. Please don't make this difficult." I looked at Dante's piercing blue eyes and was more than just a little drawn. "Enough! I have to decline. You both know I have a heavy caseload and I need to do more research to prepare for my opening statement. You can tell me all about it. There'll be another time I'm sure." I gave them both a quick hug and picked up my things and left. I knew if I lingered any longer and they would soon break my resolve.

"You're missing out," called Abir.

What I didn't know was that I would miss more than the music. I would miss the most horrifying spectacle imaginable, which would be described to me later in great detail by my friends.

*****

Dante and Abir were meticulous in telling me what happened in the park that night and although terrifying, I wished I had been there to witness it first hand. Here is their account as told to me.

Dante and Abir were on their feet and clapping along with a heavy metal rock band. The group were dressed in bizarre costumes with horned helmets and wearing Hessian type sackcloth and leather, looking just like Vikings. They pounded out the beat and my friends were enjoying the concert as much as the rest of the crowd and everyone sang along with all the band's recognised hit tunes.

Pyrotechnics lit up the night sky and laser lights danced in the heavens creating a magical show of spectacular special effects. There was a smell of cordite and sulphur to add to the scene when suddenly, a rumbling roar and crash erupted from the playing area and an alien demonic monster powered up from under the stage and shook his terrifying massive horned head. The crowd believing it to be another special effect went wild, clapping and cheering, but one by one the band members stopped playing and stared in disbelief at the awesome thundering creature sharing their stage.

The demon bellowed, grabbed a guitar from one of them and violently smashed it down breaking it apart to a wild cacophony of discordant sound. The enthralled audience surged forward in ecstasy at this more than incredible performance until the members of the group abruptly fled the stage screaming loudly in terror. The rampaging monster threw aside the equipment, as if it weighed nothing, which whistled and whined in complaint and it was only then that the crowd including Dante and Abir began to realise that this was not a stunt.

A young girl in the front row screamed as the beast

lowered his huge head close to hers and she said later, when interviewed in hospital that she could feel and smell his brimstone and fire breath. She fainted clean away. The demon picked her up like a rag doll and thrust her aside breaking her limbs.

More people screamed and tried to run away. But, as the crowd filled with fear the creature's stature grew and now he towered over the platform.

The television and film crews battled to stay filming the events in spite of the growing danger to anyone watching the terror unfold before them.

A girl who stood close to Dante and Abir - all were frozen in shock - whispered in disbelief, "What is that?"

"I don't know," replied Dante. "But, whatever it is, it seems to be getting stronger." Dante and Abir stood stunned unable to move as people flew past shouting and screaming in a chaotic frenzy. The music had now ground to a complete halt. People yelled in terror as they tried to escape the monster that was now busy demolishing the stage and wrecking the lights.

One or two braver souls took out cameras and mobile phones to capture the sickening events as they unfolded. A few risked everything to film the creature before following the fleeing throngs and trying to escape. Some were lucky and others weren't.

The thing, whatever it was, stepped out into the fleeing masses and he cast aside audience members, snapped their necks and threw them to the ground as if they were nothing but matchsticks.

A young man who was smoking a joint, close to Abir, was open mouthed in wonder, and still believing that it was some sort of stunt muttered, "Cool!"

The rest of the throng scrambled past him, pushing him over and he was trampled underfoot as people tried to escape. His neck broke and his face twisted to one side. It was clear that he was dead.

Dante took the girl's hand and urged her to run but the fearsome monster stretched out his obscene hands and grabbed her. Dante attempted to stop the demon, what he thought he could do he didn't know, but he just felt, he said, that he had to do something. It was then he was caught off balance and flung against the wrecked stage where he sank into unconsciousness.

The monster tossed the girl into the fleeing crowd. She stumbled to her feet and ran. Abir seeing the mayhem all around him fell down and played dead. He told me that he desperately tried to quell his shaking limbs. He breathed shallowly trying not to let a muscle move. He forced himself to remain still and not make a movement. He said it was one of the hardest things he had ever done.

It was then the hideous being started to shake his huge horned head as if trying to clear it of something. He raised his massive hands to his head and held it tightly as if suffering some enormous agony. The echoing cry of a name sounded out. It reverberated around the park. It seemed like the word, "UTKENA!" and the shriek of the name could be heard over the pandemonium. Abruptly, with a howl of anger and waving his long knotted fingers with their black talons he disappeared and sank down into the bowels of the earth, back from whence he had come.

The remaining scene was one of carnage and mangled bodies. Fire services, ambulances and police all arrived together and shook their heads in incredulity. What they were being told by the witnesses that had remained didn't make sense. The injured were taken away to hospital and the police tried, unsuccessfully, to impose a blackout on news reporting until they had it figured. They didn't want panic or mass hysteria to deal with as well. Abir, however, was not the only one reluctant to lose the scoop. It was a request that was impossible to enforce with television cameras filming the show.

No one knew why the creature had suddenly departed back to the hell it came from. I learned much later that this, too, was due to Cornelius Phipps.

*****

Cornelius faced Utkena in the dripping, dank gloom.

"Why did you call me back?" rasped Utkena angrily.

"We don't want to show our hand too early."

"I was just flexing my muscles."

"You will have your moment of glory," assured Cornelius.

"With more fear generated my power will increase. Soon, I will be strong enough to go out in daylight," threatened the monster.

*****

The furore that followed this horrific event was dramatic to say the least. The press and local news stations were full of the story. Concertgoers had filmed the rampaging monster on their mobile phones and vied to sell their short footage to anyone who would listen and pay. Press reporters converged on the park and fought to interview witnesses. Shock spread through those that lingered in shock at the event. The news of this devastating appearance filled the news channels and the TV stations, on the news, chat programmes, everywhere. Speculation was rife about who or what it was.

I had just finished planning my opening remarks for the case I was working on, so I made myself a coffee and switched on the television. I sat in stunned silence as I watched and heard this monster roaring and destroying all in its path. My hand flew to my mouth as I caught sight of Dante being hurled against the stage and lying very, very still.

My hands began to tremble and I could feel tears begin to smart in my eyes. The live update followed with a female reporter describing the events, as behind her ambulances gathered to remove the casualties and the dead. The Police tried to move her and the other news crews on but they were reluctant to leave the scene.

A central telephone number came up that people could ring if they were concerned about anyone attending the concert. I grabbed a pen and scribbled it down. I could hardly tear my eyes away from the screen. I snatched my phone and dialled, "Damn and blast! The bloody line was engaged. I kept trying becoming more and more frustrated. Then the woman on screen mentioned that the majority of casualties had been moved to the emergency ward at Mission Hospital. I didn't think twice. I grabbed my coat and keys and left. I had to find Dante.

I ran out of my apartment and scooted down stairs to the street. I hailed a cab and made my way to the hospital and forced my way through television crews, reporters and cameras. They were all trying to get that scoop on the tragedy in the park, so much for a police lock down and trying not to panic the people.

I searched around me and through the milling throngs of people saw the information desk and tried to push my way through. Miraculously, like Moses and the parting of the Red Sea, folks just moved out of my way and I was able to approach the desk with ease.

The bespectacled female receptionist looked up and appeared to ignore others who hurled questions at her. "Yes?"

"Dante Burgham, where can I find him, please?"

She rummaged through her admissions' sheets. "He's in the Medical Assessment unit. He should have come back from Xray. Along the corridor, area J."

"Thanks."

I rushed along the corridor, voices pounded in my head. I knew I would have to learn how to turn them off or else go mad. I could hear people's thoughts, feel their pain and their fear. People were crying but my concern was Dante.

I turned into area J - titled Fractures and Dressings Clinic and hurried to the waiting room where I saw Dante with Abir. Dante was just signing some paperwork. He turned as I called his name, "Dante."

The welcome look in his eyes spurred me on and then I saw his arm. "Whatever happened to you?" I asked in shock when I saw the sling.

"It's not serious. I was lucky. Others had much, much worse. Many are in hospital and some are dead. It was unbelievable. If I hadn't seen it with my own eyes…"

"Have you broken anything?"

"No, it's black and blue with bruising; a very bad sprain. When that thing caught hold of me and threw me he nearly crushed my arm. I hit the wrecked stage and twisted my arm as I landed. It will heal."

"I played dead," said Abir. "It seemed the safest thing to do."

"Come with us to the park," said Dante.

"We'll never get through the police tape, but yes, we think you should see the mess left behind," added Abir.

"I saw some of the footage on television. It was unbelievable but we will never get there now. It's far too late and the Police will be everywhere. Tomorrow after court. Meet me outside and we'll go then, agreed?"

"Agreed," said Abir, "I could do with a good night's sleep after those horrors. And you need to get some rest, Dante."

"I am eager to see what everyone is talking about. We'll go tomorrow," I asserted. "Come on let's go."

We made our way back through the hordes of people. The hospital had never been so busy, not since 9-11.

Once in the crowded street, filled with anxious friends and relatives seeking out those admitted to hospital it seemed all the cabs were taken or filled up.

"We need to get you home," I looked at Dante's pale face and I was concerned. Then from nowhere a yellow cab turned the corner. A thin man dressed in jeans and a vest flagged it down. I sighed in frustration and the young man opened the door looked across at us and said, "Here, you take this one. There'll be another along in a minute."

We accepted it gratefully and piled in. I insisted we take Dante home first, then Abir and finally me. I paid the driver and went into my block.

Once inside my apartment, I put on the television news channels flicking from station to station. They all had the story and arguments were raging about what exactly had happened. Because of the chaos that abounded and people fleeing to escape none of the footage of the demon like monster was particularly clear. Theories were put forward ranging from the beginning of Armageddon and God's wrath to some kind of religious sect that had conjured up the devil. I knew the demon was familiar, a creature with huge horns featured somewhere in my past but so far the memory escaped me. I had a strong feeling that the answer lay in my Indian heritage. I would sleep on it. Tomorrow I would work at remembering, and tomorrow would be here soon enough.

I had successfully made my plea in court the next morning for the prosecution. The presiding judge refused the miscreant's request for bail; my extra research had been worth it. As soon as I could I left the court. Dante was waiting for me outside the courtrooms with Abir.

"My car's outside but Abir will have to drive. Can't use my arm properly yet?"

I hopped in the back and we drove to the park and surprisingly or perhaps not so surprisingly we found a parking spot and made our way to the concert grounds.

There were plenty of macabre sightseers and thrill seekers jostling to get a look at the mess that had been left. We approached the police cordon.

I couldn't believe the scene of devastation that greeted us when we could finally see into the grounds and view the wrecked stage. Police had erected yellow crime scene tape all around the site. The news blackout had not worked and the horrific event had made headline news. People everywhere were speculating as to what or who had caused this. Was our country really facing Judgement Day? Foreign journalists had also arrived. The news story was attracting world media attention.

I picked up a piece of the broken backdrop that had strayed out of the enclosure. It was gouged with scratch marks. "What the hell did that?"

"I've never seen anything like it in my life," replied Dante nursing his injury.

"There's a huge story here. If the paper will let me cover it; I'm waiting to have it confirmed," gushed Abir. "Oh, I know other papers have the story but they don't have *mine*."

"They should do," I answered. "You were there. Nothing like first hand experience for grabbing the attention," I said. I studied my friends' faces, "You both saw it. Did it remind you of anything?"

"The horned God," said Dante and shivered. "The devil. Except it had a tail like a snake. It was scaly and its eyes…"

"I don't know," said Abir. "But, I'm sure I've seen something like it before in Indian folklore."

"That's just what I was thinking. There's not a lot we can do here. Let's get to the library and see what we can find."

We left the park and headed for the Central Library and settled at a table in the reference section. We each searched a section and returned with armfuls of books. We covered the table with tomes on Indian myths, legends and culture.

I flicked through the pages of each book in my pile but nothing attracted my attention. As I completed one I discarded it into a common pile on the next table. None of us spoke as we ploughed our way through the pages. I glanced up at the wall clock it was eleven-twenty in the morning and we had already been at it over an hour.

Dante turned a page of a picture book of mythical creatures and demons and shrieked excitedly, "There! That's it! That's what I saw."

Abir and I craned our necks to get a look and Abir agreed, "Yes. You're right. That's it!"

"That's the monster we saw at the concert," asserted Dante. "Definitely."

An elderly gentleman who was reading quietly looked up and frowned at the noise. I read the description avidly, "A demonic monster who comes in many shapes and forms…"

"Utkena!" exclaimed Abir.

The gentleman put his fingers to his lips and shushed him.

I continued in a whisper, "Sometimes as a serpent with horns… sometimes…"

"We need to get everything we can find on this thing," asserted Dante.

Now we knew what we were looking for we all returned the other books to the shelves and rummaged through the rest of our pile and took out books of legends that featured Utkena and we began to read.

Time ticked on and eventually Dante yawned and looked

at the clock. "Where has the time gone? All this is fascinating, but I have to get back. I've got an appointment in thirty minutes. A new client, I daren't be late. I'll have to leave you to go through the rest. Catch you both later?"

Abir nodded and continued reading. I looked across at Dante and smiled shyly. His gaze lingered on me and I couldn't be certain but I thought there was something in his eyes that had not been there before. I felt myself go hot and I knew I had coloured up. I hurriedly averted my gaze and returned to the books. Was I mistaken? Had I actually seen something? Was that a look of longing? I dismissed the idea as stupid and returned to the task in hand,

Abir was poring over a book of legends, "I didn't realise that our nation had such an amazing heritage."

"If this brings you back to us then something good will have come from that spectacle. My grandfather always says that from every negative will come a positive." I watched him turn another page, "What are you looking at now?"

"I remember this." He tapped the page, "The Legend of the Daughter of the Sun."

"Yes, me, too. It fascinated me when I was a child. The promise of being able to bring back the souls of the dead and let them live again. Powerful stuff."

"If it was true, you could bring back your mother and father."

I stared ahead wistfully, lost for a moment in that thought. "That was my childhood dream… Do you remember when we were kids, sitting around the campfire listening to the Medicine Man? We would feel the firelight flickering on our faces and feel the heat."

"Oh, yes. He had a way with him and could tell a story like no other. I recall being rapt in wonder hanging on his every word."

"Remind me, again. Tell me the story as you remember it, not from the book."

"Let me see." Abir scratched his head and chose his words carefully, "Ah, yes… such was the jealousy of the old mother Sun against her brother the Moon that she wanted to kill our people who smiled at the moon's soft light but squinted and frowned in her bright rays."

"Yes," I whispered softly, "It was incredible; the flames from the fire grew and pictures formed in the fire. Just like magic. And we never questioned it, just totally believed."

"I know. I was in awe as the Medicine Man retold the story handed down through generations."

"And his words accompanied the actions in the flames." It was the same magical talent I had seen in the Sweat Lodge but I had almost forgotten this childhood experience.

Abir paused and continued, "Every day when the Old Sun reached her daughter's house she would send down such sultry energy that fever broke out and people died in the hundreds."

"Yes!" I exclaimed. "We saw in the flames people crying and burning up in the searing heat. People struggled to move the dead bodies and there was much weeping and wailing."

"The humans went for help to the Little People, friendly spirits who said the only way to save themselves was to kill the Sun. Magic was made to change two braves into snakes who went up on the winds of air to wait for the Sun to arrive."

"I was captivated by the next part of the story," I whispered.

"When she came, the spreading adder was blinded by the light and could only spit out yellow slime. The copperhead discouraged by the adder's failure crawled off in defeat." Abir stopped as he struggled to remember the rest of the story.

I was absorbed in my own reverie and how I had felt as a child when Abir shouted out making me jump. "I remember! They went again for help and another brave warrior was turned into Utkena a large, fierce monster with horns on his head. And another was sacrificed to become a rattlesnake."

I completed the tale, "Still they didn't succeed. The rattlesnake bit the daughter, who died and the Sun locked herself away and wept turning the sky dark."

Enjoying the memories Abir leapt in to finish the story, "But Utkena grew angrier and more dangerous all the time. He became so venomous that if he wanted to he could look at a man and the whole family would die." Abir concluded pointedly, "He was banished to the end of the world."

"Except now he's back," I said.

I sighed and continued to study the legend. I pored over the pictures, an artist's impressions of the demon and I was instantly transported back to my childhood. "The Cherokee people missed the Sun."

"And went for help to the Little Men."

The elderly gent in the Library slammed his book shut in frustration, scraped back his chair and left the section frowning. I could see him speak to the Librarian at the desk and watched him point across at Abir and me.

Too late, I saw the Librarian proceeding toward us, disapprovingly. She wore owl-shaped spectacles that seemed too large for her face. I knew what was coming.

"I'm afraid I shall have to ask you to leave," she ordered crisply.

I tried hard to suppress a smile as we fled toward the exit. We giggled as we ran down the steps. Abir suddenly stopped.

"What happened next?

"When?"

"In the legend."

"Oh, the Little Men told the Cherokee people that they had to bring back the daughter from the Ghost Country in the Darkening Land in the West. Seven men were to make a box and carry a sourwood rod."

"Oooh, yes. And when they reached there the ghosts would be at a dance. They had to strike her with the rod, put her in the box to bring her back to the land of the living. But they mustn't open the box until they got home."

"But, of course, they didn't listen. They let her out and she became the Red Bird. The rest of the legend, you know. You see, you remember more of your heritage than you thought."

"I do, don't I?" smiled Abir with pride. "Do you honestly think it's possible to bring back the dead?"

"I don't know. I really don't know." The idea filled me with trepidation and wonder. If it were possible, what would be the implications and repercussions of such an act?

Chapter Eight

At home

Things sadly had escalated at home. My grandfather spoke with me on the telephone, "Sanjukta, Union, my heart is heavy. The company that tried to drive us out is back in business and buying up land."

"Land Shift?"

"Yes. Like father like son, the son is pressuring all of us who still remain to sell."

"So, Cornelius Phipps is following in the wake of his father, Max, is he? We'll see about that."

"Yes, many have already given in. He is offering extraordinary amounts of money. I cannot persuade them to stay against such wealth. The money is a fortune to them. They can buy new property elsewhere. It is the end of our little collective."

"And you?" I was almost afraid to ask.

"No one will force me to sell the precious land we worked so hard to buy. But I can see why so many have given in. It has been a long hard fight through the years but the son is offering so much money it is hard to refuse. Over inflated prices makes me think there is something more valuable than oil here… But…"

"But?"

"But if the community is gone then I too may have to rethink."

"Grandfather!"

"Union, I watch in sadness as our previously peaceful settlement is stolen away. Houses and land destroyed and replaced by the nodding metal-headed robotic machines, which drill for oil. Oh, I know I am stubborn. I find it hard to let go but perhaps that is no longer wise."

"Oh, Grandfather. Don't say that."

"I speak the truth. I could buy somewhere else, with land

to breed my horses but I wouldn't be so close to my old Cherokee roots and hunting grounds."

"Just hang on, Grandfather. We are building a case against Cornelius Phipps, here in the city. He may have to give the land back."

"Then my friends will be angry. He has paid them well. But I will wait before I make any decision until we speak again."

"How bad is it?"

"My and Inola's properties are the only Indian owned homes left. There is one other vacant house still left standing. Curiously, Cornelius Phipps has settled himself in there. Now, I do not know whether it is to oversee the drilling or whether there is a more sinister reason for this, I am more than a little puzzled. But, I believe I will learn the truth and a sign will be given to me."

I could hear the sorrow in my grandfather's voice.

"Sanjukta, as I gaze out across my land I look beyond to a wasteland. Nodding dog heads work in the distance like dinosaurs dipping their heads to drink, silhouetted against the perfect midnight blue of the dark sky."

As my father described the scene I could picture it all in my head.

"I watch as Cornelius stands on the porch of the empty dwelling and stares out at the starry heavens. The sound of crickets chirruping fills the air and mixes with the distant sound of machines. We will speak again my granddaughter."

He put down the phone terminating the call. I sat in my chair and closed my eyes. I needed to know what was happening and I settled down to meditate and transport my spirit home. I had learned through meditation and study with my grandfather how to 'view' places many miles away. It was a difficult task and didn't always work. I needed to focus.

I set up a CD of nature sounds and lit some white sage and drifted into that semiconscious state that allowed my spirit to roam free.

As my astral body flew through the miles I was able to see what my grandfather had described. It was as he had said and more. I saw the ruined vista, the wellheads, the empty houses and deserted streets.

There was a faint rumbling roar underground, which mingled with the metronome tap of the oil head drills as they bored and pumped.

The crickets abruptly stopped singing.

The moon glowed brightly that night until a cloud passed ominously turning the face of the mystical planet leprous and diseased. A wolf howled in the distance and the calm of the night was gone. The dark had filled with tension. I had linked my mind with my grandfather's. Both he and I could feel the union and the abnormal tension, and I knew he was worried.

The rumbling of the ground had brought me out of my meditation and I could no longer see. I had a terrible feeling of foreboding but there was nothing I could do. I sat back in my chair and tried to think through and make sense of everything that was happening.

*****

On the boundary of the original land men were working into the night. They heard a deep throaty rumbling roar reminiscent of a fleet of Harley Davidsons that tracked across iron rails.

One of the experienced oil workers, the foreman Curt, mopped the sweat from his oil-smeared face and shouted to the others, "Get ready, men! Sounds like a gusher."

The team braced themselves in readiness to cap the flow when it spurted up. The rumbling intensified and the expression of expectation on the men's faces changed as the noise continued, it drew nearer and was unrecognisable. The unfamiliar sound alarmed them.

"Don't sound like no gusher I've ever heard," shouted a worker who finished his sentence in a cry of fear as Utkena erupted from the borehole and bellowed in rage. The men were transfixed in horror. Their eyes were wide in disbelief at the monster in their view.

"We've bored into hell itself," shouted Curt.

Utkena shook his massive horned head. His serpent

tongue flicked in and out. His scaled body writhed and he stomped his cloven-hoofed feet. His eyes like a goat emitted an evil light. His cruel fingers with black talons curled and flexed. He raised his arms in defiance and triumph and made a fist before turning his huge head and eyes on the men before him.

The workers recovered their voices, found their feet and fled screaming. Utkena grabbed at Curt, lifted him up, shook him and snapped his neck before he tossed him aside. As the men ran for their lives Utkena grew in stature.

The screams of terror from the men carried on the wind. A louder more deafening roar punctuated the men's cries and Cornelius shuddered. He checked his gun holster for comfort and stepped out into the now alien dark toward the terrible noise.

Onacoma listened and watched uneasily. He heard a number of vehicles race off at great speed and saw Cornelius disappear into the night. Everything was eerily quiet except for the metronome clunk of the oil pumps.

Cornelius stepped up his pace and walked along the track to the wells. A pickup came hurtling toward him. He flagged it down; the vehicle slowed but didn't stop. It was full of frightened men. Cornelius shouted after them, "Where are you going?"

The reply came back, "Anywhere but here."

Cornelius jumped out of the way and watched the last truck disappear in a cloud of dust before resuming his steady trudge. He halted again and the crickets sang once more. He continued on and eventually arrived at the wellhead and searched around. He saw Curt's broken body and peered into the gloom. He could just make out the shape of Utkena with his massive horns and gingerly stepped out to meet him.

Utkena's voice boomed out in its scratchy raspy tones, "You have come." Cornelius nodded and whispered, "Yes."

"What do you want of me now?"

"My wife and son."

"Then come."

Utkena picked up Curt's body and flung him into the abyss that had opened up beneath his feet, and beckoned

Cornelius to follow him along another path that wound down deeper into the earth.

Cornelius braced himself and began the descent through the ground. Soil tumbled in around him and he grabbed handfuls of vegetation and roots to stop himself from slipping to the rocky floor.

Utkena was now a much larger beast and his powerful, muscular legs powered down the winding tunnel. Cornelius followed trying to banish all doubts for his actions from his mind. They plodded on going deeper and deeper into the innermost part of the earth and not a word was said.

Cornelius wore a helmet with a light that had begun to flicker, he stopped, "We've been walking for hours. I need to rest."

"I forgot. You mortals are weak," rasped Utkena. "We are almost at the entrance to the Darkening Land. Once we have scaled the cliff and I have shielded you from the tower's terrors there will be a two hour trek for you to the Ghost Country and Box of Souls."

Cornelius paused, "And then?"

"You will have the vessel to carry your wife and son home. Then, you must return without me... and plan your trip carefully, now that you know the way."

"What about you?"

"I am not allowed to abet in the removal of souls. That is a human privilege. Besides, I have other plans."

The two climbed the sheer cliff face that stretched upward and Cornelius plodded on unaware of the terrors he was about to face. The tower loomed with its grizzly circling flying creatures.

His journey was hazardous and the dangers that presented themselves were offset by Utkena's powerful presence but Cornelius knew the next time he travelled this land, the cliff and labyrinth of passages he would be alone.

Utkena shielded Cornelius as they passed the tower and were dive bombed by the vicious creatures known as Quarms. They trudged on into another channel before finally emerging from the claustrophobic tunnel into an underground cavern. A barren landscape stretched before them. In the distance a small clump of trees with branches like bony fingers clasped together, huddled next to a rusty coloured stream. One tree stood out. It stood so tall that the others were protected by its shade.

Utkena stopped and announced, "Usunhiyi. We have conquered the Darkening Land. Now, on toward the Ghost Country. See!

Utkena pointed to the tree. Cornelius looked at it in awe, "The Sourwood tree that crosses the circle of Elders."

"There you will find the key that unlocks the tunnel to Tsusginai, the Ghost Country."

Cornelius was filled with renewed enthusiasm and urged, "Come on!"

"I can go no further. The rest is up to you."

Cornelius looked questioningly but Utkena roared, "Go! I will wait here."

Cornelius could barely contain his excitement and moved on toward the trees. He was enveloped by a mysterious mist that sprang up from nowhere as he walked on. Utkena roared in triumphant glee.

*****

Troy held an in depth conference meeting for us on Cornelius Phipps and what we had gathered to date. We spent most of the morning going through the evidence we had accumulated and searched out those, who we thought would be prepared to stand up in court and testify as many prospective witnesses were reluctant to come forward or were running scared. He was now drawing the meeting to a close. Steadman and Mason's arraignment was after lunch.

"If we succeed, we can put an end to his rogue landlord dealings. That will stop one arm of his activities."

"Steadman and Mason will go down, without a doubt," said Dante. "Especially with the forensic evidence against them and CCTV footage."

Then, Troy had a warning for me, "You'll need to watch your back, Sanjukta."

"Meaning?" I answered, putting my case notes back in the file.

"We have no proof, but it's believed that more than one person has suffered a convenient accident when they proved to be a thorn in Cornelius' side."

"That's why so many of our witnesses won't take the stand." Dante put his arm around me. "But, whoever tries to harm you will have to go through me first."

As he spoke I felt a shiver run down my spine.

"Right! Enough of the negativity. Let's get some lunch and get into court. Sanjukta? You go and get 'em, Girl."

Troy's faith in me was more than I had in myself. I needed to recharge my energy but couldn't stomach a big lunch so I elected to enjoy a chicken fajita wrap and sit in the park to ponder my opening statements to the judge.

Looking calmer than I felt I made my way to the courthouse. It was busy. Mason and Steadman stood with their lawyer. Troy stood next to me and instructed, "You do this, Sanjukta. It's all yours."

I stepped forward and made my case, citing a catalogue of incidents, which gave cause for worry that I felt both men would be a flight risk.

The Defence Attorney tried unsuccessfully to counter my arguments. Things didn't go well for them as the Judge pronounced his judgement concluding, "I am therefore remanding you in custody without bail until a trial date is set.

Troy and I shook hands in delight. However, the agitation of Steadman and Mason was apparent and I couldn't fail to hear the staged whisper of Steadman to his lawyer, "Get a message to Cornelius… now. Tell him something needs to be done about that half-breed woman attorney. Tell him…" and his tone became more threatening. "If we go down, he goes down with us."

An officer of the court and a policeman came to take them away but Steadman turned back and shouted at me, "Lady, you better watch your back!"

"Yeah!" added Mason. "Cos we're getting out of here!"

The Judge rapped her gavel and issued a warning, "Mr.

Steadman, Mr. Mason. I should be careful of what you say in front of witnesses."

The men were taken away still hurling obscenities. I felt a prickling of unease manifesting in my stomach and wondered where Cornelius Phipps was now, and what he was doing. Was he still at my home or back in the city?

*****

Cornelius was back at his family home. He was standing in his study staring at an ornately carved wooden box with an intricately designed key. He turned to a picture of his wife and son gracing the wall and spoke in hushed tones.

"Soon, my darlings. Now, I have the tools. Soon." His eyes filled with tears and he hiccupped back a sob.

The irritating ring of the telephone bell interrupted his misery, demanding to be answered. He picked it up, "Phipps," and listened, a vein in his temple began to pulse. His response was curt and to the point, "Tomorrow at ten. Same place."

He put down the receiver and stared stonily ahead, his previously distressed demeanour had fled to be replaced by one of concentrated thought.

Chapter Nine

Rampage

I stood making a coffee when my doorbell rang. I went to the door and peeped through the spy-hole. Dante and Abir were outside clutching a bottle of champagne and glasses.

"Hey, Union, open up!" called Abir knocking loudly.

"Come on!" shouted Dante leaning on my door and putting his eye to the spy-hole. I opened the door and they fell inside laughing.

"What's happening?" I asked grinning like an idiot. Their good humour was infectious.

"Put away the coffee and have some of this!" ordered Abir walking to my living room. He placed the glasses on the table and began to open the bottle of Lanson Champagne. The cork exploded with a pop and he hurried to fill the flutes.

"Abir here has been promoted, " said Dante proudly. "He is climbing up the ladder of success, has had a pay rise and moved to the Clarion. He has been promised more choice in the news items he reports."

"That's fantastic news!"

"I think so, in fact it was the scoop from the event at the park that clinched it for me. That and my expert knowledge of course," he said polishing his fingers on his chest.

Dante caught me by the waist and swung me around, "So no night in for you. We are off to celebrate. You haven't eaten have you?" he put me down and I slid down his body very aware of his proximity.

"No, I was just about to get a ready meal from the freezer."

"Well, not now! You are coming out. Here." He passed me a champagne flute and we all raised our glasses, "To our dear friend, Abir, congratulations and here's to continued success."

"To Abir!" We chinked the glasses and drank.

The bubbles tickled my nose and made me giggle. Dante tapped me playfully on the nose, "Not used to champagne?" I shook my head. "Well you soon will be. We are on the road to success, all of us. Now, come on."

"I should change."

"No, you look fine. You always look fine to me," said Dante and his eyes lingered on me.

I looked down shyly, "I'll get my coat. What's the plan?"

"We are off to Castles," said Dante.

"Castles? That's a bit pricey, isn't it?"

Abir added, "Only the best for my friends. This treat is on me!"

I went to protest but he held up his hand, "No arguments. I invited you, so please accept with good grace. Then we are going on to Chequers, my favourite nightclub to dance the night away."

"Not the whole night, I have work in the morning," I said.

"As have we all, as have we all. Don't worry it won't be too late. We'll make the last train," grinned Abir.

I got my coat and bag and walked to the door, "Well? What are we waiting for?"

"Champagne!"

"Yes, we can't waste the bubbly. Come on there's another glass each in there," said Dante.

We drained our glasses, topped them up and I must say it certainly put us in the party mood. Dante grabbed my hand. I felt a tingle run up my arm, and we dashed out into the evening air.

We caught the metro to the station nearest to Castles Restaurant where Abir had booked us a table and we had enjoyed a delicious meal and a little wine. I caught Dante's eye a few times and I felt that the look that passed between us was different, somehow; more engaging and intimate or was it my imagination?

We moved on after eating and visited Abir's favourite nightclub, Chequers. We spent the first hour chatting before hitting the dance floor. Abir pulled me up to some wild piece of music and I was relieved when it was followed by something slower and easier to move to. Dante cut in and held me in an embrace to this romantic ballad and I felt unnerved at the level of the feelings springing up in me. I looked over Dante's shoulder and Abir was winking idiotically at me. He put his thumb up in approval and I was embarrassed. The song ended but Dante still had hold of me and I gently released myself from his grasp as he bowed his head to mine. He sighed and his lips drew closer. I was suddenly filled with the urge to cough and turned my head away and cleared my throat. The moment was lost. He took my hand and led me back to the table. I could see Abir shaking his head in an almost disapproving way.

We continued chatting and Dante glanced at his watch, "Time to wind up, guys. Got to get Cinderella here home and we all have work tomorrow."

I reluctantly got to my feet, grabbed my coat from the chair and bag. We made our way out into the cool night air and the street. The chatter was free and easy as we walked on. We made our way to the underground and boarded a crowded subway car. The mood was frivolous and full of fun as we all laughed and joked together. People in the carriage smiled at our antics and Abir's very lame jokes, as we rattled through the tunnels.

"A Mexican fireman had twin boys. What did he call them?" asked Abir trying not to laugh.

"Er... I don't know... Fernando and ...think of some Mexican names," Dante prodded me.

"Um... Jesus..."

"No!"

"José?"

"Yes," he shouted, "Hose A and Hose B... get it?" We all groaned collectively and then started giggling. That set the theme for the next part of the journey as to which one of us could tell the worst jokes, and the train rattled on through the stations. Filled with euphoria from our night out we had no idea what was happening that would affect our journey.

*****

The subway train driver was driving through the familiar

tunnels on his route at his usual speed when he spotted something in the branch of the tunnel ahead. He rubbed his eyes in disbelief at the apparition in front of him and closed and reopened his eyes again. Unbelievably, the thing he saw was still there. The train was rushing toward something that could only be described as a demon from hell or someone's worst nightmare.

Utkena filled the track with his enormous bulk as he shook his massive head and roared like a demented devil. His bellow reverberated through the many tunnels that wove underground. The driver slammed on his brakes, Metal on metal screeched and sparks flew. As the train was about to collide with this monster, Utkena stepped out of view and moved to the side. The monster peered into the driver's cab and glared at the driver.

Horrified the driver grabbed at his heart as he suffered a huge and fatal heart attack. His hand, which was resting on the control that drove the train on, was knocked forward. The train's speed rapidly increased. Utkena screeched once more.

*****

The passengers plummeted forward as the runaway train gathered speed. The carriages rocked from side to side. I fell into Dante's arms and he helped me to sit as the carriage swayed and raced along. Light-heartedness forgotten I exchanged worried looks with Dante and Abir.

Two of our fellow passengers, a young woman and her son, stood in readiness to alight at the next station but to everyone's shock the train roared through the next stop leaving surprised passengers on the platform, who had been waiting to board the train, looking in astonishment as the train plunged recklessly on straight through station after the station.

Panic erupted in the carriage and Dante attempted to soothe the other passengers. "It's best if we sit tight and stay calm."

"We don't know what's happened. What if the train is out of control?" said one traveller.

"Yes, there must be a way of stopping it," said another.

People looked from one to another. It was clear that complete panic was only moments away.

The young mother was held in the grip of anxiety and her frightened expression and demeanour had communicated itself to her small child who began to cry. She tried to comfort him as his cries became louder and more alarmed. She took him in her arms and cuddled him, "It's okay, baby. Everything's okay." But the look I could see in her eyes told a different story.

Dante tried to come up with a satisfactory explanation, "Maybe the points failed or something."

An old man on his left said, "Or maybe the brakes."

Abir caught my arm and I bent my head. He whispered, "Listen! That noise. What is it?"

A terrible howl echoed above the rattling train and the carriage shuddered. I somehow knew, I had guessed at its source and made a decision. "I'm going forward." I rose and began to totter toward the adjoining carriage door, which led through the train to the driver's cab.

Abir was instantly at my side, "I'm coming with you."

"So am I," exclaimed Dante.

In fact, all of our fellow passengers nodded vehemently and followed behind me as I began to move through the violently, swaying carriage. As I forced my way through the connecting doors more and more people began to walk behind me. When each door to each adjoining carriage opened Utkena's rumbling roar drowned out the sound of the train and filled the tunnel. With each clicketty-clack of the wheel we were drawing closer to the beastly sound.

*****

In the tunnel Utkena lurked waiting to wreak his havoc. He was angry and insatiable. He stepped onto the track at the division of the tunnels and smashed his mighty hand against another subway car coming from the opposite direction that veered off from the blow and rattled along another track. He knocked the train from off its rails as if it was a toy. People inside screamed in terror as the train was derailed and it flung the passengers inside against the doors and windows. Blood from lacerated limbs daubed the windows and travellers fainted clean away. Utkena strode off boldly down another tunnel leaving the brutal chaos behind.

*****

Eventually, I arrived in the first carriage that was immediately behind the driver's cab. The train was rolling alarmingly and I was struggling to remain upright. I had quite a crowd of people behind me urging me on. Everyone was trying to steady themselves and with the train travelling at such a dangerous speed I felt that if I couldn't get the door open we would all be hurtling toward our death, and I did not want to die.

I started pulling at the handle and trying to work the lock. I swore as I tried to force it open. The train rushed onward. Then, even in the mayhem around me, I heard the soft click of a knife and froze. A scowling young man stepped forward wielding a stiletto blade he had pulled from his pocket and flicked open. The rest of the company around me all stopped; their faces filled with anxiety. It was hard to read the chap's expression. He looked none too friendly. Was this man going to rob or attack us?

He gestured with a flick of his head at the door, "Let me."

I stepped aside and the guy picked at the lock with the knife and was rewarded with a clunk. He slid back the catch. I opened the door and pushed through. The others crowded around. The train was still rumbling crazily further and further on.

I pulled back the thickset driver in his seat. He was dead and his eyes... his eyes were transfixed, glazed in the dullness of horror. There was nothing any of us could do, as the train continued to plummet on through the underground channels at a reckless, breakneck pace.

Through the windshield the train's lights illuminated the way ahead and I could see in the distance the cement wall and barriers of the end of the line looming much faster than I would have liked. I grabbed the dead man's hand from the control and eased it back.

Abir yelled in panic, "It's not slowing down!"

I glanced down at the pedals. Dante managed to haul the driver out of his seat. I quickly slipped into his place and, sounding braver than I felt, I shouted, "Brace, yourselves. Everyone!"

The accompanying passengers collected themselves and sat or crouched in the brace position. Abir and Dante were still standing behind me; I hissed at them, "You, too!" Sweat beaded on my forehead and I said a swift prayer in my head.

Time was running out, I slammed my foot on what I hoped was the brake pedal and switched off the power. The train rocked as it screeched and teetered along the remaining stretch of track. People fell in the aisles. Some screamed, others were shaking with fear and in tears, but the train had started to slow, albeit marginally, and it finally ground to a halt as sparks shot up from the metal wheels. I could see the crash barrier hurtling toward us. I closed my eyes, hardly daring to breathe. The locomotive finally stopped. I opened my eyes; the front of the train had halted just a foot short of the final barrier.

The silence seemed heavy almost deafening, but was soon replaced by cheers and jubilant applause. Dante pulled me to my feet and hugged me close. I was trembling. We held on tightly to each other. I didn't want to let him go.

The fear of our own mortality just seemed to do something to us and as he turned his face to me our eyes locked on each other. I was inextricably drawn into Dante and we gazed at each other for what seemed like an age as if time had stood still. His head bent down to mine and we shared our first kiss, which became more passionate with each passing second. The feel of his gentle soft lips on mine brought a flooding delight that filled my stomach and sent shock waves through my body. It was like nothing I had ever experienced before and I didn't want it to end, but then again, I didn't really want an audience for this very special intimate moment.

Abir whooped and said, "What a scoop!"

Dante broke off and demanded jokingly, "You talking about the kiss or the story?"

Abir nudged his arm and laughed, "Both."

I had the grace to blush and could feel the colour flooding up my neck to my cheeks. I could hardly tell Dante that this was my first proper kiss, ever. He nuzzled my neck, the feel of his lips on my skin sent shivers down my spine and all the while people were still cheering. Dante whispered, "I have wanted to do that for such a very long time."

Abir laughed, "I shall write the scoop of the century. That's if anyone will believe it."

"Too many witnesses. They'll have to," said Dante laughing. "Especially after the park… How long do you think before the emergency services get here?"

"I've been trying to ring but I couldn't get a signal on my phone. However, I believe someone has managed it," said Abir.

I suddenly came to and closed my mouth, which I was aware had dropped open, "I think we ought to make our way back through the train. It will make it easier for any rescue team and I won't feel so claustrophobic," I said.

There was a general consensus of agreement amongst everyone and we all began to retrace our steps. "That poor man. What a horrible way to die," said Abir.

"I can't imagine what was going through his mind. He must have thought that the devil had come for him, or the world was ending," I added as we walked through the eerily still train. Our fellow passengers were settling down quietly to wait for rescue, while my head was still reeling from the kiss. Dante laughed and joked with everyone else and I began to wonder if I had imagined the whole episode. That is until he took my hand and pulled me down next to him. His arm went around my shoulder and he drew me close.

Abir fished out his reporter's notebook, he never went anywhere without it, and began scribbling, editing and rewriting. He was clearly going for the scoop of the century. What's more, the strangers that surrounded me were all displaying a real camaraderie, the sort I had read about in books that only comes from a shared disaster. It was a display of real unity. Maybe I was living up to my name after all.

But what was really worrying me was the reappearance of Utkena. What did he want? How had he come back? And why? This mythical creature was real and intent on going after mankind. If this was just the beginning I dreaded what was to come. How could this monster be vanquished?

Abir's story made the front page, his headline read, 'Heroes Save Runaway Train' by Abir Noski. I had to suppress a smile as we Cherokee have never had surnames but his need to be like the white man had made him take one or make one up, but at least it had an Indian ring to it.

None of us realised the impact it would have on us. When I arrived at work the next day the press and the media deluged us, and the law firm, with attention, which was something that I didn't seek.

"Sanjukta! Is it true that you were the one who stopped the speeding train and saved everyone's lives?"

Flash bulbs popped and I tried to be polite but noncommittal, "Anyone else would have done the same."

"But, in the end, you led the way. How do you explain what happened down there?"

I ducked my head and muttered, "I can't," and fled into the office with questions being hurled and shouted at me from frustrated newsmen who were prevented from following me into the building by Security.

Dante was there to greet me, "Run the gauntlet, then?" he grinned.

"I'll say. You, too?"

"Oh yes. Guess we'll be lunching in today. "

"Yes, I shall be buying from the trolley. Can we get out at the back this evening?"

"Dad has said we can take his car, it's parked under the building."

"Good. Did you see Abir's article?"

"Great stuff, except for mentioning our names!"

"He probably thought you'd want your one minute of fame," I laughed.

"Well, I can do without it. Catch you later?"

"Sure." I smiled shyly at him and moved to my desk.

Fortunately, Abir had respected me enough not to mention my unique talent although some of the eye witness statements had alluded to the fact that this Native American Woman had such charisma that they all felt compelled to help and back me up. That I could deal with, but what I didn't want was anyone checking into my life too carefully. I was hopeful that today's news would soon be forgotten in the stampede for yet another scoop and I knew in my heart as I did last night that Utkena wasn't done with us yet.

The television station news channels were full of it. They had enough witnesses to interview and Dante and I had managed so far to escape the limelight. There was a huge ongoing debate as to the explanation of the derailment.

The emergence of a demon monster both at the concert in the park, and that this terrifying creature was now marauding the town subway tunnels was dismissed as fantasy by many. There was one theory that the scene in the park was induced by a collective drug-induced haze and that the audience had experienced some kind of mass hallucination. The dreadful carnage that had followed was deemed to be some violent knife-wielding renegade addict who had run amok on a killing spree. Another so called expert opinion theorised that the incident in the park was a special effect gone wrong and that many of the attendees and witnesses were high on hallucinogens. The discussion raged and no one wanted to believe the truth. I thought that maybe this was a good thing not to create panic. If the city knew the truth of the existence of a powerful demon loose in the city, who knew what would happen?

I read varied accounts in a number of papers and watched the news. The train incident was explained away as an unfortunate accident with the driver dying at the wheel from a heart attack. Anything else was too terrible to contemplate. No one had tried to rationalise the fate of the other train. But, my rising fear was the feeling that this battle with Utkena was nowhere near over.

Following another winning news story from Abir, after

evading the paparazzi, we all went out to celebrate again. We had another scrumptious meal and ended the evening once more at Chequers Night Club, one of our very favourite haunts. Time ticked on. I didn't have to be at work the next day nor did Dante and we relaxed to enjoy the night. The mood was both jubilant and happy as we toasted Abir in a celebratory drink. He had moved a little higher up the ladder in his line of journalism and was now being considered for the role of head reporter of news and events. He had already confided to us that he hoped to become one of the paper's top investigative reporters. His ambition was encouragement to us all.

*****

Cornelius waited in his car in a deserted alley. It was late. A gust of wind blew the page of an old newspaper along the alley strewn with rubbish that tumbled from an overfull dumpster and trashcans. Ironically, Abir's front-page story flew up and fixed itself on the windscreen of Cornelius' vehicle. He opened the window and retrieved it, screwing it into a ball before tossing it away in disgust. He watched it bowl away down the alley like tumble weed in a desert breeze.

He glanced at his watch. His contact was a few minutes late and he hissed into the gloom, "Come on, Jacko. Where are you?"

Two headlights appeared in the gloom growing brighter as the car neared Cornelius. The vehicle pulled in and stopped bumper to bumper with Cornelius' car.

The driver, Jacko, an unkempt man in his mid twenties with lank greasy hair stepped out of his vehicle and approached Cornelius who had now stepped out of his SVU.

Few words were spoken. Cornelius handed Jacko a package, "You know what to do?" He spoke curtly and looked warily about him as they conversed.

Jacko sniffed and nodded in acknowledgement before spitting onto the ground.

"And I know where she is. Been following her for a few

days now." He also cautiously looked around him and once certain that the way was clear he grabbed the packet and shoved it into his coat's roomy inside pocket.

Cornelius questioned, "Don't you want to count it?"

The man rasped, "If it's not all there, your ass is mine!" Jacko wiped his nose on the sleeve of his jacket and glared warningly at Cornelius.

"It's all there."

Jacko returned to his car and quickly reversed out of the alley toppling a trash-can and the rubbish overflowed spilling out into the alley.

Cornelius shuddered. He didn't like the man but the threat to his men and his own liberty warranted tactics that personally he didn't like. Cornelius assured himself that this was a necessity and he had no choice. He returned to his car and screeched out of the alley to get as far away as he possibly could. He needed a drink.

*****

Back in the nightclub under disco lighting and a glitter ball Dante and I were dancing to a slow ballad. I nestled into Dante's embrace with a sigh. Abir watched us from the side of the dance floor a drink in his hand. He lifted his drink to me as if to say that this was right. It was right. It felt right. I had never felt so complete in my entire life. There were still plenty of people in the club who were out for a good time although the hour was late.

Over Dante's shoulder I watched a scruffy man stride in. He spat onto the floor, much to the disgust of two girls who squealed in dismay as he pushed past them. He aggressively marched on deliberately banging shoulders with anyone in his path.

One guy exclaimed, "Watch where you're going, asshole!"

I could see that Abir was watching the man suspiciously and with apprehension. I glanced back at the focus of his attention and saw this rough looking character striding purposefully forward. I was about to say something but it was at that moment that Dante bent his head to mine, his lips parted and I felt my heart race. Everything else forgotten we shared a tender kiss. I allowed myself to melt in his arms when something inside me prodded me to open my eyes.

It seemed like the stranger was headed for me. Abir looked alarmed and was galvanised into action. He struggled to push his way through the dancing throng to try and reach me. Dante swung me around at that point and kissed me again. I felt a tap on my shoulder and broke off the kiss. The man was right behind me. I stepped to the side and to my horror I saw him draw a wicked-looking knife from his pocket. The aggressor drew back his arm to stab me as Abir alerted Dante and shouted, "Look out!"

Dante jumped in front of me and shoved me out of harm's way. I tumbled to the floor as the man plunged the knife into Dante's heart and I screamed.

Nothing could be heard above the pulse of the music. I vaguely remember Abir shouting, "Get him!"

The thug ran toward a large window facing the street. He grabbed a bottle from a surprised man, and hurled it at the glass, which broke on impact and without hesitation he leapt through the shattered window. Police sirens could be heard approaching the club as I picked myself up and ran to Dante's side. I placed my hand over the fountain of aortic blood that spurted from his body. I lifted my eyes heavenward and emitted a cry of utter anguish. The rest is a blur as the police burst in and pushed through the dumbfounded crowd.

"Please, someone help him, help Dante, please," I screamed begging them to help him. Abir tore me away from Dante's lifeless body, "Union, stop! There's nothing you can do. Let the police and medics do their work." I fell into Abir's arms and sobbed uncontrollably. I felt as if my world had ended.

The pain that filled my heart burned through me and a total feeling of hopelessness and helplessness surged through me. I was numb; I was angry; I was devastated. So many different emotions raged inside me but I was left feeling bereft and wanting to be alone. Ironically that was the one thing I could never be. People tried to comfort me and all I wanted to do was to push them away.

Abir threw his coat around me and dragged me away. I don't remember much I was in such a daze but I believe we took a cab from the club after the police had taken our names and addresses. I was beginning to understand how some victims felt in the light of such an atrocity. It was no good Abir telling me it would make me a better lawyer and other platitudes. I wanted Dante back!

By the time we reached my apartment and had got inside I couldn't be still. I knew I was being unreasonable. Abir was trying to calm me but I just wanted him to go away and to let me be by myself. I knew that knife was intended for me and I grew more and more distraught wanting to pull out my hair, anything to feel physical pain other than the emotional agony I was experiencing.

I threw off Abir's coat, goodness knows where mine was, and at that moment I didn't care. I ripped off my shrug that was drenched with Dante's blood, his life force given for me. Tears stung my eyes and face as I shouted, "It should have been me!"

"It wasn't your fault." Abir tried to reason with me to make me understand.

I was so consumed with anger. I must have looked like a mad woman as I dragged my fingers through my hair now untidily showering my shoulders.

"Listen, Sanjukta. It was not your fault."

Telling me that over and over again did nothing to help and I yelled back at him, "Tell that to his parents." I pounded my fist into the wall so hard that the plaster crumbled and my fist bled. I didn't feel it. I began to slide to the floor as a warning knock came from the apartment next door and then I dissolved into sobs.

Abir, bless him, was trying his hardest to be gentle with me and I wasn't making it easy. "You can't blame yourself."

I searched his eyes, and I was just a little calmer now, "He gave his life for mine. No one is worth that!" I managed to murmur.

"It's the killer, you should be blaming."

My voice had dropped to a whisper. My strength seemed to have drained out of me, "No. I blame myself." Then I became enraged once more, "If it wasn't for this stupid power…"

By then I needed to destroy something, hurt something. I pulled myself up and ripped a framed photo from the wall depicting Dante and me on the courthouse steps after celebrating a big win. I smashed the picture on the floor. The glass and frame shattered and I fell against the wall as another warning knock came from next door. I slid slowly down until I collapsed in a crumpled heap on the floor, totally drained. The realisation that my love was no more was too great to bear and this time I allowed Abir to hold me as I broke into heartrending sobs that was an outpouring of my bitter grief.

"We were just beginning to…" But the rest of the words stuck in my throat and I was unable to say anymore.

Abir held me tight as I whimpered in his arms and he stroked my hair, saying gently, "I know… I know…"

Chapter Ten

Back to my roots

It was a miserable day, the light in my world had been cruelly stolen from me and yet the sun had the audacity to shine. The sky was cloud free as if even God didn't care. How could such a sad day as Dante's funeral be so spectacularly beautiful? It just didn't seem right. It should have been grey and dim and dreary with rain to match my tears and thick grey clouds to mimic my heavy heart.

All this raced through my mind as we stood at Dante's graveside and listened to the minister. I stood in between Abir and Dante's parents. I was aware of the desolation of Grace Burgham, Dante's mother. Her anguish reached through her husband Troy and penetrated my soul. Her quiet understated elegance and dignified solemnity even at this terrible time was an inspiration to us all. I just stood silently and numb with pain. Abir was at this point reduced to tears.

I barely heard what the minister had said and struggled to focus on his final words.

"We pray that justice will prevail and that with your strength, Lord, you will help to ease our sorrow allowing us to treasure our loving memories of Dante. Dante whose name means best friend and who was a good son, too. A light has gone out; without so much as a flicker, and all we have left; is the precious memory of how brightly it burned; the warmth he gave us, which will be felt for years to come. Amen."

Friends and relatives chorused quietly, "Amen."

At this Dante's mother stepped forward and placed a rose on her son's casket. "Sleep peacefully, my son. Until we meet again."

I followed and did the same blowing him a kiss and whispered, "Goodbye, my love. I was born when you kissed me; but I have died now you've left me and I have lived but a few weeks while you loved me," before I returned to Abir's side. Grace just remained standing there, staring at the coffin covered with three roses, and the deep trench in which he would be buried.

It was then that Grace's apparent composure crumbled and she began to weep. Her tears fell freely as Dante's casket was lowered into the earth. Troy stepped forward and clinched her in his arms and with the mutual exchange of unspoken emotion he, too broke down and began to cry.

I felt my expression freeze as I clung to Abir's arm and the rest of the burial service finished in a dirge before the funeral procession made their way back to the transport that would take them to the wake at Troy and Grace's upscale home.

There were a lot of guests. Dante had touched so many people's hearts in so many ways. The celebration of Dante's short but eventful life was recognised by us all. The event went on for four hours and finally Grace and Troy accompanied two of the last guests to the door as Abir and I cleared away empty cups, saucers, glasses and plates to the kitchen. I had to feel useful and needed. It helped with the pain.

Abir placed a stack of empty dishes on the counter top and forced me to face him, "Talk to me, Sanjukta." I turned away but he gently pulled me back and his concerned eyes searched mine. "Union, please…"

I tried to explain about the ferocious pain in my heart and the coiling dread of despair that churned inside me. "I can't face them, Abir. Dante was their only child. He was my best friend and I hoped we would…" I stopped and pulled away from him finding it difficult to reveal the conflicting emotions in my heart. "Now, he's dead, because of me. And we will never know…"

At that moment Troy and Grace entered the kitchen and I am sure they heard my last words. The depth of my grief communicated to them and I saw them exchange a knowing look as they moved further into the room and approached us. Grace took my hand and held it tightly. She extended the other to Abir and did the same.

"Please, let's have some coffee."

I couldn't believe that she was so gracious in her sorrow. I nodded and Grace urged Troy to usher us into the sitting room while she put on the coffee. We acquiesced and sat primly in the sitting room while we waited for the coffee to percolate. There was not a lot to say and conversation was difficult. I allowed Abir to speak for both of us. He exchanged pleasantries and reminiscences and I listened trying to keep a lid on my feelings.

Grace entered with a tray, "Here we are. Just what we all need. Something to perk us up."

I remained silent while the coffee was poured. The sound of the liquid splashing into the cups was surprisingly loud and over-rode any conversation. I was aware of a drone, a buzz of conversation. I knew they were talking about Dante but I was lost in my own world watching a video film reel of my lost love and all we had shared together. I don't know how many cups of coffee I drank. My ears and eyes were closed to all around me. How could I be in a room with people I cared about? And yet I felt so horribly alone.

"Sanjukta?"

I suddenly realised Grace had been talking to me and I hadn't heard a word she'd said.

"Sorry? I was miles away…"

Grace leaned forward, "Dante adored you." She paused slightly and moistened her lips before continuing, "You were the best friend he ever had." She nodded at Troy, "We could both see how close you were becoming."

I struggled to remain strong at their words but I could feel Abir studying my face. I stole a quick glance at him and could see genuine concern etched on his face. I took a deep breath as Troy continued.

"That's right. You did everything you could to save…"

"No." I interrupted his flow. "Dante is dead because of me. I will never forgive myself."

Grace attempted to console me, "No. You're wrong, Sanjukta. It was a crime, a horrible, horrible crime. You were not the one to wield the knife."

At that point I could feel my head buzzing, I stood up

fearing I would faint clean away, "I'm sorry, Mrs. Burgham, I don't mean to be disrespectful."

Troy spoke up, "Why, Sanjukta... Dante did the same thing you would have done in his place. He..."

I interrupted again, "No, you don't understand. He'd still be alive if it wasn't for my..." I checked myself and announced, "I think it's best if I leave the firm."

Troy was shocked and saddened. He rose to face me, "No, no. The firm needs you now more than ever... I need you there."

The thought of the kindness of Dante's parents in the light of all that had happened was more than I could bear. I just couldn't face any of them anymore. I turned to leave and whispered quietly, "I'm sorry, Troy," and walked toward the door.

"Sanjukta?

I kept walking.

"Abir, speak to her please."

I didn't respond. I couldn't; my face was frozen in a mask of grief. I stopped momentarily at the door before I opened it and whispered again, "I'm so sorry."

Abir ran after me calling, "Sanjukta, Union... we need you." But his words fell on my deaf ears and I hurried away to lick my wounds and drown in my own despair.

I got out of the apartment with its hurt and anguish and I ran; ran as if my life depended on it and in that lonely run I had time to think. I just wanted to escape the city with all its memories. My power of uniting those of a good heart behind me now seemed more of a curse than a blessing and I wanted to flee back to my roots.

I ran all the way to my apartment. I couldn't face public transport with people's eyes on me sympathising, pitying or wanting to help. I needed time alone. I quickly packed a bag and looked around my smart fashionable home and wondered if I would ever be back? Time enough to sort out my belongings and sell the property when I was better able to deal with it. I grabbed the phone and rang the coach station. There was a bus leaving in two hours that would take me back to my grandfather and I booked a one-way ticket.

Feeling calmer, now and more composed, I rang the local cab company to take me to the station. The taxi arrived in good time and I was lucky that the cabbie was taciturn and no more wanted to talk than I did. I paid my fare and lugged my overfull bag to the ticket office where I collected my ticket before moving to the stand to wait for the bus. I averted my eyes from others in the queue signalling that I didn't want contact and didn't want to talk and I waited for the Greyhound bus to arrive.

The weather had undergone a startling change. Now the sky had turned an ominous grey and rain clouds were rolling in from the west. The driver with his droopy moustache opened the hatch under the bus and began loading the passengers' bags. He said hardly a word, which suited me fine.

As I stepped on the footplate of the bus the first spots of rain began to fall. I walked along the gangway aisle and found my seat next to the window and kept my gaze fixed there. I was staring blankly at the outside world but not seeing anything. I don't even remember the bus filling up with people or the driver starting the engine.

I watched the rain tumbling from the sky and traced the raindrops on the window that ran down the glass, which matched the silent tears that coursed down my face. I didn't realise there were any more tears left for me to cry.

The driver must have switched on the radio and a poignant ballad filtered into my consciousness. It was a song that I loved and had shared with Dante that triggered memories of happy times together.

My mind played those times like a film reel in my head and I watched myself running around the University athletic track with Dante joining me, which was our first meeting. His voice filled my head as I recalled the times we discussed our hopes and dreams over a bottle of wine in his study and how I felt when his hand lingered on mine and the sound of his laugh, deep and throaty with a catch that made my heart turn somersaults. I sighed as I thought about our first kiss on that speeding runaway train that we had succeeded in stopping and our celebrations as we won our first case together. I heard Dante applauding me and his voice rang around in my head, "We're a winning team. That's for sure."

I closed my eyes to shut out the images and his voice that I knew would cruelly haunt me forever. Whenever I would smell his brand of shampoo, see someone with a cheeky smile, hear someone singing off key, I knew I would think of Dante.

I finally drifted off to sleep with the sound of the song in my ears and the comforting rumble of the bus' wheels. It was good to sleep. I hadn't slept properly in over a week, but that worry drifted from my mind as I relinquished myself into the realms of dreams. I am sure I would have many more sleepless nights but for now peaceful sleep was upon me even if only for a couple of hours.

I awoke with a start and looked out of the window. It was now daylight and the bus was arriving at the station. I had reached my destination. My heart was still heavy and I had this pressing feeling in my head that was building up as if to explode and my stomach churned uneasily with accompanying nausea. I knew I was supposed to move on from this tragedy, but it was early days yet. However, I believed that I would never recover from Dante's loss. And I was tired, tired emotionally and physically. I desperately needed a full night's sleep.

I moved like an automaton down the aisle and off the coach to collect my bag and searched around for a taxi to take me home. I didn't feel the need to communicate on the trip and the driver respected my wishes.

We drove silently through the dusty town, into the countryside and onto Onacoma's land. It was heartbreaking to see the once thriving village from my childhood so desolate. The cabbie pulled up by the access gate and I alighted, paying him.

"Didn't think no one lived out here anymore," said the taxi driver as I tipped him.

"No, it looks that way doesn't it?" I replied.

He drove off speeding away in a cloud of dust and I stood there motionless scanning the landscape. There was nothing to see there to lift my spirits or fill me with hope. Oil wells stood where once families had lived. Their rhythmic clanging permeated the air as did the smell of industry as the metal-nodding dogs robotically did their work.

I opened the gate and walked back along the track to my grandfather's house. Something must have alerted him to my arrival, maybe it was Saskia slumbering on the porch of Inola's cabin, who gave out a succession of small barks, or maybe it was that indefinable link that we had between us. I don't know. All I know is he emerged through his front door and stopped as he saw me approach.

I could see the stress of fighting Land Shift had taken its toll. His bronzed but weathered face was now creased with the wrinkles of old age, worry and wisdom. His eyes lit on me and a single tear rolled down his cheek from his rheumy eyes.

I continued walking slowly toward him but unable to bear it any longer I dropped my case and ran into my grandfather's arms. We embraced and the wealth of his love injected into me and I crumbled in his arms.

I could see Inola peering through the window of his living room at me and bowing his head in understanding. He came out and petted the now quiet Saskia as he observed our reunion. Inola strode to my dropped bag and picked it up taking it into the cabin's porch. Onacoma put his arm around my shoulders and led me onto the veranda.

In the haven of my home my grandfather stepped back from me. He rested his weary hands on my shoulders and fondly brushed the hair from my eyes.

"Let me look at you." For some reason, I was unable to meet his steadfast gaze and averted my eyes. His face clouded with sorrow, "What is it? Has city life changed you? Are you ashamed of your people? I know the village is gone but…"

I placed my hand gently on my grandfather's mouth to still his words. "No. No." I replied vehemently, "It's just…"

"What? What is it? What is this cloud that surrounds you that steals your light? Please, tell me, what is it?"

I swallowed hard. How could I explain my feelings when

I was still so horribly confused and damaged by all that had happened? I struggled to find the right words, "It's this... this... It's me. I'm not worthy, I can't..."

Onacoma would not let me finish. He held up his hand, "Sanjukta, Union, you are chosen. It is the will of our ancestors. Come, my granddaughter."

He picked up my suitcase, took my arm and urged me inside. It didn't escape my attention that he acknowledged Inola with a look as if to ask him for privacy. Inola nodded his head in understanding, a worried look on his face and he retreated to his own cabin.

We went inside. It was as if my despair had infected him and he soothed, "Come, Granddaughter. Unpack your things. Your room is as you left it. We will eat. Food in the belly helps us to rationalise our thoughts. We will not talk now. Tomorrow. Tomorrow when the sun is up we will walk and talk and you will tell me what is troubling you, my little one."

I almost laughed when he said that and managed a smile. He had called me 'little one' and yet I was tall for a woman. Suddenly, life seemed simpler. I fell into my role of granddaughter and a child wanting to please her grandfather.

Onacoma was true to his word. He didn't question me but surrounded me with his love and for the moment I felt safe. Tomorrow would come soon enough.

Secure in the sanctity of my room I was able to relax. I felt safe and protected even if the cloak of despair was still lying heavily on my shoulders. Although my sleep was still troubled I knew that I was entering a period of calm and that Onacoma's wisdom would enfold me and guide me.

I lay on my bed that had been mine from a child and remembered my years growing up, reliving my memories of my life and what I had been born to do. In spite of all the good things that had happened I still felt that uncertainty about my future and wondered indeed, if I had a future. Was I like a wounded animal going to hide myself away until I healed, even though I felt that, that time would never come? With these thoughts spiralling in my mind I finally fell asleep.

At first light I heard someone arise and move about. I opened my eyes and was slightly disorientated before I realised where I was. I got up and showered. The water cleansed me from my journey and seemed to wash away part of the clinging shroud of melancholy. I turned the temperature down slowly, finishing with an invigorating burst of cold water that chased away all remnants of sleep and I stepped out to dry myself and shook my mane of thick hair that needed the warmth of the sun and the gentle wind to dry it. It made me yearn for the outdoors.

Onacoma called, "Breakfast is here when you are ready, Sanjukta."

I came out of my room and sat at the table and smiled at my beloved grandfather, "Pancakes. I might have guessed."

"They were always your favourite."

"And no one can make them like you, with a berry compote and honey."

He grunted in that satisfied way he had that I knew so well and he sat with me while I ate. I was really quite hungry. I hadn't eaten properly in a long time, not since that fateful night. Food just turned my stomach but at least for now I could appreciate and be thankful for the little things in life.

I ate my fill and drank my grandfather's special blend of coffee and we sat quietly together. Onacoma rose and stared out of the window at the rising sun and beckoned me. "Now. It is time. Let us walk."

I took my fringed buckskin jacket from the coat rack and we left the cabin together. We walked out to the edge of his land now surrounded by the irritating thrum and screech of working oil wells the sounds from which filled the air. We reached the place where the village once stood and I gazed about me in sadness, "This is the very spot where Ned's antique shop stood. Isn't it?" Onacoma nodded silently. "Where is he now?"

My grandfather hesitated a moment before replying, "His heart gave out. He passed away after they tore down his building. He was a good friend to your mother."

I turned to him, puzzled, "You didn't tell me he'd died."

"You have been busy fighting for our people's rights. Ned would not have wanted that to be interrupted."

A wave of anger surged through me. I stooped and picked up a stone and threw it hard, "He put his faith in the wrong person. You all did."

My grandfather turned me to face him and looked deeply into my eyes, "I was afraid this day would come." He strode off leaving me wondering what he meant. I chased after him and we walked together. Surprisingly, we were comfortable, once more in each other's company.

He pointed out different areas to me of what had once been and now had been taken. The land was mostly barren dotted with oil wells and across the vista only three houses remained.

"You have seen what is left. Now it is time to return. And you can tell me what has brought you back and why your heart is so troubled."

"I don't know where to start…" Onacoma said nothing, his wisdom prevailed and he listened. "At first I thought this power bestowed on me was a thing of wonder to be valued. It brought me friendship," I swallowed hard, "I was never alone and it has helped me fight injustice in many forms." I stopped walking and speaking.

My grandfather stopped with me, "But?"

"I found love, for the first time. My best friend…"

"Dante?"

"Yes, our friendship had blossomed and we were so in tune, fighting for the same things when some…" my voice cracked and for a moment I couldn't speak. Onacoma said nothing. He waited patiently for me to continue. "You see… a man came to execute me … and Dante gave his life for mine." I couldn't say anymore and I choked back a sob. My grandfather put his hand on my shoulder in silent understanding.

We walked back together and entered the cabin. I turned to my grandfather and hugged him, "I'm sorry, Grandfather, I…" my voice trailed off as again I became choked up with emotion. I released him and walked back into my bedroom. "I need to rest."

"Are you hungry? I can prepare…"

"No, no ... Not now." I fled to my bedroom but I could feel my grandfather's troubled eyes upon me.

In the sanctity of my room I knew I would be here for a long time. For the moment I couldn't see a way forward but I believed that here, in my home, is where I would find my way again.

In my room I could hear Onacoma preparing a meal and I was aware of voices. Inola had come to share in my grandfather's repast. I felt I was being churlish in retiring to my room and the scent of the fish did smell delicious.

I came out and yawned, stretching my arms skyward.

Onacoma's face wreathed in smiles, "You have changed your mind."

I smiled, "How could I ignore such tantalising aromas? And then again, it would be good to speak with my Uncle Inola."

"Come and sit down. There is plenty," smiled Inola, "And fresh bread baked by my own hands."

We sat down together and enjoyed the fish that Inola had caught and I attempted to bring some light-hearted conversation into play, "Perhaps you will share your special fishing spot with us."

Inola nodded eagerly, "Of course, but I expect it is one that you already know."

I worked hard at being amiable and although I am sure my grandfather and Inola knew that my mood was forced, the rest of the evening passed relatively pleasantly and I tried, I really tried to put aside my grumbling thoughts of gloom. Eventually, however, I took my leave, tossed my napkin down and retreated to my room. I had made an effort to be normal, whatever that meant, but apparently not as successfully as I would have liked, for I had witnessed the concerned looks that passed between them. No matter, I couldn't think anymore. I was tired and hopefully sleep would come more easily after a decent meal.

It didn't and I tossed and turned.

The days all blurred into one and were spent in much the

same order. We walked and talked of nothing significant. I avoided further talk of Dante and what had happened. I could feel my grandfather's compassion for me and his worry about my future but the time I was taking out here was just what I needed. Whether I would find my drive or ambition again I didn't know but I was sleeping less fitfully and my skin had lost its pasty look and my hair had regained its healthy sheen and glow.

Most afternoons we sat on the cabin porch in hand-hewn chairs in silence except for the drone of the oil wells. On one such afternoon, Inola's dog, Saskia scampered onto the porch and sat at my side. I rubbed her back setting her back leg off into a frenzy of scratching, which made me laugh.

"It is good to hear you laugh again. Your laughter is like the fresh mountain water that runs through the rocks and cascades harmoniously like the music of tinkling silver bells."

At that moment the telephone inside rang. I knew, somehow, I knew the call was for me. As Onacoma rose and reached for the door handle I stopped him, "If that's for me, I am not here."

My grandfather looked pleadingly at me, "Please, Sanjukta. You cannot turn your back on the world."

"No."

I was nothing if not stubborn. He stiffened momentarily, a pained look on his face and entered. I heard him say, "I'm sorry, no. She is not ready to speak with anyone yet."

I felt then at that moment that I had let everyone down, my family, my friends, my colleagues and most of all myself and I needed to get away. I rose from my seat and strolled off in the heat of the sun and into the countryside beyond the drilling.

I found myself walking a familiar trail that wound through the forest. I stopped at a babbling brook and sat, deep in thought, when I became aware of another presence. A mountain lion was watching me from a short distance away. I turned to face the creature and our eyes locked as if we were in union.

Eventually the cougar padded away and I continued on

the trail. An eagle flew overhead and landed in a tall pine. I couldn't help but notice it and I studied the magnificent bird for a while before setting off again. The eagle took off and circled screaming, flapping its massive wings.

I strode off with renewed energy and began to scale the side of a mountain with an effortless ease, which surprised me after my time in the city, and all the time the eagle was circling and watching me. I felt at one with nature. The trip into the wilderness was like the cleansing of my soul. It was uncanny, I felt somewhat better and I had a feeling that something was about to be revealed to me.

As I climbed higher, I became aware of just how precarious a position I was in. The rocky ledge on which I was standing was of shale and not very safe. I felt it could crumble at any time. I knew I needed to climb higher and find an alternative route down. I caught hold of a tussock of grass and hauled myself onto a path of sorts, as I did the shelf on which I had stopped disintegrated and tumbled down the precipice. I took a deep intake of breath in realisation of how dangerous a position I had been in and I scoured around me for another way down.

The eagle above my head called again. Its cry startled me and I slipped on the grass and rocks. I stretched out my hand to save myself but the ground was unstable. Why I had come this way I didn't know? I should have known better. Onacoma had taught me to be aware of my surroundings and nature. I had climbed in some sort of foggy fugue, recklessly forgetting the fundamentals I had been taught.

The stones slipped some more and tumbled down the cliff hitting rocks and creating a small landslip. I started to slide. I knew at that very moment that I didn't want to die. I wanted to live. I also knew I had a purpose in life and one I would follow once I was ready but was that chance going to be snatched from me, now?

I clung by my fingertips to another small ledge that I had managed to grasp but my legs dangled in fresh air. I tried swinging my feet up to regain a foothold but it was proving difficult and I was getting tired. I didn't know how much longer I could hold on. I cried out feebly. There was a sound above my head and two timber wolves stood on the rocky outcrop. They whimpered softly in their throats and looked down at me.

My heart pounded in my chest as one pushed forward and bowed its head to my face. I could feel the creature's breath on my cheeks and see its ferocious, sharp canine teeth and lolling tongue. It lunged forward grabbing a mouthful of my buckskin jacket and began to tug. The other wolf did the same on my other side seizing me by the shoulder. I had the horrible feeling that I was to be their next meal as their saliva began to drip and drool.

They pulled so hard on my jacket that it began to tear but with strength found from somewhere I gave one last kick and with the leverage from these animals I managed to place my foot on the jutting rock and with the animal's help I scrambled up to where they were. They whined softly at me as I lay at their mercy. By now I was crying and shaking with fear. The larger of the creatures and the blacker of the two licked my face before raising its head to the sky and letting out a mournful howl. Its smaller, grey companion joined in the song and satisfied with their announcement they padded off and appeared to leave me.

I pulled my knees up to my chin and sat huddled there for a while before rising and finding a better route back. I was shaken but grateful that these wondrous creatures had given me my life. I had always known that the wolf was my totem animal and this proved it. I also had a strange feeling that I would see one or both of them again.

I searched around and noticed a small track leading down the cliff that was accessible with care and much safer to hike down. As I set off, I felt eyes on me and turned to see the wolves following at a discrete distance. I knew then they were watching over me to ensure I reached the forest floor safely. I felt brighter than I had in a long time and set off with more peace in my heart, which had replaced the pressing despair that had so debilitated me. But, still I was not ready to return to the world of work and men. I knew I no longer wanted to die but I was not ready to be pushed back into the law firm and I knew I needed to escape even from my grandfather and family roots. I needed solitude to assess my future. I needed to think. I knew I had to leave my childhood home. Where I would go I was not sure, somewhere… anywhere I could be alone.

It was taking me longer to get home than I expected and I was nervous about facing the chief. My mind was racing as I made my way back to my grandfather's house. He studied my expression and saw the holes in my jacket but he stopped himself from quizzing me. I could see that he was burning to ask questions about where I had been and what had happened but I wasn't ready to talk, yet. I felt selfish and ungrateful, and even a little guilty, but knew what I had to do.

That night I tossed and turned in my sleep. I dreamed. It was so vivid. Dante and I walked side by side, and hand in hand, through the remains of my childhood village. The oil well pumps screeched and droned as we spoke.

Dante was enthusiastic. He let go of my hand and danced at the side of me, and in front of me entreating me, as he walked backward facing me, "We can still win this fight, Union… No! We *will* win this fight."

We passed Onacoma, who was standing on his porch. He waved cheerfully, nodding in approval at the two of us with a broad smile on his face. He mouthed words at me that were all in slow motion. I could hear his voice inside my head, "You are the chosen one."

I turned to my grandfather, smiled and returned his wave. But when I turned back Dante had walked on and had slipped into a pit of quicksand. He rapidly sank to his shoulders. His arms were above his head; he waved them and cried out, "Help! Union! Sanjukta… Help me."

I sprinted toward the pit of sinking sand but I was just too late. Dante's words faded and he sank out of sight, as I arrived at the edge of the pit. "NOOOOOOO!"

I sat bolt upright in my bed. Beads of sweat covered my forehead. It was like losing Dante all over again. It was then that knew exactly what I had to do. My thoughts were crystal clear. I rose from my bed and packed my belongings. I had to leave and I had to go now. I took pen and paper and scrawled a note to my grandfather, which read, 'Dear Grandfather, I am sorry to leave in the dead of night but I have to come to terms with the direction of my life and at the moment I have little belief in myself and do not know what I want. I am not worthy as you seem to believe. I am weak: I do not feel I can bring honour to our nation at the moment. I love and respect you but I do not love and respect myself. Please be understanding. Don't try to find me. You know that I will return at some point, I am just not sure when. Love and blessings, Sanjukta.'

It was bald and to the point. I hoped he would forgive me. I left it on my pillow and slipped out cloaked in the secrecy of the night.

It was a long trudge to the coach station. As I traipsed the dusty road, which saw little traffic, I was lucky enough to hitch a ride with a truck driver headed for town, who dropped me off and I bought a ticket for the first bus that was leaving. I worried what my grandfather would think when he knocked on my door in the morning. I could imagine his sorrow when receiving no answering call from me; he would open my door and see my perfectly made bed and my room devoid of my things. I blinked back my tears. I didn't want to upset him but I had to find myself again and reassess my future. I needed to do that on my own. Ha! I smiled grimly, would I ever be able to do anything alone, ever? Even my lift into town was more than fortuitous; I couldn't ignore that fact.

I boarded the coach and headed for the back where I could stretch out if need be as there were few passengers. The bus journey was uneventful and slow. However, I didn't sleep I was lost in my thoughts, guilt and concerns for my grandfather.

We arrived in a small Tennessee town. I gathered my bags from the driver and scanned my surroundings. I spotted a flashing room for rent sign down the street and lumbered toward the building, dragging my case but feeling more my emotional burdens that now weighed heavily.

As I trundled down the main street I passed two ten-year-old boys fighting. Several children surrounded them, cheering them on. I stopped and stared, and sighed wishing they would cease and make up. The two boys suddenly stopped wrestling and hitting each other and to the watchers' surprise they shook hands and harmony was restored. I walked on and the children's eyes observed me. Like the pied piper they followed me as I strolled on down the street.

The red brick constructed motel was a little run down. I entered the tiny front office and the bell on the door rang behind me. An elderly man looked up from reading his newspaper behind his desk.

"Can I help you, Ma'am?" he drawled.

"Yes, please. I'd like a quiet room, non smoking away from the sound of traffic."

"I think we can accommodate you. Don't get much traffic build up round here, no how." He grinned toothily at me. "Here, can you fill this in?" He handed me a registration form. "How long are you intending to stay?"

"I'm not sure. Can we take it a week at a time?"

"Sure, we ain't full up no how, and I don't expect to get many visitors until hunting season starts. We can sort you out."

I checked into a room facing the back road and unpacked my things. I gently removed a snake rattle, my medicine bag and two photographs wrapped in white deerskin: one of my mother, Louella and one of Dante. I placed them on my bedside table and climbed into bed.

Hours passed and day turned back to night. I sat up in my bed, switched on the bedside light and picked up my magical accoutrements. I studied the snake rattle and the photos of my mother and Dante. What they would reveal to me, I didn't know but they gave me a comfortable feeling of calm.

I replaced them before turning off the light again and I lay down staring pensively up at the ceiling, waiting for my eyes to become accustomed to the dark. A neon light flashed on and off, blinking irritatingly, outside my window. So, it seemed I wasn't to enjoy the complete blackout of the countryside. I hoped that I would sleep.

My dreams were becoming more vivid and emotionally disturbing, I knew my ancestors were communicating with me in my dreams, as I was unwilling to accept their influence and their given signs to me during the day. I always had been stubborn.

I dreamt of my grandfather in full Indian Chieftain dress. The sun was rising over the forest and he stood at the edge of the river that ran through it. He waded into the crystal clear running water and recited Indian prayers in Cherokee as he methodically dipped his body into the water seven times. Gazelles came to the water's edge with mountain lions and buffalo. They watched my grandfather and settled down together taking it in turns to drink from the refreshing water. I sighed in my sleep I knew what this meant.

Then, I was travelling through space and time. The stars in the galaxy whizzed by me and I was looking in at Abir sitting on his bed. He was surrounded by books on Indian folklore and legend. Some lay open at pages with pictures of Utkena staring out. Abir looked troubled. He reached for his phone and dialled a number. My grandfather answered. I heard their conversation as Abir asked after me. I could feel my grandfather's disappointment when he replied that I wasn't there and he didn't know where I was. I heard the sorrow in his voice and I felt his pain. I watched as Abir replaced his receiver and buried his head in his hands and I felt even more ashamed and even less worthy.

I woke with a start and knew what I had to do.

I rose at sunrise and left my room and the boarding house with my backpack strapped to my back. There was no one around it was too early in the day. I stopped at the edge of the dusty town street and pulled the rattle from my pocket. It felt as if it had a life of its own. It remained quiet in my pocket but when I deviated from the path it would jump about in my clothes until I changed course. At first, I would remove it and watch the rattle tail flick. It would stop when I altered my path. Now, I understood its significance and the message it was sending me I tucked it away and continued on my journey.

I knew my grandfather had instrumented this and would be mirroring my actions with affirmations of his own. So, I began to jog out of the town and into the forests that encircled this place. I wound my way through the dense woods and although out of breath with a sharp stitch in my side I didn't stop until I reached a small clearing with a clear babbling stream running through it. I leant forward placing my hands on my knees to catch my breath and heard my grandfather chanting in Cherokee as he faced the dawn of the morning. My head swam giddily and filled with images. The accompanying vision showed me that he was again in his tribal dress. He methodically dipped his body into the water seven times as he had in my dream when he faced the east and the rising sun.

The rattle was still in my pocket but nevertheless I pulled it out and stared at it. It seemed to imbue me with the strength I needed to continue and was unquestionably the link between my grandfather's psyche and my own. As I drew this conclusion the rattle from the snake appeared to move on its own, as a kind of affirmation and the sound it made and the movement of the scales was communicating to me.

I wrapped it once more in the deerskin and returned it to my pocket. I studied the gurgling stream, watched the colours change in the water where the light played through it, as it bubbled, frothed and splashed over the glistening rocks. The air was fresh and smelled strongly of pine. I took a deep breath and closed my eyes for a moment feeling that indescribable freedom and euphoria, which comes from being in the wild and the privilege of being at one with nature. When I opened eyes moments later; the headiness was gone and a grey wolf came out from the undergrowth and stood at my side, while an eagle flew down and alighted on the branch of a nearby tree and watched me.

I could feel Onacoma's presence and amazingly, I could see him standing perfectly still meditating. He still faced the sunrise and I knew he had sent these envoys to me, to watch over me.

There was something familiar about the wolf. It was the expression in its amber eyes. I was certain that it was one of the wolves that had accompanied me on my previous trek into the wilderness. The wolf began circling me as if trying to gain my attention and the eagle flew up. It swooped and dived overhead. The two creatures called to each other respectively with a howl and a scream and enticed me to follow them. I seemed powerless to refuse. I was compelled to follow them. They led me deeper into the woods.

Trusting in my visions and in nature I continued into the depths of the forest and up to the base of a cliff. In the rock face was the entrance to a large cave overhung with vines and brushwood that was not immediately obvious. It was here the wolf stopped. It turned and fixed its eyes on me as the eagle landed on a craggy rock and watched. I turned to face the wolf, locking eyes with him. It was willing me to enter the cave.

Decisively, I entered the mouth of the cavern and went deep inside followed by the magnificent grey wolf. We went further and further into the cave and its ever-growing darkness as the sunlight no longer penetrated through the rocky passage. I fumbled in my pack for a light and struck a match to light a candle I had brought with me that would help me to see my way in.

Grotesque shadows flitted and flickered around me but still I pressed on albeit cautiously, watching where I placed my feet and avoiding the anaemic blind insects that scuttled away into crevices and small holes. Undaunted, I explored deeper. Five minutes into the stony tunnel I came to a cavern with a high cathedral ceiling. Ledges like hand-hewn shelves jutted from the passage walls and it was here I stopped and settled. I built a small fire from the kindling and brushwood that littered the cave floor. And from my back pack I produced a bedroll sleeping bag and made a makeshift bed on bracken and springy heather that seemed to have been collected for me and just lay in a crevice at a fork in the tunnel. I rested my backpack against the wall and practised some deep breathing to calm and centre myself.

I settled on my bed by the flickering fire. The wolf sat at my side. There was an unseen and unspoken bond building between this beautiful canine creature and me. I looked deeply into the wolf's orange amber eyes. Images of us running wild and free together filled my mind. I knew we had known each other in a previous life. Finally, the wolf slept at my side infusing me with his bodily warmth. We lay together for about an hour until little voices woke me, voices, which bounced off the cave walls and filled the air. I sat up and several small figures appeared at the edge of the darkness, where the firelight didn't reach.

The wolf at my side stirred and awoke. He yawned loudly. The animal wasn't alarmed but stretched and sat up. He stared at the small figures. I watched as the visitors stepped into the flickering light of the fire.

They were the Little People, Native American Indian miniature people from our legends, only two foot tall. They had shapely bodies and long hair that almost touched the floor of the cave. A tiny middle-aged male whom I later discovered was called Astila stepped forward and addressed me. "Who are you to seek us out?"

"I am Sanjukta and I come to seek your help."

"Sanjukta, sometimes called Union. We have heard of you. What do you wish?"

"I need the tools to defeat Utkena but I also yearn to return my love and friend, Dante to the world of the living."

Astila frowned and formed a huddle with the other Little People. They spoke in hushed tones and frequently glanced back at me as I watched them curiously. Astila took the hand of a small Indian female whom I assumed, rightly to be his partner. They separated from the rest of the group who retreated to the back of the cave.

"I am Noya, wife of Astila," she indicated her husband. "The Great Spirit is with you. He blesses your work."

"I have no work."

Noya was silent. Astila plucked a feather from his belt and handed it to Sanjukta and said, "You have work."

Noya continued, "You will bring pride to your nation. But to achieve your aims you must return to the world of the white man."

Astila looked at me thoughtfully, "You ask much to bring your lover back." He paused and said pointedly, "Be sure it is what you want."

I had no hesitation, "It's what I want."

There was silence in that cave as we all assessed each other. Finally, Astila nodded his agreement, "Then it will be." He jerked his head at Noya who still eyed me. "Tell her," he instructed.

"To defeat Utkena and scourge the land of his evil you must work alongside your mortal enemy," said Noya.

I was aghast, "Cornelius Phipps?"

"Together, and only by working as one can Utkena be controlled and confined to the caverns of death beneath the ground."

Astila snapped his fingers, "You will need these." He beckoned to another younger female. She brought an Indian talisman on a thong and placed it around my neck joining the rune necklet from the Cherokee museum shop.

Two more little people, a male and a female, carried an ornamental knife and slid it into my belt. Once they had done this they scurried back to the wall.

Noya made a mystical sign in the air in front of me, "Our magic will surround and protect you. The power of the universe is with you."

Astila added, "As long as your intentions are honourable."

I nodded slowly in understanding as things became clearer to me. I no longer doubted. I believed wholeheartedly in my heritage and what was required of me but I couldn't help but ask again. "And Dante?"

"First, complete the journey together. Help each other. Then, with Dante, you will succeed."

The little people seemed to dissolve into the cave walls. Nothing fazed me now. I trusted all I had ever learned as a child at the medicine man's campfire and I knew his teaching to be true. Of that I had no doubt and now I had to go back to the city. But first I needed to see my grandfather. He deserved to know what was expected of me and I wanted his blessing. I packed up my things and kicked sand over the fire to douse it and travelled back through the cave.

It was with renewed vigour that I trekked back through the dense woodland and tramped the dry roads returning into town toward my lodging. The faithful wolf accompanied me but on the outskirts of town he licked my hand and loped off into the bushes. The connection I had with this critter was both mystical and incredible, and I knew I would be seeing this same animal again.

I arrived at my room, packed up and went to the motel office to check out.

"You're leaving?" the old man asked as he prepared my bill.

"I have to return."

"Well, I sure am sorry to see you go. Will you be back?"

I shook my head, "I don't think so. Sorry."

"It's a strange thing but with you around I have felt so much calmer. Things have been better everywhere. It may be a coincidence but I don't think so. You've kind of brought harmony into my life."

I smiled and paid him. I believe he looked quite disappointed when I turned away from the desk.

"Whatever you're looking for, I hope you find it," he added, "Good luck!"

I thanked him and made my way to the bus station where I bought the ticket that would take me home.

The bus was fuller this time but I still managed to find a window seat where I could sit alone. I was going home. That thought alone lifted my spirits. However, the journey was tedious and dragged on. The difference this time was that I was now eager to return and see my grandfather. I felt rejuvenated as if I had a purpose, which I did. It was good to have something to live for again.

The rumble of the Greyhound's engine was soporific and I began to nod off in the comfortable warmth of the coach. It was a dreamless sleep and for that I was grateful. By the time we arrived at my destination, night had fallen. I collected my luggage and backpack. I was glad that my case had wheels and that little effort would be required to get it home.

This time I didn't take a taxi. I needed to walk and I somehow knew I would be greeted by a faithful friend. How I knew this I didn't know. I just did.

I strolled out of town, past the drinking bars and gentleman's club, where a police car sat on patrol. I trundled on. The night sky was clear and the moon and stars lit my way. The road ahead was straight. The route dipped down and then up to a junction where the highway divided. Sitting at this spot sat my friend. He rose to meet me and wagged his tail in greeting and allowed me to ruffle his fur. We walked on together in union.

Some thirty minutes later we reached the access gate to Onacoma's land. I opened the gate and began my walk along the dirt track through the wasteland that had once been lush and green.

Onacoma's cabin loomed in the distance and I could see the form of my grandfather sitting on the porch in his rocking chair. The way he was sitting, hunched over and peering up at the starlit sky denoted his sorrow. My companion stopped and howled softly. An answering cry came from the hills and Onacoma brought his eyes level and stared out into the darkness. It was then he saw me approaching. He jumped up to greet me all traces of his previous sadness vanished and he stretched out his arms to me, exclaiming joyfully, "Sanjukta! Union!"

I hurried to meet him as he stepped out to meet me and we embraced. It was good to feel my grandfather's love surround me. He held me tight and I could feel the wetness of his salt tears on my cheek.

I said bleakly the words he wanted to hear, "I am so sorry I hurt you, Grandfather. I needed to find myself and regain my confidence and now the time is right. I must return."

"I knew you would come back. I had faith. I knew you would make things right."

My canine companion watched the encounter and as we walked to the cabin he settled down outside to wait. Saskia rose from her slumbers on Inola's front porch. She was getting on in years and she gently snuffed the air. The strong scent of wolf assailed her sensitive nose and she growled softly. I called out to her, "Stay, Saskia. All is well." And the old dog obediently lay back down and returned to her sleep.

We stepped up onto the veranda and I explained to my grandfather all that had transpired, concluding, "Therefore, I must face my enemy and make him my friend."

Onacoma nodded, "The peace of the Great Spirit goes with you."

Our attention was caught by the trail of a shooting star that traversed the sky. It was an omen, a good omen, we believed.

The telephone inside began to jangle, impatient and insistent on being answered.

I said, "When two worlds collide chaos reigns."

"Unless they avoid catastrophe by travelling side by side."

I noted the wisdom of my grandfather's words before entering the house, wheeling my case, to answer the persistent ring of the phone leaving Onacoma to study the night sky and the messages contained in the heavens, which he could read.

"Union! Thank God."

It was Abir, bless him, he had been phoning my grandfather regularly to find out if he had any information on my whereabouts. The news he had for me made me realise I needed to act fast.

"We need you to return. Troy is in despair and the case against Cornelius Phipps is due to be heard shortly. It has been postponed because he knew how important it was to you but the DA is on his back and so Troy is moving forward with it, with or without you."

"You have to stop Troy," I urged.

"Stop him? How?"

"Anything to delay him. Make him wait, at least until I get back, please."

"I'll do my best," Abir assured me. "When will I see you?"

"Soon," I promised.

I ended the call and went back outside to my grandfather, "Troy finally seeks to indict Cornelius for all that he has done. I must return."

"But tonight, we will eat and we will talk. You will share with me about your totem friend there." He indicated the wolf.

I nodded and tucking my arm in his we went into the cabin together.

Chapter Eleven

Back to the City and Utkena's Wrath

My enemy, as described by the Little People, Cornelius sat morosely in a booth sipping a beer facing a hard looking man with a scarred face. They were deep in conversation and speaking little above a whisper so that no one would hear their discussion. The man looked rough and someone not to be trusted he was relaying information he had gleaned from the District Attorney's office.

"It was hard but I think they have more than enough to indict you and close down your business operations in the city. And more than likely the oil business, too."

Cornelius questioned him closely, "So, our whole operation is in jeopardy?"

"They've sent for that whiz kid female lawyer, Sanjukta. She has evidence. She's arriving in town tomorrow morning, early. They've parked her car outside the station. I've got a team watching it."

"Then you know what to do."

The man nodded, "I'll fix this and her."

Cornelius dismissed the man and ordered another drink.

*****

I had travelled by train through the night to arrive in the city. The dawn was breaking and it promised to be a beautiful day. Troy was standing on the platform waiting to meet me. He took my bag from me and set it down before hugging me warmly.

"Thanks for coming."

"Forgive me, I had a crisis of faith and now I have a job to do. We need to hold fire on the Phipps case. Just for a little while."

"I don't know if I can do that..."

"Please, just let me get home and I'll call you."

"Then, you'll be staying?"

I smiled, "For as long as it takes."

Troy handed me some car keys and a small file. "Your vehicle is parked around the back of the station in Maiden Street. Those papers list the evidence for the indictment. The full case file, if you need it, is at the office." He sighed and hoarsely whispered, his voice choked with emotion, "It's good to have you home, Daughter. I kept up the maintenance fees on your apartment. Settle back in and I'll see you tomorrow."

With that he left me and strode off, clearly not trusting himself to say anymore. I extended the handle on my case and pulled it with me toward the station's exit and Maiden Street.

The back road was quiet and seemingly deserted. It was good to see my Kia Sorrento sitting waiting for me. I unlocked it, packed away my luggage and got into the driving seat, tossed my purse and the Cornelius Phipps file on the passenger seat. I closed the door, started the engine and set off.

I looked in the mirror and a BMW X5 pulled out from its parking place and followed me. I observed the driver in my rear view mirror. It was no one I recognised. He appeared to be scanning the road around him to see if anyone was watching. I saw him give a nod to his front seat passenger as if to say, 'Get on with it.' It was then I caught sight of the passenger pulling out a gun. He screwed on a silencer. I knew I had to move, and quickly. But, the BMW seemed fixed on my tail and suddenly accelerated, ramming me hard in the back and shunting me forward.

I glanced back quickly and spotted another man in the back, who was leaning in between the driver and passenger. He, too, had a pistol and was talking to someone on his cell. The man in the front aimed his gun at my head, I swerved quickly avoiding the shot, which shattered my wing mirror. In doing so I scraped a parked car but there was nothing I could do about that now. My tyres began to smoke and scream as I struggled to get ahead. A crossroad was fast coming up and the BMW was still on my tail. I could see it was going to try and ram me again.

A Lincoln screeched through the crossroad in, I supposed, an attempt to cut me off but I made a sharp right turn into a street preceding the crossroad, which was now blocked.

A nanny pushing a stroller was waiting to cross the road but leapt back as I came thundering past. She then stepped back into the road but was forced back by the BMW and Lincoln that were both now chasing me. I had never before paid such close attention to what was happening behind me on the road, using all my mirrors to try and deduce what their next move would be. I had to make snap decisions and try and shake my pursuers off. I glanced around swiftly and bolted up another side street, made a hard left and struggled to keep control. I clipped a Dodge Neon and its car alarm blared out loudly. My heart was now thumping and I was beginning to sweat. I was unable to access my phone in my purse for help. I was on my own. If ever I needed a miracle; I needed one now.

Both vehicles were in hot pursuit, they had wound down their windows and shots were being fired at my fleeing car. I was only just managing to keep my Kia on the road. Again the BMW rammed me hard from behind shunting me across a T junction and spinning me around. I reversed and took off in the opposite direction at great speed down the other side of the road. I'd be okay as long as another car didn't approach in my lane.

My mind worked quickly and as the pursuers started to catch me I backed into a side road, spinning my car, which careened off down yet another side street. I was no longer certain, where I was or where I was going I just had to keep one step ahead of them. As I sped off, narrowly missing my pursuers, they slammed on their brakes and collided crumpling their hoods. This did little to stop them and they were soon after me, once more.

I turned onto the main city street, recovering my bearings and questioning whether they would have the nerve to continue their assault in such an obviously busy public place. However, it didn't seem to deter them and I headed toward the River Bridge with both cars still in hot pursuit. I could only assume that these were more of Cornelius' henchmen.

I studied the action behind me in my mirror and the BMW came dangerously close to ramming me again so I speeded up to avert disaster and switched lanes. A blue Ford Focus dropped in behind me effectively stopping any car from battering me from behind.

The vehicles in the adjoining lanes kept pace with me, and the driver on my right looked across at me and nodded in support. It was as if I was barricaded from harm by the other vehicles around me. I gasped in understanding but the Lincoln's driver was not to be thwarted; he pulled onto the hard shoulder passed the car protecting me then darted in front and slammed on his brakes trying to stop me.

A Dodge pickup that seemed to come from nowhere sideswiped the Lincoln, shunting it into the next lane where it spun around several times. Cars were honking and swerving to avoid this near disaster. I clocked the Lincoln's driver hitting his steering wheel in anger and exasperation as he struggled to right his car and continue the chase.

I was now flanked by the pickup and a series of vehicles on both sides and behind, which formed a protective escort around me. The BMW cruised to the shoulder and raced on trying to pass this convoy and get ahead of me. The passenger of the enemy vehicle leaned out of the open window and aimed his gun at me, just as the traffic lanes dwindled to two as we reached River Bridge.

The Lincoln forced its way through and passed the BMW, which had been rammed by a Chrysler. An Impala travelling in the opposite direction crossed the median and tried to block the Lincoln. It shoved the Lincoln into an erratic spin and made cars swerve out of the way as they hooted at the Impala.

Now my Kia was exposed to danger.

Three more cars entered the combat and drove in formation to rally around my Kia. The Lincoln's driver tried to evade pursuit and recklessly changed lanes on the bridge. A red Corvette steered in front of the Lincoln and blocked its path. The Lincoln's driver swerved abruptly and because of its excessive and dangerous speed was unable to stop. It nosedived off the bridge and into the water below.

I continued on toward the end of the bridge, unimpeded and uninjured.

The BMW's driver fiercely spun his steering wheel and resumed his chase. He revved his engine until the tyres screamed and smoked. In my head I could hear him swear but I knew that I was not yet safe.

A Malibu hurtled onto the bridge and joined the BMW in pursuit. I could see in my mirror that one man was hanging out of the window as they crossed the bridge and raced after me. Now that I had my bearings I knew exactly what I was going to do and in spite of my heart stopping manic and twisting fear I managed a grim smile.

I kept an eye on my internal rear view mirror and watched the BMW as it dodged and weaved through traffic. As I came off the bridge I put my foot down hard, flooring it, and darted past cars. Swiftly, I turned right down a side street trying to lose the pursuers.

Tyres squealed in complaint as both cars chased me down another side street. This time my grin was even broader, "Come on then, you bastards! Bring it on!"

I barely managed to keep ahead. I floored the Kia once more, twisted down an alley, blazed past dumpsters and out the other end and continued for another block where I spun to a controlled stop to face the oncoming cars. They continued toward me and screeched to a halt. I was facing them head on and saw the BMW driver's eyes widen in shock. The other henchmen in the car were waving their arms around and clearly shouting their orders at the driver to get the hell out.

I afforded myself a chuckle as I faced the enemy cars as a Matador would a bull. I revved my Kia but didn't move. The Malibu and BMW were stuck, unable to retreat or move forward. Blocked from behind with no escape route their eyes gazed in horror at where I had halted. I had stopped in front of a police station where officers were swarming out and into the street. Some piled into squad cars. Six officers approached the BMW and Malibu.

Now, I could grab my purse from the adjacent seat. I took

out my cell and checked a number from the file and dialled. It was answered quickly.

"Phipps."

"Cornelius? Sanjukta. We need to talk."

*****

Under the city in Utkena's tunnel lair the horned monster faced the Shaman who had helped, Cornelius' father Max.

"You betrayed me."

The Shaman stood frozen in fear.

"To white men."

The Shaman apologised nervously, "My intentions were good. I thought it would bring you recognition and honour."

"It angered me. As the Cherokee nation angered me many moons ago. I will turn men's hearts to stone as I turn your body to granite."

The Shaman raised his hands protectively to his face. Utkena's malevolent eyes lit with an evil fire that penetrated the dark and surrounded the Shaman with an energy that fused the cells in his body turning him to stone. The Shaman's scream of terror tapered to nothing. Utkena smashed his huge hand into the granite statue, which crumbled and bled.

Satisfied Utkena strode away and roared, "I will have my revenge. I call upon the Furies of Nature to do my bidding."

Through the cavern, strange mocking laughter was heard and five Furies, beautiful women type creatures, in Hessian rags, with talon like nails and tangled hair followed fawningly after Utkena.

The demonic monster marched on following a tunnel that led to the mouth of a cave overlooking a partially deserted beach area. Further along the sand children and families enjoyed the sunshine. The scene was one of calm and serenity.

The Furies spilled out of the cave at the feet of Utkena, who growled, "I urge you. Turn the sea into a boiling tempest, drown the flatlands in a violent surge and you will have done well."

The Furies screeched with delight and raced to the water's edge their ragged clothes billowing in tatters like a vampire's tattered cape flying behind them. They gazed at the cloudless sky. Collectively they exhaled streams of mist and fire. Clouds bubbled up and changed a beautiful summer day into a picture of a wild tempest. The sea boiled and churned angrily. People scurried to pack their things and raced for cover.

An eleven-year-old girl watched the sea in fascination. Her mother called for her to follow the rest of the family.

"Lexi! Hurry… Come on!"

Lexi was transfixed, watching the strange pattern of the tide as it retreated toward the horizon. Fish were left flapping on the sand. Lexi stopped staring and turned to her mother and shouted, "Mommy! I've seen this before, in Geography class. A tidal wave is coming."

Her mother saw the intent look on her daughter's face and didn't argue. She grabbed Lexi's hand and ran up the beach.

"High ground. We have to get to high ground," shouted Lexi.

They scrambled off the sand and ran up the beach road to a hotel several stories high. They gathered people as they went. Others ignored them and laughed at their extraordinary behaviour.

On the horizon a towering wall of water powered toward the beach. The Furies played in the surf and laughed dementedly.

A young man climbed on the roof of his three-storey beach apartment. He used his mobile phone to film the water that raced toward the land. He scanned the beach with his camera phone and barely discerned Utkena standing and turning at the cave entrance before disappearing. "What the… ?"

*****

The next day the papers were full of the story. The media backed up claims that there were no warnings for this terrible disaster. They were calling it a freak wave rather than a

Tsunami. Everyone was talking about it at the law offices where I was headed for a meeting with Troy. I was hoping to buy some time and check on Cornelius' whereabouts. Cornelius had been less than cooperative on the phone and had disconnected the call refusing to pick up when I rang back. I knew that some P.I.'s had been tracking his movements and daily routine. I needed to speak with Cornelius urgently, face to face. But, I couldn't reveal my true intentions to my boss I just hoped that he would trust me enough to go along with my request.

I entered the boardroom and slapped down the Land Shift File and the personal data on Cornelius Phipps. Troy looked questioningly at me.

"Troy, I know we need to go after Phipps with everything we've got and the DA is anxious to proceed but..." I hesitated.

"Yes, but?"

"Can you give me some time?"

"Why?"

"I won't lie to you and I cannot explain, at least not now, but as a favour to me, can you give me a week? Just one week, please. I promise I will be back."

Troy frowned and sighed ruefully, "I don't know... the DA has been on my back already." He looked at my earnest expression and something made him give in. "I can try and stall him."

"Please."

"One week you say?"

"Yes, one week and I need to review the information on his surveillance, his habits etc."

"You're not going to do anything stupid, are you? We're sure he's at the back of the attempt on your life. We believe he's trying to kill you."

I sighed, "I know. Just one week, please. That's all I ask." I waited while Troy considered my request.

He finally spoke, "Very well."

I heaved a sigh of relief, "And I need to take the week off work."

Troy raised one eyebrow but I didn't give any

explanation. "Phipp's file is with my secretary. Wait!" He scrawled a note to his secretary giving permission for me to take the file. I grabbed his authorisation and hurried out.

The secretary didn't bat an eyelid as she handed me the notes. I took myself off into my office and devoured the contents. I glanced at my watch. If I left immediately I would be likely to catch Phipps at his morning coffee stop. I hurried out and made my way to the diner listed in his file. It was now ten-twenty a.m.

I took my car and punched the zip code into the Satellite Navigation. Luckily it wasn't far from where I worked and there was room at the front of the building to park so I pulled in and entered. I searched the place with my eyes and spotted Cornelius in a corner booth sipping coffee. I waved away the attention of a waiter wanting to seat me and assured him I was joining someone. I stepped across to the booth and sat opposite him.

Cornelius looked startled as I sat down, "We have to talk."

"I have nothing to say to you."

"You need to hear this."

"Speak to my attorney."

I lowered my voice, "I can help you."

"You can help me by getting your half breed ass out of here."

"Just listen…"

"Look, I don't give a shit. If you don't leave I'll sue you for harassment."

"Please, just hear me out. You don't want what I know to be public knowledge."

Cornelius looked at me scornfully, "You think?"

"I'm talking about the Box of Souls."

Cornelius' mouth dropped open, and after a stunned pause he said in a measured tone, "Keep talking."

Time ticked on, we talked solidly for an hour and a quarter.

"I am not making it up. You know the truth of the legend. But, if we don't stop Utkena you will have no life with your wife and son and nor will anyone else. Mankind is doomed."

"That's somewhat melodramatic."

"Look at the evidence. Look at what he has already done, and he is getting more powerful. Please." I pressed him and tried to persuade him to join forces with me. "We have to do this together. There is no other way."

Every time the waitress approached with fresh coffee we would fall silent until we had our refills. We would wait until she had moved onto another table and I extended my hand, "Do we have a deal? You'll listen to what I am going to propose? Think about it and meet me, again. Yes?"

Cornelius nodded reluctantly in agreement and we shook hands. His grip was firm. There was no limp wrested nambi-pambiness about it. "When?" he asked.

"Tomorrow. I'll meet you here at ten. I'll drive and we'll talk with no other ears to hear."

Cornelius nodded, "Okay."

We were interrupted by a news flash that filled the screens of the TV's placed strategically around the diner. A news reporter announced, "We have exclusive footage of the tidal wave or what some describe as a freak wave that struck the East Coast without warning. There was no seismic activity but the disaster was captured on one man's mobile phone, which we bring you now."

A short grainy film played with the reporter describing the ferocity of the water. Cornelius and I watched as it played out before us. As the film scanned the beach I spotted the formidable shape of Utkena in the distance, "Did you see that?"

He nodded, "Utkena… I never meant… I don't want innocent people hurt…"

"Never mind. We have to stop him. And we can only do it together. He will soon be too strong to stop or for you to control. Are you with me on this?"

Cornelius set his mouth in a hard line and I wasn't sure if he would agree or not.

Finally, he acquiesced, "Let's do it. No more talk. We will leave tomorrow." I still wasn't sure if he was being sincere. But, I had to trust him. There was no other option and no other way.

"I need to prepare. I'll meet you here tomorrow as arranged. And bring the box," I ordered.

"What I don't understand is why you would put your life at risk?" He eyed me questioningly.

"My boyfriend is dead because of me. I want to bring him back as you do your wife and son."

"So you believe in the box's power?"

"Yes. I believe, now. And it makes sense to join forces."

"But Utkena..."

"We must stop him ... together. Follow the rules of the Little People. It's the only way. Agreed?" I asked him again.

Cornelius finally nodded, "Agreed."

I believed him this time and left the diner. I had much to do before the next day when our quest would begin. My preparations had to be meticulous.

I rang my grandfather when I got home and was surprised when he told me that Abir was there visiting with him and Inola. Apparently, he didn't know that I was already in the city and had travelled back to see me. And it seemed he had a change of heart regarding our heritage as they had sat together in the morning sun.

I could envisage the scene as my grandfather related the events to me.

"You see, Abir admitted that he never knew or fully understood what it meant to be Cherokee. It was all a game as a child and his schooling educated the mysticism out of him. I have stressed that all that mattered was that he had returned to us and I told him that I was convinced that he will bring glory to our nation, like you, and bring pride to our heart. I told him I was sorry that he had missed you." My grandfather fell short of saying anymore about the meeting and went on to more mundane things.

It was then I heard the rest of the conversation in my head. I heard Inola's teasing tones as he told Abir, "In you, brave one, he sees a future for our tribe and his family line."

Abir must have been surprised but understood what was meant as he responded, "Union... Sanjukta doesn't think of me like that. Not in that way. She loved Dante. We are and can only be friends. It can be no other way."

I felt myself colour up as my grandfather continued to chat and yet in my head I heard the rest of his conversation with Abir. Onacoma's voice resonated in my ears, "If she doesn't want you now, with Dante gone, she may turn to you. The Great Spirit has shown me she will wed. But to whom? I do not know. That is the mystery."

The voices in my head were so clear I missed what Abir said to me next. I bid him goodbye and as I replaced the phone I had an image of Abir shaking his head in disbelief. And my grandfather silently turning his face to the sun and letting the warmth bathe his face. I wondered how I would greet Abir the next time I saw him. I would have to hide what I knew.

The next morning Cornelius was on time. We drove to a private airfield where Cornelius had his own plane and after stowing our bags and other necessary items we boarded the small craft. The pilot informed us that it was a two-hour flight as we had a good tail wind to push us along.

Cornelius and I sat in uncomfortable silence hardly exchanging a word. Finally I spoke, "For this to work we have to be civil to each other. We can rely on no one on this journey but ourselves. Can we at least call a truce?"

Cornelius nodded grimly and said begrudgingly, "Okay, but don't expect me to turn into your best buddy. We have issues. Those issues stay out of play and anything learned on this trip stays with this trip. Agreed?"

"Agreed." My main focus was on ridding the world of Utkena and I reminded him of this. "Our uniting together is to stop Utkena and what he plans to do in our world."

"And to bring back our loved ones."

"If it's possible."

"It's possible. My father wouldn't have spent the time and money he did if it was only a myth."

"How will we get to the house without being seen?"

"Don't worry. There is a landing strip east of the oil field and under the foreman's office is a basement with a tunnel that leads straight to the cellar of my house and from there we start the beginning of our journey."

"I will need somewhere to change and prepare. We must have this venture blessed if we are to succeed."

Cornelius looked at me scornfully, "I don't know about that. But you do what you feel you need to do."

The rest of the trip was comparatively smooth and we landed just as the pilot had predicted, collected our things and made our way to the foreman's office. There I readied myself for the task ahead. I took out my change of clothes, my amulets and other important items and my face paint.

Later that same day, we stood at the entrance of the tunnel that would take us on the first part of our dangerous journey. Cornelius clutched the key to the Ghost Country and the Box of Souls, which he had tucked under his arm.

He faced me. I was wearing full Indian dress and my face was painted as I had painted it years before for my trials and tests of initiation. I carried with me my Shaman mystical tools, a runic talisman around my neck, the miniature medicine pouch necklet given to me by the Little People, my ornamental knife, prayer feather and rattle, which were all tucked into my belt.

He bent down and placed the box and key in his rucksack and strapped it on his back after removing a flashlight to light our route. This cast strange fluttering shadows on the rocky walls.

My heart was thumping. I did not know what to expect. I extended my hand, "We understand each other?"

Cornelius hesitated then he took my hand and shook it, and said firmly, "We have a deal."

We stood there a while longer weighing each other up. This was no time for me to have doubts. Cornelius took the lead and walked away down the gnarled tunnel full of strange, peculiar shapes and winding bends. "This way."

Water dripped and moss grew freely on the walls in green murky clumps. I stepped out after him. As we progressed through the dark passageway the twisted forms in the rocks came to life. The beautiful Little People emerged, as would a butterfly from its cocoon. More and more of the tiny beings poured out from the crevices. Astila dashed to my side.

"Union! Sanjukta!"

I stopped.

"Be not afraid. Utkena will not hamper you, yet. He's causing havoc in the world of men. You will need to deal with him later. But, perchance you do meet, do not look him in the eyes. His power is greater now and his poisonous glance will turn you to stone. Be warned."

"Thank you my friend."

By now Cornelius had stopped and he, too, saw all the little people. If he was amazed, he didn't show it but waited patiently for us to continue.

Astila indicated him and spoke in words that he could hear, "You do well to unite. If you work for the good of man, rewards will come, for both of you. We will be watching."

The Little People scurried back down the passageway and vanished into the rocks, once more. I was surprised that Cornelius didn't question me on their appearance, but he didn't, and I didn't offer any further explanation. We plodded on in silence as the rocky cavern narrowed and the ceiling began to close down on us. I fought my feelings of claustrophobia as a pungent smell hit my nostrils. I recognised the scent of guano.

"Bats," said Cornelius. "Watch out!" His voice reverberated around the cavern disturbing the roosting critters that began to chitter, swoop and fly. I held onto my hair not wanting any of them to get tangled in my tresses. Whether it was an old wives' tale or not, I did not want to take the risk. I shared some of DH Lawrence's loathing of bats. One squeaked as it dived around my head; of course, its internal radar would keep it from hitting me but that knowledge didn't take away the fear. The small Pipistrelle bats didn't bother me, they were quite cute like mice with wings but these were vampire bats and lived to suckle on warm-blooded animals including people and I was not, nor ever had been a fan of Dracula.

We walked on and the rocks started to change colour. Where water monotonously dripped from the cavern roof and ran down the walls the surface of the rocks had become luminous. Although looking eerie they actually helped to light our way.

Our path dropped down further taking us deeper and deeper into the earth and the low rocky roof forced us to crawl on our bellies. We squeezed through a very narrow gap before emerging into a weird and alien landscape.

Rainbow water cascaded into a rocky magenta pool. Glass like leaves tinkled in a sudden breeze scattering large pods that had fallen from them. They rolled at our feet as if caught by a whirling dervish.

Cornelius stopped and pointed, he took a swig from a water bottle that I passed him. "There! The Darkening Land."

We both looked in awe at the mystical landscape like nothing I or any other human, apart from Cornelius, had ever seen. We stared at sombre Nimbus clouds in deep gentian violet, which skirted a stark forbidding expanse of scenery that looked as if it had come straight from a Gothic or science fiction horror movie.

Skeleton trees with burnt spiky fingers twisted up to a barren cliff topped with a crooked tower where strange flying creatures circled endlessly. Twin moons shone silver blue amidst angry burnt orange stars. Malevolent shadows danced grotesquely on the cliff's edge.

The earth was blood red and littered with many varied coloured crystals. Strangling blue vines criss-crossed the veined rocks that bordered a twisting path that writhed its way toward the forbidding tower that stood like a sentinel guarding the land, on watch, to prevent anyone from entering or leaving and betraying its presence.

Cornelius indicated the route we should take. "The Darkening Land; we'll scale the cliff, pass the tower, if we can evade the flying creatures, and travel to the plain where the Sourwood Tree crosses the circle of Elders. There a waterfall of corrupt dreams falls into the pool of disillusion. That's where I found the box."

"And then?"

"Behind the waterfall is the Tunnel of Damnation, which leads to the Ghost Country."

"Tunnel of Damnation?"

"Where your worst fears are realised."

I frowned. I didn't like the sound of that.

Cornelius continued, "No one has ever survived the journey. Are you sure you still want to travel on?"

I nodded, "We have to stop Utkena. There is no other way. We will go on."

Cornelius nodded grimly.

I studied the rocky cliff face that was drawing closer with each step. It would be a hard climb.

*****

In the world of men, which seemed a million miles from us, Utkena was preparing to ravage a theme park. Terror was about to turn a happy day out for families into a living nightmare. It was a typically fun-filled day at a crowded amusement park where excited children tugged at their parents' arms and pleaded with them to move onto the next ride. Music and laughter rang out amid the background of roaring roller coasters and screams of pleasure from the thrill seekers on board.

A gang of teenage boys with one of the group's little brothers approached the largest of the roller coasters. Chad the youngest and just twelve years old followed the others reluctantly his face filled with fear. Sixteen–year–old Phil motioned to his friends, "Come on. Get a move on or we'll never get on."

The rest of the guys rushed to join the end of the line. Chad held back and grabbed his brother, Brett's arm. "You go ahead, I'll wait here."

"Don't be a pussy!" groaned Brett.

Phil looked back and grumbled, "What's the hold up?"

Chad looked up pleadingly into Brett's scrutinising eyes, "Just go, man. I can't do it."

Brett shook his head derisively, "Look, get your ass in line. I told Mom you were a big baby. Yet, you've always got to hang around me and my friends."

Another of the guys, Andy, called out in irritation, "You guys coming or what?"

Brett hit Chad in the arm in frustration, "Go on!"

Chad hesitantly joined Phil and Andy, followed by Brett.

Chad shuffled awkwardly along in the queue, clearly unhappy at being forced to join his brother and friends.

The ride was situated quite close to one of the main parking lots and a tram shuttling guests from the cars to the amusement park gate suddenly rippled and swerved as if it would from a minor earthquake. The guests laughed as if it was a planned gag but the rumble stretched into the park and to the boys waiting in line. Chad looked even more uncomfortable while the other boys geed each other up.

The lads were now nearing the front of the queue. Above the deafening roar of the roller coaster and screams another slight rumble was heard.

Phil looked up at the sky, "Man, I thought it wasn't going to rain till tomorrow."

Andy looked up at the clear blue cloudless sky, "Looks okay to me." He ruffled Chad's hair teasingly, "Right, big guy?"

The older guys laughed at Chad's solemn demeanour and terrified face.

The roller coaster screeched to a halt. Shaken riders exited as others rushed to grab a seat, guided by two ride attendants.

Phil and Andy scrambled to win their place in the coaster's coveted front seat. Brett shoved his little brother, Chad, in behind them and then slid in next to him. The gang all joked and laughed except for Chad who was now frozen in fear, as they fastened the seat belts. Brett turned to his little brother and shrugged his shoulders warning him, "Maybe this'll teach you not to follow me around all the time!"

The giant roller coaster took off slowly then gathered a little speed. As they climbed the first steep incline the boys raised their hands in the air. Chad grasped his safety bar.

'Clang, clang, clang!' The roller coaster made its way to the top, then plunged down the first huge drop. Brett looked at Chad as they rounded the next curve in the track his fearful expression had disappeared and changed to one of pure delight.

The roller coaster followed more curves and bends then

began the next colossal incline. This time Chad was the first to raise his hands. So intent on the ride, none of the boys noticed what was happening in the fairground. People stumbled off rides as the ground shook again. Some exchanged nervous looks as they realised that the ground was trembling.

The roller coaster approached the top of the second monumental drop. Riders jostled in their seats screamed. Some realised that there was a problem but the boys were still blissfully unaware.

Suddenly, Utkena reared his ugly head. He pushed his head right up through the ground near the roller coaster ride and upset an ice cream cart at the park gates nearby. People scooped up children and hightailed it out of the theme park.

Utkena roared.

The weakened roller coaster structure slowly gave way as it buckled. The front section of seats were ripped from the track. The first few carriages dangled from the track's edge. Hysterical riders saw Utkena next to the giant framework as chaos erupted below. The park was suddenly full of screaming men, women and children.

Utkena lunged at a neighbouring parachute ride and spun it with his massive fingers. He bellowed in delight as people were thrust from their seats and propelled through the air.

Phil, Andy and Chad hung from the front seats of the coaster. Brett reached for Chad but couldn't stretch far enough. Chad slipped further away as Brett called out to him, "Hold on… You're gonna be okay."

Phil and Andy slowly managed to clamber to safety. Brett left his area of relative security and climbed to his brother's rescue. He was in a precarious position but just managed to grasp Chad's hand. Phil and Andy enlisted the help of other riders to form a human chain to help bring the two brothers to safety. People cheered urging Brett on and when Brett reached Chad he pulled his brother close and hugged him tightly, his street credibility was all forgotten. Chad clung on gratefully to his big brother, who was trying to hide the tears streaming down his cheek. The people went wild at the reunion.

Sirens were heard approaching in the distance but everyone's attention was now focused on Utkena. They stared in disbelief and dismay as he plucked a Park Security vehicle from the street and crushed it in his enormous hands.

Utkena delighted in his victory as the mangled metal tore into the living bodies inside and blood oozed out through the broken glass. He howled in pleasure when the ground rumbled. But his time it was not of Utkena's doing. His appearance and disturbance of the ground had triggered seismic activity.

The ground trembled and structures shook. The park became an even more chaotic scene. People tried to flee, rides ground to a halt. The Ferris Wheel stopped turning and left filled chairs stranded and swinging dangerously at the top. The Helter Skelter cracked, split and tumbled. Dodgem cars crashed and flew into barriers and out of the arena. Park goers screamed and ran in fear for their lives.

Utkena shook his head in glee and roared dementedly. He spied a little boy on the ledge of a smaller children's roller coaster. His blood lust had grown and driven by his exuberance and rage he reached out for the child as the boy's father tried desperately to haul his son to safety.

The earth's rumbling increased; the ground beneath Utkena cracked revealing a huge fissure. A water main burst and erupted from the ground. It was like a scene from a disaster movie. The water turned to steam, as it was seared by the heat from below, and a huge vacuum was created, which sucked Utkena back into the ground and the yawning crevice was filled with the falling debris and machinery of park rides.

Then just as quickly as the terror of the quake had begun the dreadful shuddering subsided. It had left a mass of destruction behind.

*****

That same afternoon, Abir's luggage waited as a cab driver took the bags to his vehicle. Abir hugged Onacoma and Inola and said goodbye.

"I planned to stay a few days, but…" a puzzled frown was on his face, "Something is calling me back to the city."

Onacoma looked from Abir to Inola, "We understand. Sanjukta will need you at her side."

Abir walked toward the cab and paused to wave at the two men before getting in the taxi and setting off for the airport.

The frown didn't leave his face and he was silent for much of the journey. The trip was quick and Abir paid the driver, collected his bags and was relieved to see there was no queue as he went to the check in desk to collect his boarding pass. He passed through Security with ease and made his way to the departure gate where he sat with a group of people waiting for the same flight.

Together they watched footage of the Amusement Park disaster on one of the small TV screens dotted through the airport. Abir leaned forward to hear what the reporter was saying.

"Although most park-goers say it felt like an earthquake, some report seeing a huge monster like creature."

A brief barely discernible blur of Utkena was seen on the screen. The lady next to Abir almost spilled her drink, "Damn!" She turned to Abir, "Did you see that? I saw it. I know I saw it. There's a monster on the loose!"

Abir slowly nodded his head and said almost to himself, "I'd recognise Utkena anywhere."

"What did you say?" snapped the lady. "Some psychotherapist guy is saying it was all a mass hallucination from the hysteria. I don't believe it. I wasn't there but I saw it, too. The camera can't lie."

Chapter Twelve

Dangerous paths

Cornelius and I had trudged along the winding path to reach the forbidding cliff face. With each step that we took I began to feel more heavily depressed and uncomfortable. I began to doubt myself and our mission.

The alien terrain of the Darkening Land was stark like something out of a futuristic fantasy movie. The sky's hues graded from deep gentian violet to indigo with any number of shades in between. Ominous, rolling clouds bursting with water that never fell, churned above, sometimes stealing the light from the twin silver blue moons that shone with a weird eerie glow. The ground underneath our feet was blood red as if stained from the drained bodies of many warriors and gloom showered down from the purple turbulent sky. I could hear the clash of steel in battle and cries of soldiers as they were slashed and cut to the ground. This land was filled with pain.

Every so often fissures would rip across our path revealing glowing molten lava in many colours that bubbled and spurted up. The heat was unbearable. We had to leap over these chasms that would mysteriously heal as if they had never been there. I began to wonder if they were real or some sort of mirage.

I felt as if we had been walking for hours and each plodding step was increasingly heavier as if we were trekking through desert sand that clung to our feet and weighted us down as would cement boots. The cries of a million lost souls rang in my head and rocks seemed to live and breathe sprouting blood drops, which sizzled and puffed fire.

The frightening skeleton trees seemed to develop a life of their own as they attempted to pluck at our limbs and impede our journey and I could swear that I heard snorts of derision as deformed branches scratched against the terrifying cliff face, a cliff face that we had yet to climb.

I stepped back to catch my breath and to discern the best footholds and places where I could safely scale the unforgiving cliff.

Cornelius saw my defeated expression, "I'll go first. I've done it before."

I didn't argue. I watched him climb. He was surprisingly agile for a city man. Once he had got into his rhythm I began to follow at his heels. We had managed to successfully negotiate the first leg of the climb and I felt my spirits beginning to lift when Cornelius' foot slipped sending a shower of loose stones tumbling down the cliff. Some hit me and stung my face. I bit my tongue and tried to avoid looking down the drop of the deadly precipice.

He shouted out, "Don't look down! There's a small ledge off to my right. I will try and reach it and rest a moment."

I watched him struggle as he tried to swing his foot onto the rocky edge and haul himself up but he almost missed his footing and part of the shelf he was trying to reach broke off under the force of his kick and plummeted down the escarpment.

I heard him grunt with exertion and could see the sweat beading on his brow. He finally clambered onto the relative safety of the ledge and sighed with relief. He pressed his back against the rocky wall and closed his eyes. I looked up but was blinded by a dusty avalanche of small stones that cascaded around my head.

He called out again, "Come on. Your turn now."

I took a step and wedged my foot securely in an indentation in the rock and stretched for the ledge to haul myself up but my fingers, moist with sweat, slipped and I was unable to get a grip. I misjudged my next step and lost my footing. In panic and unable to find a handhold I thrust my free hand into a small crack in the rock face and gasped to get my breath. There was a strange buzzing sound as I scrabbled futilely, hanging by one hand but oh so tantalisingly close to the safety of the ledge.

A swarm of metal helmeted black and red hornet like creatures surged angrily from a small crevice and began to attack me. I blinked as they dive-bombed my face and I looked up in supplication to Cornelius who stood frozen on the rocky platform. I couldn't read his expression.

"Cornelius!" I entreated. "Help me!"

Cornelius stared in horror at the winged army and remained completely immobile. My situation was as desperate as it could have been with the creatures tangling in my hair and trying to thrust their sharp, prickling stings through my clothes whilst others focused on using these burning stings on my hand, which was struggling to maintain its grip on the ledge. I realised that this onslaught could be heralding my death if Cornelius refused to come to my aid.

I screamed his name again, "Cornelius!"

My cry for help spurred him into action. His face twisted into an ugly grimace as he stared with uncertainty down at me. My single handhold was becoming weaker and the thought crossed my mind that if he stamped on my fingers I would tumble into the abyss and no one would know what had happened to me. My fingers slipped further when suddenly Cornelius bent down and firmly grasped my arm. Agonisingly slowly Cornelius managed to pull me up onto the small ledge. He breathed heavily with the exertion and neither of us spoke for a moment.

The army of soldier insects retreated back into the cliff and I collapsed in a heap at Cornelius' feet to nurse my wounded hand, which was coming up in angry red weals and bumps. "For a moment there, I thought you were going to let me fall," I croaked huskily. My mouth was dry with fear.

"For a moment I thought so, too," admitted Cornelius.

"Then again, we have to travel back this way," I muttered.

Cornelius raised an eyebrow, "Then again, we might not."

I swallowed hard. I was not feeling confident and at the back of my mind was the fear that perhaps this man would be my death knell, my nemesis.

*****

Many miles away, a prison officer, Lyle Sutton was driving his SUV to work and chatting on his cell phone. He was a big man and seemed in good spirits as he talked with his wife, he glanced back at the rear seat almost as if in need of reassurance as he glimpsed a large box sitting there. He grinned, "Yep, I got it. I'll assemble it right after work tonight."

Lyle's wife, Marie chatted on the cordless phone as she rinsed the dishes before loading them into the dishwasher. She tossed down the dishcloth and twirled around, "Jimmy's going to be so excited. You got the one he had his eye on, right?"

"Sure did... And I got him a padlock so no one can take it this time."

Lyle drove to the prison gate entrance, showed his ID and continued on. He parked his vehicle and stepped out, still talking, "Mum's the word. The bike's a surprise."

His wife clattered about as she finished loading the dishwasher, put in the detergent capsule and closed the door, "I know. I know."

Lyle strode toward the entrance to the prison, a sign above the door read: Employees Only. "Okay, babe. I'm at work now, I got to go. Love ya."

"You be careful and be well."

Lyle laughed and flipped his phone shut as he entered the penitentiary. "She always says that. What the hell can happen to me here?"

He clocked in and made his way to the second floor when on the stroke of nine the doors on that level opened automatically. Prisoners stepped out of their cells and formed a line. Lyle, together with several other guards led them to the exercise yard.

As the prisoners and guards exited the building into the compound's recreation area the ground erupted. Utkena appeared forcing his way up through the tarmac. He was angrier than ever and he knocked down anything and everything in his path.

Sirens and alarms blared as Utkena shredded a tall electrical fence. The wires tumbled down, snaking and shooting sparks everywhere but Utkena felt no pain.

A guard in a tower aimed at the monster and hammered

shots out from his automatic rifle. Bullets bounced off the demon. He grew stronger, taller and angrier with each hit. One swipe of his giant hand propelled the guard through the air and toppled the tower.

"What the hell is that?" shouted another sentry.

"Damned if I know and I ain't waiting to find out, " screeched a prisoner.

Chaos reigned in the yard. Prisoners both scared and excited attempted an escape.

Lyle and other guards drew their weapons and gathered together some of the inmates near the basketball hoop. Utkena roared and grabbed one of the prisoners. Lyle shot at the demon, which dropped the prisoner and then turned his anger on Lyle. He seized the officer from the ground and bellowed. Lyle struggled to free himself as Utkena stomped off toward the city.

*****

In the Sutton's home kitchen, Lyle's wife, Marie watched a small TV as she prepared dinner. A news flash caught her eye. She turned up the volume as her son, Jimmy entered. "What's up, Mom?"

"Shh!" Marie nodded at the television and they listened to the report together.

"This is just in. State and local police have been called to Lesley Prison. First reports indicate a possible riot. Some prisoners have escaped. Residents living nearby are being asked to stay inside and lock all doors and windows."

Marie gulped back her tears, "Oh, my…"

Jimmy grabbed his mother's hand, "What about dad?"

Marie pulled her son in close to her and stifled a sob, "He'll be okay, pumpkin." She kissed Jimmy's head, "He'll be okay." She paused and added, "He has to be."

*****

Cornelius and I had finally made it to the top of the cliff where there was a whirling, whistling wind. We each stopped to catch our breath after the arduous climb and moved on, leaning into the ferocious wind that strived to push us back and force us off our feet.

"The wind will drop once we reach the tower," shouted Cornelius above the howling screech as the elements tugged at our clothes and us.

"But then we face other dangers," I answered with trepidation.

We struggled on passing a small black obelisk with a strange inscription. It caught my attention and I paused a moment to scrutinise the symbols that looked like Indian petroglyphs.

I ventured closer and felt compelled to touch the rock carving. My fingers dipped into it like quicksilver. I stepped back in shock as if I had been burnt. The rock rippled like the surface of a pool and Astila stepped out to face us. He handed me a medicine bag and raised his fingers to his lips as if imparting some huge secret. It was hard to hear above the cacophony of the wind.

"When the quarms come to feed on the organs of sight, unroll the bag and hold high in the wind. The gossamer strands will divert their flight, disorientate them, and mask you from view. It is a shield that can only be used twice. Use it with care. You must hurry for Utkena is intent on destroying the world."

The little man jumped back into the obelisk and faded from view.

"Organs of sight?" I questioned.

"Those little flying creatures," Cornelius indicated the cloud of critters circling the tower, "Are quarms. They are there to blind you, to eat out your eyes so the path is kept secret."

"How did you avoid them before?" I asked curiously.

"Utkena was with me."

We moved on toward the harsh, menacing and crumbling tower that stretched up to the threatening sky where the quarms circled and screeched. Cornelius pushed forward into the howling wind after he placed goggles over his eyes to shield them from the quarms and the swirling dust.

I began chanting a Cherokee mantra of protection, as I had been taught by my grandfather. I shook my Shaman rattle and looked about me. One of the brown leathery skinned steel-eyed quarms spotted us and gave a blood-curdling shriek. The creature dived down to Cornelius' head and gnawed at his goggle straps. I plucked the flapping creature from his head, which flapped and hissed. It screwed its head around and spat yellow venom at me. I shielded my face. The yellow spittle singed the skin on my arm.

The creature's screech of anger alerted the rest of the quarms, which descended rapidly. I knew we were in trouble.

Cornelius yelled, "Quick! The medicine bag! Hurry."

I feverishly ripped open the bag and struggled to unroll it. My hands were shaking like some alcoholic bag lady. I could see one of the terrifying creatures hurtling toward me its vicious beak leading it straight to my face. One of the laces snagged on my ring and I hurried to free it. I felt the wind from its scaly wings fan my face just before I managed to free the gossamer strands and hold it aloft. The threads streamed out and flew around Cornelius, who had crushed up tightly to my back, and me.

The magical yarns effectively masked us from the attacking quarms who screamed in fury at being denied their delicacy of human eyes.

From under the rocks and stones crawled armoured black scorpion type creatures, which milled into a protective defensive line behind Cornelius and me. They waved their pincers in the air and a quarm dived down to them but they latched onto the hapless creature with their sharp claws, drew up their deadly stings and fatally pierced the critter's body stinging it to death.

The other quarms seeing the demise of their fellow killing machine retreated to circle the tower once more. A platoon of the strange scorpions waved their pincer claws menacingly. They bunched together to protect our pathway so that we could move unimpeded to safety. We walked on.

The sandy ground rippled like mercury that had bled out. It was hard to walk bunched together. As soon as we had travelled far enough from the tower I was able to wrap up the threads and I repacked the magical shroud into the medicine bag and placed it into my backpack.

We plodded on and the moons turned violet and the sky became a midnight blue inky colour. Cornelius pointed ahead, "The circle of Sourwood trees. That's where we'll make camp."

I nodded, he had been here before; I hadn't. I was in his hands. "I'll find some kindling. We'll need to make a fire."

"Don't wander too far. It's not safe." He pointed to a shadowy swirling mass filled with pinpricks of light, "The Ghost Country lies through there."

"Are you sure you don't want to press on?"

"We need to rest. We will need all our strength and we need to eat." Cornelius hesitated.

"Was there something else?"

"This place, where we are now…"

"The Sacred Circle?"

"It's not as safe as it seems."

I looked at him questioningly, "Go on."

"A strange mist is known to envelop this area bringing illusion and deceit. Don't believe all you see and hear."

A shiver ran down my spine. I attempted to collect some brushwood for a fire. I needed to do something, to be busy and not to have to think about what Cornelius had just said.

Cornelius undid his bedroll from the backpack and a small primus stove, which he lit while I made up a small fire in the hope it would chase any evil mist away. He rustled up some corned beef hash and beans and I stared thoughtfully out into the ink black night that was dotted with tiny specks of starlight.

We finished our meagre meal and cleared up. "We must sleep," said Cornelius. He stuffed his ears with some wax earplugs and settled down to sleep. I made sure I had my Shaman knife by my side and kept all my magical accoutrements close to me and tried to rest, firmly closing my eyes to the strangeness of the dark that had crept around me.

I turned erratically in my sleep as a whispering voice invaded my dreams bringing me to an uncomfortable drowsy wakefulness as if in a nightmare state. I peeped through my eyelashes. An alien fog had surrounded us and began to take form. I closed my eyes firmly trying to blot everything out when a familiar voice coursed through my mind and I partially opened my eyes and saw a shadowy figure gaining substance or was it a trick of the light? I gasped as I saw the strong features of Abir and heard his voice urging me to wake, "Sanjukta, Union! Wake up!"

I opened my eyes wide and searched the dark then rubbed them in disbelief, Abir?"

"Ssh! You'll wake him." The figure indicated the sleeping Cornelius.

"What are you doing? How did you get here?" I was trying to reconcile myself with seeing my old friend but questions tumbled through my mind, how did he find me? How did he avoid the quarms?

I was given no chance to think my thoughts through as he spoke quickly, "Hurry. It's all a trick. He brought you here to kill you."

"But…"

Cornelius began to stir.

The voice became more urgent and insistent, "Quickly before he wakes."

The voice echoed in my brain pleadingly, begging me to finish Cornelius before he finished me. Almost as if my will was being sapped I felt the knife in my hand. I stole from my bed and began to sneak across to where Cornelius lay.

"Go on! Do it!" hissed the voice.

Cornelius propped himself up on his elbow and saw me approaching with my raised blade. I saw the alarm in his face as he read my tortured expression and I stopped.

The voice hissed, "What are you waiting for?"

I had time to think back and remembered the time on the cliff when Cornelius had saved my life and I hesitated, "If he'd wanted to kill me, he could have done so before this."

Cornelius spoke quickly and assertively, "That's right. On the cliff face… I could have let you fall."

"Ah, but there would have been the danger of being found. He wants no evidence and no witnesses. Trust me."

The voice had turned oily with fawning supplication.

I was confused, this man was my enemy the other was my friend. But I had come here on a quest to serve mankind. Who should I have believed? My mind was clouded with uncertainty. I couldn't seem to think straight.

Cornelius kept his eye on me and the knife and whispered, "Ask him something. Ask him something only you and he know."

Abir's voice came back at me, "Don't listen to him. He's just stalling. Kill him or it will be the end for all of us."

I held still I knew my face was a mask of confusion and hatred. I lifted the knife higher and moved closer.

Cornelius was now panicking, "Sanjukta…?"

I stopped and fired a question at who I thought to be Abir, "Tell me what was it that first made us friends?"

The reply came back instantly, "That's easy, your courage and strength. You could fight like a man."

I pressed him with another question, "What happened to us when we met Chitto in the clearing with the others?"

The figure stopped to think as the memories flooded my head.

"When you stopped me spying on the girls as they bathed?"

I tried to force the images from my mind and focused, "No! We were fourteen."

Cornelius interrupted my flow and ordered me, "Don't think about it. He can read your mind. Think of something unrelated."

"You saved my life," said the figure more confidently.

I emptied my mind and concentrated hard, "How?" I filled my head with memories of the snake pit and how the ritual had changed.

The figure of Abir seemed to struggle desperately to read my mind and then his face lit up in glee, "You bit the head off a rattlesnake that was going to attack me."

I turned from Cornelius, and brandished my blade at the figure as I moved toward him. He started to back away.

I shouted at him, "Wrong!"

The figure hissed in defeat and snarled revealing vampire-like teeth and then imploded into a puff of smoke.

I stepped back to Cornelius and sheathed my knife, "Sleep or no sleep, let's get out of this place." I offered him my hand and pulled him up.

We hurriedly packed up our things and set off into the all-enveloping dark.

Chapter Thirteen

The Ghost Country

Cornelius and I walked with trepidation to the swirling indistinct mass ahead of us. We knew it was the portal to the Ghost Country but neither of us knew what to expect either in it or beyond it. A slight breeze blew the leaves on the shrubs that bordered the ever-turning circle of mist and light. They tinkled like glass bells in the soft air.

The wind grew stronger and billowed around us the nearer we got. It pulled at our clothes and buffeted us toward the mystical entrance. We exchanged looks and Cornelius prodded me, "Go on."

I tried to step forward but was repelled by the vicious wind and an invisible shield. Cornelius took the key he carried and held it out and the force field dissipated to nothing. I looked at him. What would await us on the other side? I had no idea. I needed to dig into the well of courage that was hiding from me that day.

"Never mind," Cornelius grinned humourlessly and pushed past me. "I'll go first." The tumbling wind blew his hair from his face and his skin rippled and stretched as if in a wind tunnel. He shouted, "Geronimo!" and stepped inside the vortex and vanished from my sight.

I gulped hard and followed. I seemed to be twisted and thrown into a moving rotunda that took my legs out from underneath me and somersaulted me out through the other side where the disturbing wind was no more. All was still. I stood up and was visibly shaken.

Cornelius was sitting on the ground next to me. He rose and dusted himself down, "What kept you?"

I had to admit that humour at this time was quite welcoming in view of what we had already been through.

The Ghost Country seemed to be a place in permanent twilight. The landscape was a shadowy grey. The trees and vegetation were indistinct in colour and shape. A path stretched before us of well-worn roughly hewn stone with silver moss that spread freely across the surface cracks.

In the distance we could see light, a distant tunnel of light with rhythmically jumping rainbow beams that beckoned and called to us in our hearts. We could just discern mystical shapes that danced in a magical mist where the colour transcended the normal and was brighter and more vivid than any that man could create. This was of the Gods.

Cornelius grew excited, he indicated the alluring colourful and illuminating barrel portal. "That's where we're headed."

I stood there enraptured. I felt it calling to me, "It's beautiful," I sighed.

"That's the danger. At the edge of the Ghost Country drifts the souls of those unable to find their way. The newly dead dance together before proceeding to the light, where paradise awaits."

"What's the danger?" I asked puzzled.

"That we won't want to go back."

We moved on treading the grey and silver path. As we walked I had a vision. My thoughts were so vivid I wondered if these fleeting events that worked into my memory were real or imagined. In my mind's eye I saw the horrific image of Utkena striding along a deserted highway. He was marching past homes and farms where residents on catching sight of the demon ran to take cover. He plodded on clutching a man wearing a prison officer's uniform in his gigantic hand. The image reminded me of the film King Kong where that huge gorilla held onto Fay Wray.

I gasped. Cornelius asked, "What is it?"

"Utkena. He's moving on toward the city."

"How do you know?"

"I can see him… in my head. He's got a prison officer… no wait. He's flung the man down. He's lowering his head and horns and is going to march on the city. We have to succeed." This knowledge and how it had come to me strengthened my resolve and spurred me on.

Cornelius nodded and we paused as haunted figures and faces flew past us, souls in torment searching for a way back to the living. The terrible moaning and wailing they made was heart rending and frightening. Faces looked gaunt, grey and harrowed. They opened their mouths and despairing cries echoed out. They reminded me of Edvard Munch's iconic painting, 'The Scream'.

I ducked swiftly as a phantom shape with wizened features like an old crone almost swept right through me. We hastened our steps where this place of lost souls terrified and frightened me. An eerie silence suddenly encompassed us. Even our footsteps seemed muffled, blanketed in the half-light. I didn't know what to expect when an eagle screeched overhead and swooped from the gloom and hovered above me. A melancholy wolf howled and materialised from the murky depths and padded at the side of the two of us.

The appearance of these creatures deflected the impact of the ghostly shapes whose faces were locked in the terror of death. We marched on past these spiritual wrecks and the light began to brighten and warm as we emerged from the dull clinging fog into the pink light of love.

Musical harmonies whispered on the wind and grew louder as we approached a circle of dancers. The light was beautiful and the feelings it brought with it were joyous and free. I rubbed my eyes, never had I been anywhere so lovely. I glanced across at Cornelius whose jaw had dropped in wonder.

He suddenly became alert and prompted me, "Find him. Find Dante."

I scanned the many dancers of different ages and gender that were all bathed in an ethereal light. They were wearing fine silken robes that floated as they moved and then I saw him. My heart almost stopped. I wanted to run to him and hold him but I knew we had to follow the correct procedure or it would never work. "There he is. See!"

I pointed him out and Cornelius followed my finger and urged me, "We must be quick. As he nears us you have to strike him to put him in the box."

Cornelius removed the box from his pack and I took out a hand carved sourwood rod and waited for the right moment.

All of the dancers were blind to us and only involved in the dance.

The circle of dancers moved round and Dante approached. I moved like lightning and struck Dante on the shoulder transforming him into an orb of brilliant blue light, which darted and zoomed.

Our watchful eagle swooped after the orb. Its great wings swept it into the open box. Cornelius closed the casket with a flourish and the dancers continued, oblivious to what had just occurred.

"Now what?"

"We must proceed to the tunnel, walk through the light and find my wife and son on the other side."

"But, how can we keep Dante in the box when we trap the others?"

"I don't know, but we have to try. I'm sure we can manage. The point is, we must not open the box on the return journey, no matter what they say. Once we reach our country we can release them safely to live again."

"It sounds simple enough," I said then hesitated when I saw Cornelius' expression.

He looked me straight in the eye and said quietly, "But, it's never been done!"

I took a deep breath and stepped forward. I was gratified that Cornelius walked with me alongside the wolf and the eagle. We stopped at the opening to the rainbow tunnel and exchanged a glance and as one we stepped inside.

The tunnel swirled with a myriad of tiny rainbow dancing lights and bathed us in its colours, which were tangible and warm like a soft fabric, which allowed us to walk as if on air. We travelled on through this miraculous tunnel, which filled us with euphoria. As we travelled on the voices from the world of man that had filled my head were stilled. No more could I hear Abir and Troy wondering at my location and what I was doing. No more did I hear of the evil and havoc that Utkena was unleashing. I was calm, serene and at peace.

The tunnel progressively brightened. Bird song and laughter became clearer as we neared the entrance to the Land of Souls. I had never felt so completely at ease but I knew this could be a dangerous state of mind and Cornelius' warning came back to me, 'We won't want to leave.'

As if I had spoken the words aloud Cornelius said, "I've never felt so good. It's as if there are no troubles left in the world that love cannot conquer."

I had to remind him, "We have to focus on our mission and not get caught up in the ecstasy of this place."

I watched as Cornelius shook his head as if trying to clear it. I saw him taking some deep breaths. I assumed it was to try and centre his mind.

We stepped into this world of love and light.

Cornelius turned to me, "You wait here. If I'm not back in thirty minutes, leave without me."

I checked my watch and was amazed to see the hands racing recklessly around the dial, "But…"

"Here, there is no time," he explained, "You will have to gauge it. Do as I say, and save your friend."

"But I need you to stand with me against Utkena if I am to succeed," I protested.

Cornelius studied my face before replying crisply, "I know." I watched him stride off toward a range of rolling hills and meadows and settled myself by a small waterfall where nature spirits danced and swam. I was entranced at their beauty, their tumbling hair, ethereal figures and silvery, tinkling laughter. Oh, how I longed to dive in and swim with them but I knew that would be a mistake and possibly bind me to them in this wondrous realm.

My friend the wolf sat at my side. The warmth and softness of his fur as I ruffled it chased all questions and worries away. As we sat I saw something moving behind the curtain of water and to my delighted surprise saw my mother, Louella, emerge with my handsome father, Ridge. They both shone with an extraordinary light that radiated out and into my heart.

My breath caught in my throat and I could barely speak such was my emotion at seeing the mother I had never met or known. I managed barely a squeak, "Mother, is that you?"

She laughed, as she crossed to me, and the sound was like a thousand harmonious scales played on a baby xylophone.

Louella offered me her hand and pulled me to my feet. A warm glow pulsed up my arm at her touch and I wanted to cry.

"Sanjukta, my daughter. Let me look at you."

I gasped as she held me by the shoulders and I could feel this amazing heat emanating from her hands and travelling around my body, healing me and making my hornet stung hands whole and clear, "You are beautiful. We are so proud of you, of all you have achieved and all that you will do for I have seen your future."

My father hopped lightly on the stepping-stones to join us and added, "And it is a good one, my daughter."

I suddenly had a brilliant idea, "Come back with me, please. I have the means."

My father gazed into my eyes, "But, why would we want to leave paradise?"

"Here there is no prejudice, no hatred and everything is born of love," said my mother simply.

"Then I will stay."

My father shook his head, "It was our time. It is not yours. You still have much to do."

"But, I never had a chance to know you. That was taken from me most cruelly."

"We will visit you in your dreams," my father assured me.

My mother gestured to her chest and head, "And you will carry us in your heart and mind."

I was beginning to feel tearful, "But why? Why would I want to leave you?"

"Because of this," and as my father spoke he waved his hand across the curtain of water, which became a living moving screen depicting the world of men and Utkena rampaging through it.

His monstrous bulk was tramping toward the city and far behind him the man that he had flung down in prison officer clothes, Lyle struggled to stand. He brushed himself off and checked his injuries. His trouser leg was soaked with blood, he stepped forward and a grimace of pain crossed his features. It was clear his ankle was damaged or sprained and yet the man managed to take a few steps, even though he winced in agony. He peered into the distance after the demonic monster intent on striding toward the city. I could hear the man's thoughts and determination as he made a concerted effort to hobble after Utkena.

My mother turned her loving eyes onto me, "Utkena must be stopped. He wants to destroy everything and everyone."

My father added, "You are the only one who can do that." He waved his hand again and showed me the broken fairground, the wrecked prison and the fawning creatures that played in the wave of a Tsunami. "You and Cornelius. You must unite and do this together."

"But, what if Cornelius doesn't return? What then?"

"He will."

"But where is he? What is happening to him?"

My father changed the fluid screen once more and I could see Cornelius walking through this beautiful land, as if on a cloud of happiness. The delight on his face was evident for anyone to see. He reached a valley of flowers and closed his eyes and inhaled their fragrant scent. The sound of a babbling brook and tranquil music filled the air around him. It was if I was in his heart and with him. I caught my breath, feeling his joy.

Rabbits and deer stopped at the side of the stream and Cornelius opened his eyes. He watched the creatures in awe and stretched out his hand to pet the small roe deer. But the animal darted away. It remained tantalisingly close as if it wanted Cornelius to follow. Follow he did, chasing after the creature as it scampered ahead.

He crossed over a hill where an even more enticing scene awaited. Before his very eyes I could see Cornelius' face as he spotted his wife and son sitting in the grassy meadow in the shade of a strong oak tree.

I was mesmerised and eager to see what happened next. A light breeze blew his hair as he called out to them.

"Suzanne! Jon!"

For some reason they did not appear to have heard him and I felt Cornelius' heart begin to pound in his chest as he ran toward them. "Suzanne… Jon… It's me. I've come to take you home."

His wife and son finally looked up at him and smiled. His son was the first to speak. "Dad! I knew you would come."

"We both did," sighed his wife.

Suzanne rose to her feet and clasped her husband in her arms in a loving embrace and tears formed in her eyes. She whispered, "I am so sorry. I should never have done what I did."

Cornelius soothed her, "That doesn't matter now." He released her and hugged his son. "I was so proud of you, Jon."

"I know, Dad. I know."

"Come... Let's go." As he said these words a distance sprang between them. Cornelius looked puzzled.

Suzanne glanced at her son and back to her husband, "Oh, Cornelius. I'm sorry. We're happy and at peace here."

Cornelius floundered, uncertain what to say, "But you... but I came to..."

Jon interrupted his father's confusion, "She's right, Dad. We're both where we want to be. It was my time. If it hadn't been Iraq it would have been something else: another tour of duty, a car accident, a fatal illness. I'm not meant to return."

I could feel Cornelius' agony that squeezed at his heart.

"And I know what I did was wrong," said Suzanne. "But, my life would only have continued a few more months. It was all meant to be."

Cornelius started to plead, "But, I love you. Without you my life is empty."

Suzanne and Jon slipped a little further away. She stretched out her hand and was suddenly, back at his side. She tenderly brushed aside his hair that was ruffled by the gentle breeze and tumbled across his forehead., "You must go back without us, my darling."

"But, Suzanne...?"

"Oh, Cornelius. You make my heart ache, but you have to return and leave us here."

"But..."

"It is your destiny. You were never meant to be like your father. He was a tyrant."

"I don't understand..." Tears were now streaming down

Cornelius' face and I could taste the salt in them. He was completely crushed.

"There is a monster loose on earth that only you can stop. You and your Indian sister."

"We've seen the future, Dad," said Jon.

"Your future." And in words that echoed those of my parents Suzanne added, "And it's a good one. Look out for a woman called Ella. She will bring joy to your life once more."

At that moment Suzanne moved back to Jon and a further distance lay between them. His wife took Jon's hand and they stepped backward.

"Stop! Wait! Don't go!" pleaded Cornelius.

His son and wife chorused, "Goodbye. We love you." They blew him a kiss and began to fade.

"No!"

Suzanne and Jon continued to fade until they could no longer be seen and Cornelius wept, "Come back! I'll stay here, with you."

The voice of Suzanne was heard on the breeze, "It's not your time…"

I watched as Cornelius sobbed, a broken man and my love went out to him. I could see him struggling to compose himself. He marched onto the tunnel where we had entered. My father spoke, "Quickly, follow him. He sees nothing but his sorrow. He will be tempted to stay."

I felt Cornelius spirit rush past me. He didn't stop but strode on into the tunnel and toward the Ghost Country. I had no time to say my goodbyes but the image of my parents standing lovingly together watching me would remain with me always.

"We love you, Sanjukta and we will visit you in your dreams." They stepped back behind the curtain of water and vanished.

I sped into the tunnel after Cornelius. I could see him ahead of me but it was as if I was deliberately being delayed. I found it hard to walk. My limbs felt like they were covered in treacle and I had to focus hard to move ahead, one foot in front of another. Cornelius had now reached the place where the dead danced and I struggled on, able to see him but not get close.

A beautiful woman suddenly appeared at Cornelius' side. Her voice was haunting and enticing, "So, you want to stay?"

He nodded miserably and I yearned to push through the sticky air mass that was holding me back. I heard his voice, "Well, yes, with my wife and…"

The seductive female sidled up to him and short, sharp prongs on her skimpy clothing tried to attach to Cornelius, "You can stay with me." She beckoned him provocatively, "But, you must come of your own free will…"

Cornelius looked around, "But, my wife… my son…"

The woman arched her back and purred seductively, "Come…"

I struggled against the sticky strands from this thick molasses and finally burst through in time to see Cornelius stepping toward the female spirit as if hypnotised. I flew out from the rainbow tunnel my feet running in the air and I floated down and shrieked out, "No, Cornelius! Don't be fooled."

My voice made him turn but he seemed unable to react or move. The woman latched onto his arm and the little prongs from her clothing began to work their way into his.

The eagle, which had been circling let out a warning cry that snapped Cornelius from his stupor. I raced to his side and begged him, "Don't do this. We must be strong, strong together, remember?"

Cornelius looked at the alluring female that seemed to be fawning all over him, enveloping him. He gazed back at me as I continued, "You will go home with me and bring honour to Suzanne and Jon. Please."

A miraculous change came over him and he struggled to extricate himself from her grasp. I caught his arm and tugged helping to free him from this encompassing evil. Once he stood alone the woman began to spit and she screeched in anger reforming into the vampire figure from before. Cornelius' eyes were still latched onto this wraith and I had to drag him away from this temptation.

The wolf who had been with me at the waterfall waited

patiently at the tunnel opening and snarled at the figure, which dissolved into mist. The air around us was filled with hysterical mocking laughter.

Chapter Fourteen

City cases roll on.

Troy was embroiled in a pile of case files. He closed and tossed one down. He sighed and swung his laptop to face him and opened it. It fired up immediately onto the Yahoo home page and he clicked on 'News'.

The headline story had newsreel footage of Utkena's widespread damage. Troy was drawn to the pictures of devastation on his computer screen when his secretary tapped on his door and opened it.

"The D.A.'s here to see you."

Troy pulled his gaze away from the screen and smiled, "Great. Send him in please." He hurriedly minimised the news clip to sit in his dock for later and rose half way to greet Robert Meade and shake his hand. "Hey, Rob. Glad you could make it. I imagine things are buzzing down at City Hall." Troy nodded at the computer screen, "I've been following the news."

Troy indicated a chair in front of his desk for Rob to sit.

Rob sat; his expression was gloomy, "The mayor wants us to call in the National Guard. The thing is, no one really knows what we are up against."

"Terrorists?"

"No, they've ruled that out."

"Well, in the meantime," Troy paused, "I have some good news." He tapped an oversized file on his desk. "It looks like we have an open and shut case against Cornelius Phipps." Troy passed the large file to Rob, who opened it and thumbed through it. "And that's just the beginning."

"Nice work. I'll finally get to put that scumbag where he belongs."

"Yes, I just wish Sanjukta was back to see this. She worked so hard on this case."

"Yes. Where is she?"

"I don't know. Even her friend, Abir hasn't been able to contact her. We are all quite worried. She promised to be back in a week and I have been holding out with this for her return."

"Hm. Not to mention the fact that she would be a huge loss to your firm."

"I have a feeling she'll be true to her word. She'll be back."

"I hope you're right."

*****

At that moment, Cornelius and I trudged the path we had crossed before carrying the box containing Dante's soul. We knew how dangerous this land was and ahead of us we could see the tower and the quarms circling it.

I could tell that Cornelius was in emotional pain and hoped that it wouldn't cloud his judgement. He turned to me, "You still have the pack?"

"The cloak of protection?"

Cornelius nodded, "Yes."

I patted my Shamanic pack. "It's here."

"We'd better prepare." He covered his anguish well and his tone was firm and flint-like, "Just ahead by that boulder. We will stop."

Together we marched on into this desolate, Godforsaken, barren land.

A quarm spotted us approaching and dived down, leaving the tower and hurtling toward us. The eagle that was still with us flying overhead swooped down on the creature before it could reach us.

The shriek from this alien being attracted the attention of the others who came to the stricken creature's aid. I watched in fascination drawn to the horrific act being played out before me.

"Quickly!" yelled Cornelius. "Hurry."

Alert once more I wrested with my pack to remove the roll. Above us a battle raged. The noble eagle was outnumbered and suffered fatally in the attack. He plummeted to earth in a flurry of feathers. The vicious critters quickly devoured the eagle's eyes and then began on the body. This feeding frenzy gave me some precious time.

I was all fingers and thumbs, shuddering at what was happening. Cornelius grabbed the pack and held it aloft, which unrolled and shielded our wolf friend and us from the quarms' sight. For the minute we were safe. We struggled on. It was difficult to keep our arms up, especially in the growing wind that raced around us.

The world of men and visions from them filled my head. I knew I was seeing events as a way of spurring me on to complete the quest. I could see the Prison Officer, Lyle barely walking. He stumbled along a deserted highway when he spotted a car at a crossroad up ahead. Re-energised he speeded up and waved at the driver. The young man at the wheel did not appear to see him and turned the corner. Lyle limped to the middle of the road almost defeated but drew enough energy to shout and wave madly.

The driver caught a glimpse of the Prison Officer in his rear view mirror and exclaimed, "What the…?"

He hurriedly turned his vehicle around and raced back to pick up Lyle and they sped off toward the city.

I knew in my heart they were moving on toward Utkena and terrible danger and that thought pushed me on.

My exhaustion forgotten I sprinted to the cliff and looked down. Cornelius wrapped up the gossamer threaded shield and joined me, "Ready?" I asked. He nodded "The wolf? Where is he?" We looked around but neither of us could see the creature. and so we gingerly clambered over the top and began our descent.

The climb down was proving as difficult as the climb up and I struggled to find the correct handholds and footholds. My foot slipped and I sent a shower of stones tumbling down the cliff and froze, desperately trying to regain my equilibrium.

As I stopped a fierce knocking came from the inside of the box. Dante shouted, "Help! I'm suffocating. Let me out."

My heart hiccupped when I heard his voice and I whispered, "Dante."

He heard me and questioned, "Sanjukta? Union? Is that you?"

I tried to placate him and also still the tears that rose so freely at the sound of his voice. "I can't release you yet. We're on a cliff. It's too dangerous."

But Dante was in a panic, "I'm claustrophobic. My heart will give out. I need air. Please." I hesitated. I never knew that my friend was claustrophobic and I could hear his distress as he began to whimper.

Cornelius stopped his descent and shouted at me warningly, "Don't do it. Remember what happened to the daughter of the Sun."

I set my mouth in a determined line and refused to listen to Dante's pleas. I just kept repeating the words from the legend as I recalled them and I called out, "Dante, my friend, I can't. For if I do you will die."

He knocked even harder as if trying to break free but the further we travelled down the cliff the fainter the knocks became. "Cornelius?"

He could hear the anguish in my voice, "No! You must be strong."

"But what if he dies in there?"

"That's a risk we have to take. You cannot set him free."

I slipped down the last few feet of the cliff and grazed my hands in the process and tumbled to the ground. Cornelius jumped down and helped me up.

"The box has gone very quiet," I whispered.

"I hope it stays that way until it's safe to let him free. Then we will see whether or not it is all a myth," replied Cornelius.

I nodded and miraculously, our friend the wolf appeared, he must have found his own route down the cliff and he was unscathed by the quarms. He padded alongside us as we travelled on.

Cornelius and I traipsed back through the twilight to the circle of elders. We were both exhausted and in desperate need of sleep. It would not do to let our guards down now, so we walked on to the tunnel that led underground to the basement of his property.

The tunnel was damp and dripping I slipped on a patch of moss and almost dropped the precious box. If it hadn't been for Cornelius it would have smashed and then who knows what would have happened? We pressed onward. The tunnel wound around and gradually sloped up. The dark was becoming oppressive, we had little light to guide our way, but the wolf remained with us at every step. Eventually, we reached the ladder that would take us up into his house.

Cornelius went first and I shivered, what if he were to lock me in down here? How would I escape? Who would know of my whereabouts and what would happen to Dante? I tried to chase these unforgiving thoughts from my mind and I was almost surprised when he extended his hand for the box and set it through the hatch on the floor next to him and then offered me his hand again to help me up. I flushed guiltily at such uncharitable thoughts.

"Cornelius, what about our friend the wolf?"

"Can you lift him?"

I was surprised that the animal didn't flinch but allowed me to put my arms around him and I succeeded in raising him aloft. His paws scrabbled on the edge of the wooden flooring and he sat at Cornelius' side and waited.

I clambered up and tumbled onto the floorboards and scrambled up dusting myself down.

"What now?" asked Cornelius.

"I suppose we should get outside and make our way to Onacoma's cabin."

Cornelius nodded curtly and stepped to the front door. I picked up the box, which felt heavier as if there was some substance inside. Cornelius led the way. We walked in silence toward the Chief's house. As we neared his porch a light wind sprang up from nowhere and whirled around us. The wolf sat down and lifted his amber eyes to me. It was a sign.

Cornelius and I eyed each other and in silent agreement we nodded to each other. The time was now. The box was set down on the dusty track. I knelt down beside it and ever so cautiously Cornelius touched the latch and unhitched it. The lid flew open.

A blinding light flashed before us. We shielded our eyes in the brilliant glare. We heard a whirring whizzing sound and tentatively removed our hands from our eyes. When we did we were stunned to see Dante standing before us.

Cornelius whispered in awe, "It worked."

Dante stared lovingly at me, "Union!" He opened his arms. I fell into them.

We embraced and he kissed me passionately. My eyes pricked with hot, salt tears, "I thought I'd lost you for good." I sighed.

"Why? What happened?"

"Don't you remember?"

Dante looked puzzled, "I recall dancing with you at the club and then... and then... a man pushed his way through to us. He had a knife. He wanted to kill you and I... I..."

"You took the hit for me," I finished.

"But how? I... How did I get here and..." Dante lifted his silk shirt and examined his body, "I don't understand there's no mark... no scar..." he looked quizzically at me. Then he glanced back at his apparel. "What am I wearing?"

"We can fix this, don't worry."

"But, why am I wearing this and why is there no sign of the injury?"

"I don't know whether you'd believe me if I told you."

"And..." he looked at Cornelius, "What's he doing here?"

"It's a long story."

"I'm listening." It was then he saw the wolf, "My God, what's been happening here?"

"He's nothing to worry about; he's a loyal friend who has journeyed with me."

I was just about to try and explain all the events when from under the wooden porch two of the little people appeared and ran toward us. It was Astila and Noya. Dante just watched and listened, totally lost for words.

Astila called my name, "Sanjukta, Union! Now is the time to fulfil your destiny. You must gather the people around you to face Utkena but only you..." he turned to Cornelius and held his gaze, "Only you, Cornelius can send him back. As *you* summoned him so *you* must make him retreat."

Cornelius looked helplessly around him while Dante watched in wonder, "But how?"

Astila pointed at the Box of Souls, "The box carries another power, the power to shrink fear. Open it in his presence and sprinkle the ground with this." Astila handed me a pouch filled with herbs and seeds.

I hesitated. I knew I should have known better but I couldn't help myself, "But they're just herbs, herbs and seeds."

"What can a bunch of herbs do?" snorted Cornelius derisively. "This is Utkena."

Gradually Dante began to understand something of what was being said, "You mean, we are going up against Utkena?" I nodded and he continued, "Great! We're facing a monster and all we have to fight with is next season's vegetable patch."

Noya held up her hands to halt the dissent. We stopped and listened to her, "You must be strong. And you must believe. Listen carefully. Engraved on the casket is a mantra, which you must repeat. Say it, over and over. But, remember do not look directly into his eyes or you will become stone."

"How will I know when to do it?"

Astila said firmly, "When Utkena's eyes turn red."

The door of the cabin opened. The Little People scurried away and retreated back under the porch as Onacoma emerged. His face was serious. But, when he saw Dante with me his face crumpled into a joyous grin.

The wolf rose up and shook himself. He seemed satisfied as if his vigil had ended. The animal licked my hand, and wagged his tail before he trotted off into the countryside. Onacoma stepped down to us and exclaimed with elation, "Dante!" They embraced and then my grandfather turned to me. His voice was mellow and strong belying his age, "Sanjukta… you have done what no living person could. But now the time has come for you to fulfil your destiny. Abir called." Onacoma's tone became more serious as he gravely announced, "Many are dead."

A piece of tumbleweed blew past as the wind gathered strength, "A storm is coming. The fight for the survival of mankind is in your hands, yours and you," he pointed to Cornelius. "Redemption will be yours if you join with Union and do as the Great Spirit directs."

Cornelius was silent. At first I thought he was changing his mind, but he drew himself up to his full height and faced Onacoma head on. "I will try and…" he stopped. It was clear these next words did not come easily to him. "I am sorry. Sorry for all my father did and sorry for my stupidity, callousness and greed. My only defence is that grief does strange things to us all."

Onacoma nodded, "It does, indeed. But now you have a chance to make amends and right the wrongs."

Cornelius extended his hand to my grandfather, "Forgive me. I did not handle my sorrow well. I have done more wrong than you know."

Onacoma took his offered hand, "That is of no matter now. Now, you must put things in order. And hurry. Time is running out, for soon Utkena will be so powerful he will be unstoppable and will grind our world to dust."

"Yes," I asserted, "We must return to the city. Are you ready?"

Cornelius smiled grimly, "I'm ready."

"What about my clothes?" asked Dante. "I can't return like this." He gestured to the light silken almost transparent robe that he wore.

"Come." Onacoma urged Dante to follow him inside while we waited. Cornelius and I didn't talk. There was no need. We each had our own concerns and needed this silent time to think.

A few minutes later, Dante came out of the cabin with Onacoma. I gasped. Dante looked so handsome and so… so Indian. He wore a fringed buckskin shirt and denims. He was carrying a mirror. He held it up to my face and grinned, "You may want to rethink your makeup."

I stared at my reflection and laughed, "I'd forgotten. Full war paint might scare the natives. Give me a minute." I ran into the lodge and dashed to the bathroom, which still housed cleansing wipes and scrubbed at my face. I finished with a refreshing cold wash, which served to chase away some of my tiredness. I looked in the mirror and muttered, "You'll do!" A quick brush of my hair and a dab of lip-gloss and I knew I looked better. I ran outside to the others.

"I shall come, too," said Onacoma.

"No." I insisted. "We will need you here in case we don't succeed."

My grandfather seemed to accept what I said and urged, "Go now. Quickly. And come back to me safely, my granddaughter. How will you get there?"

I looked at Cornelius as we had flown here. He said, "We can get a car in town."

"No, take mine. It is parked by the gate," said Onacoma. He tossed me the keys from his pocket, which I caught.

We said no more and began our walk back to the access gate and where Onacoma had left his car. He walked with us and watched as we walked to his vehicle.

"I'll drive," said Cornelius as he opened the driver's door and sat. "That's fine by me. I'm exhausted," I said as I sat next to him.

Dante settled in the back, "I will take my turn and then you can both rest."

I looked back as we drove away and saw my grandfather's worried expression. I knew he was wondering if we would all return alive.

Chapter Fifteen

Back to the city

We drove back towards what we all knew would be a devastated city. Dante was full of questions, which I attempted to answer as best as I could. The story I told him must have seemed like something out of a children's fairy tale storybook but he appeared to accept it. He knew me too well not to.

As we travelled into the unknown we discussed what we needed to do from what we had been told.

"The box is paramount," said Cornelius, "We must open it and repeat the inscribed mantra."

"But how will we know when to sprinkle the herbs?" asked Dante.

Cornelius said firmly, "When his eyes turn red."

"But we can't look in his eyes," reasoned Dante.

That set me thinking and then I smiled, "I have an idea."

Cornelius turned his head from the wheel. "Tell us."

"Make a stop at a convenience store and I'll show you. But for now let me sleep." I curled up and tried to rest. I was exhausted and I knew I would need all my energy to face Utkena as would we all.

Cornelius switched on the car radio and a live broadcast recounted the terrifying events taking place in the city, which filtered through to me as I tried to sleep. Cornelius put his foot down. We were in a hurry.

He skidded to a halt on the outskirts of a conurbation and the sudden action brought me to wakefulness. "You wanted a supermarket?" Cornelius asked.

I was a little groggy and rubbed my eyes. "Yes, how much cash do you have?"

"I don't have anything," said Dante sheepishly and laughed, "There are no pockets in a shroud!"

"Cornelius?"

Cornelius dug in his pocket and pulled out his wallet, "Here." He pulled a hundred dollar note out. "Is this enough?"

"That will do. Come on," I jumped out of the car and ran into the store. Cornelius and Dante exchanged a glance and followed me inside.

I searched down the aisles and stopped to ask an assistant, "Do you have any sunglasses?"

"Aisle three at the far end."

"Thanks." I dashed to the named aisle and hurried to the end. Dante and Cornelius joined me.

"Sun glasses? Why do we need sunglasses?" asked Dante.

"Not any sunglasses, mirrored sunglasses," I replied.

"I think I know where you're coming from," said Cornelius, slowly.

"Good, grab all the mirrored ones you can find on the stand."

We soon depleted the stand of all the mirrored glasses, took them to the front of the shop and the cashier, where we dumped them on the counter.

"Do you have anymore?" I asked the confused assistant.

"Um... there may be some more out back," she said.

"Good. We'll take all you've got."

"What?"

"All of them and quickly please we are in a hurry," added Cornelius.

The assistant came back and rang up fifty pairs of mirrored sunglasses.

"Cornelius, pay the lady."

Cornelius handed across his money and waived the fifty cents change, "Put it in the charity pot."

The assistant did as she was bid and scratched her head in bewilderment as we hurriedly left the store.

"Right, Dante, you drive. Cornelius and I need to sleep."

Dante slipped behind the wheel and we sped off again toward the city.

The main square in the centre of the city was one of chaos and terror. Crowds of people were fleeing the normally bustling square. Screaming mothers scooped up crying children. Taxi drivers abandoned their cabs where they stood, some were left with the engines still running, blocking the street and causing mayhem as escape routes were closed off. Men shouted in fear, turning every few yards in disbelief of the horror following them ravaging the buildings and destroying people who had stumbled and fallen.

A tide of people packed the sidewalk. They were desperate to get away from the pursuing monster, Utkena, whose power had grown. Like a leeching vampire he had fed on the fear of others. His stature had grown and the hideous demon was now towering to the rooftops of the surrounding buildings, and he was able to peer in at workers trapped inside their offices. He roared in venomous rage and shook his massive horned head, as was his way.

Utkena lifted his foot above the roof of a vehicle. The driver barely managed to escape from his seat as Utkena stamped violently with one of his huge cloven-hoofed feet on the top of the car, crushing it to the ground. The screech of disintegrating metal delighted him and he bellowed in anger as he saw his quarry from inside the vehicle flee.

He flailed his powerful sinewy arm into the side of a skyscraper advertising a Broadway show. The walls of the building crumbled and the wires from the neon sign sparked and crackled before snaking free.

An escaping car struggled to find a route out of the danger zone. Utkena peered down at the vehicle, no more than a toy car to him and grabbed it. The terrified driver screamed as Utkena slammed the car into the side of an occupied office building. Windows shattered and Utkena reached in. With an almighty roar he plucked a hysterical woman from inside and slapped her down. The car was now balanced precariously through the broken building window. It slipped back down the wall, screeching and sparking as it fell and smashed into a fire hydrant.

Water gushed and people jumped back. Their faces filled with puzzlement and revulsion as they saw a new enemy come to aid Utkena's rampage. The Furies rode the spouting wave of water spraying into the air. The female entities laughed in delight as they swiped their talon-like nails at the crowd. Their eyes glowed with a feral, inhuman light and people attempted to run.

Utkena's tantrum increased. He glared his fatally poisonous stare at a businessman, complete with briefcase and umbrella, who was rooted to the spot. The man's mouth dropped open in horror as he gradually turned to stone.

The earth and tarmac cracked. A horde of metal helmeted red and black hornets, the same ones we had experienced on the cliff face in the Darkening Land appeared at Utkena's side. Now there was another evil terror to face. They swarmed around people who were running for their lives, stinging, blistering and singeing their skin with their cruel barbs. People screamed in intense fear as the stinging mutant insects surrounded them in black and red clouds. The creatures' vicious corkscrew stings penetrated their skin and some folk fell down, paralysed by the toxins. Other people who foolishly looked into the eye of hell were frozen and turned to stone. The Furies violently inflicted their avenging havoc on the people that were now petrified stones and smashed them to dust.

One pair of feet, mine, steadfastly and stoically moved against the thronging tide of panic, flanked on either side by two more of a good heart. My feet pounded relentlessly toward the source of the terror. And, as my feet marched on, other feet stopped, turned and joined us. We were a trio of righteous vengeance.

A brave young man skidded to an abrupt halt. His whimpering wife urged him to run with her but he stopped, turned and walked alongside me. Then the wife appeared to be filled with calm and she, too, stepped to my side, fully composed and marched with us through the fleeing masses.

Two more younger men stopped and joined us. Gradually one by one the people who were running mindlessly in fear seemed filled with calm. Their panic subsided. They joined the ranks of this growing army of rebellion that was striding to face down Utkena.

Utkena thundered past a building site. His baleful glare melted the steel scaffolding, which collapsed to the ground.

One of the builders rushed at Utkena swinging a hammer at the demented hornets, which buzzed and surrounded his head.

Another oblivious workman, who was sweeping the pavement, listening to music on his Ipod, stopped, as the ground at his feet trembled and shook. He looked up and faced the fleeing throng. A determined look spread across his features. He ripped out his earphones, snapped the head off his broom and waded in, wielding the stick at the Furies' slashing talons.

A patrolman stopped his car and faced Utkena. He shakily removed his gun and levelled it at the monster. Utkena's eyes pulsed with a red light and fixed on the weapon, which became too hot to hold. The Officer dropped it and the Furies overcame him and began devouring him. Utkena roared in enthusiasm and extreme ecstasy. He visibly grew even taller and he beat a tattoo on his chest like a gorilla in the jungle.

It was then I stopped on the corner, with Cornelius and Dante on each side and somehow Abir had found his way to us. He was full of questions and his jaw dropped in total disbelief when he saw Dante standing with us very much alive.

"No, you're not seeing things," I said. "It is Dante. I can't explain now, but I promise you I will."

Abir stuttered, "Union... The Box of Souls? Then it worked?" I nodded and he just grabbed Dante and hugged him, repeating "Wow, man. Wow!"

I had to call them to order. We needed to be organised and ready. We all stood still. "Glasses, now!" I instructed and we all put on the mirrored sunglasses to face the enemy. Abir and Dante handed the spare glasses out to all those that surrounded us.

A tumultuous crowd now gathered around us as the power of the people strengthened. Builders, workmen, office-suited men all wielded weapons of some description, in fact grabbing anything they could lay their hands on. We turned as one and faced the towering rage of Utkena who stopped his rampage and howled in fury.

What went through Utkena's demented mind when he saw

the huge tide of people surging toward him behind me at the apex of the crowd, I do not know. He must have recognised Cornelius who powered to my side with Dante and the faithful Abir. The crowd was totally united behind us. This is what my grandfather had meant and this was the destiny my mother and father had spoken about.

Dogs on the street gathered in packs to aid our crusading army. They bared their teeth at the monster who abruptly dived down and grabbed an unsuspecting man that was curled in a ball and sobbing in fright.

Using the man as a missile, Utkena hurled the man at us. He landed with a thud and skidded past us. We continued to approach, slowly but steadily, as a threatening mass. The man was helped to his feet and his sobbing stopped. He turned and joined us; the conquering horde and I felt proud, proud of my heritage, proud of my power and proud of my destiny.

I watched as the prison officer, Lyle from my vision staggered around the corner. He joined the legion of people. Even though he was injured he managed to keep in time with our progress. Behind him came the boys from the Amusement Park. They too marched steadfastly toward this demon that we had to vanquish from earth. There was power in numbers and that selfless attitude that was present in all gathered there would score in our favour, of that I was sure.

Others stepped out to join us, good men and true women, who had helped at the tenement block. And the occupants from that building, Granny Ableman using a zimmer frame walker, Joe Whitlock and the others all gathered together in union behind us as we edged our way toward the roaring monster.

This was amazing, even Lexi and her mother and those who had faced the tidal wave on the beach seemed to have turned out for the final showdown. We stopped.

Dante whispered to me, "Now what?"

I needed to be the strongest I had ever been. This was the ultimate test. I instructed him, "Remember… lift your face to him but lower your eyes. Do not look into them. I will see in the mirrored reflection of your glasses when his eyes turn red." At that point I turned my back on the hideous beast. The crowd inched forward. I stood my ground and repeated the Indian mantra over and over again, "Mannaz, mannaz. Om eim hrim klim chamundeayei vicche namah om .Om gum shrim Maha Lakshmiyei swaya" I nodded at Cornelius, who was still standing firm. It was his cue.

"Utkena, I call on you. Return to the hell from which you came. Leave this world in peace."

Utkena bellowed and began to bear down on us. The ground reverberated with the stamping of his feet. No one moved. I shouted above the cacophony of the Furies' shrieks and the monster's roars, "Dante, look down NOW! Now, look down."

Caught in the mirrored frames I could see the demon's eyes change from angry orange to malevolent red. I chanted even louder calling for me to be victorious in my quest and threw a handful of the magical herbs and seeds over my shoulder into Utkena's path.

"Open the box," I yelled above the wind that had begun to blow and was rising to hurricane pitch. Cornelius opened the casket. A whirlwind of light propelled from inside. It flew over my head. I threw more of the herbs and I could see in the glasses' reflection that the light danced around Utkena but it didn't seem to affect him. The light encompassed the hornets, which shrivelled and burned in a squealing mass. I could see Utkena grimace but he still pressed on.

Cornelius yelled, "It's not working."

Utkena screeched and beat his chest. He stepped forward as if to charge and the ground shook once more.

"Try again. Hurry," urged Dante.

I yelled, "Believe! You all have to believe." And I threw some more seeds.

Utkena's wild roar appeared to lose some power. His movement was still full of rage and determination but he had slowed slightly. This spurred me on, "Believe! Believe. You must believe." And I repeated the mantra again and again and again.

The fantastical light chased around the Furies and bound them all with magical golden chains. The demon women flailed against their controlling bonds and slowly started to sink back into the ground.

The seeds had sprouted on contact with the ground and had begun to grow. Writhing shoots twisted around Utkena's huge muscular legs, physically entwining him and drawing him back down into the earth.

Utkena's limbs turned green with the restricting foliage, which penetrated the ground and rose up his body like living chains, binding him and impeding his movement. His steps became slower until he could walk no more. He twisted and turned in dire anger but could not break free of these living bonds. His cries became more terrible as a fissure opened in the ground.

Roots from the seeds pushed into the bowels of the earth and the ensnared Utkena was slowly dragged down. He physically shrunk in stature. People stood shoulder to shoulder standing their ground led by Cornelius, Dante, Abir and me. **This** was the time and I turned to face Utkena whose eyes had now turned black. The thrashing monster appeared stilled.

There was an uneasy silence. We watched and waited.

Cornelius shouted out, "You can't use me anymore, Utkena. I am free. I order you back from whence you came. Now! Go!"

With a sudden rush of power Utkena managed to rip the gagging creeper from his mouth. A fearful cry boomed out. Momentarily it seemed he was coming back to strike a final deathblow at me. I threw the last remaining herbs directly into his face as Cornelius ordered, "GO!"

Utkena shrunk dramatically and finally he disappeared through the ground bellowing furiously as he went. Vegetation filled the void in the earth and sealed the fissure. The crowd stood with mouths agape, stunned.

Billowing clouds in the heavens formed shapes in the sky. I looked up in awe as I recognised them as my mother, Louella and Ridge, my father. I heard my mother's voice, filled with resolve, "When those of good heart unite against fear, injustice and evil, there is nothing that cannot be accomplished."

I was filled with wonder and felt my emotions rising. Cornelius started to clap. He was joined by Dante and Abir. One by one the people united together and joined in the applause. The celebration turned joyous as people greeted each other as friends. They shook hands and cheered for joy. They were united in the monster's harrowing defeat.

In spite of the half demolished buildings and the devastation surrounding us. It felt good. Tranquillity seemed to have returned. People said they felt differently, more united and together, and the city began to feel as it should be once more.

Later that same day Abir, Cornelius, Dante and I gathered together in a coffee shop. The normality of the situation was incredibly soothing after everything we had been through. It was a time of celebration. What was even more gratifying was the change in Cornelius. He was hardly recognisable as the morose arch villain who had attempted to destroy me, my people and everything I stood for.

In fact, as we sipped our lattes Cornelius made a historic announcement. "I have learned, much. More than I ever expected to at your side, Union. Not only have I stood at your side and worked with you. I have found that the one I thought an enemy has become my friend."

I nodded in agreement and Dante nodded his head in acknowledgement.

"I want to say now, to you all, that I was wrong, very wrong. What I have done I will endeavour to put right. I have had time to think and I am going to change all my company policies. No more bullying tactics. I will do my utmost to behave with integrity and obey the law."

"What about all the people you forced out of their homes?" questioned Dante.

Cornelius sighed, "I can't give them back their homes but I can help each and every one of them and I will. I promise." He paused, "And…and I will return the land I purchased from your people and return it to the Cherokee nation. The drills will be stopped, the machinery dismantled and moved. I will do my utmost to restore the ground to its former glory. We cannot risk Utkena ever escaping again."

I was quite moved and found it hard to speak. My voice quavered slightly, "No... he must remain under the ground and away from all humans forever."

Abir asked, "And the Box of Souls?"

"Will be destroyed."

Dante had a more testing question, "How are we going to explain my return to my parents? It had better be good."

I couldn't answer that at the moment but replied, "We'll think of something. I think they'll be so happy to have you back they won't worry about how we managed it."

"We still have to explain it somehow. It has to be clearly understood," said Dante.

"Then maybe we just tell them the truth," added Abir.

"My parents will be okay with that. It's the rest of the world that will be the problem."

I turned to Cornelius trying to lighten the proceedings, "And do you realise you haven't nibbled your nails once since we began this quest?"

Cornelius laughed, "You're right." He studied his hands, "I don't believe it. I never thought that would happen."

We chattered on more excitedly. I was feeling more alive than ever and was just relieved that the media hadn't become involved in the events, yet. I needed to keep a low profile if I was to continue to work. I didn't need any complications arising from the newspapers realising the significance of my powers.

We continued laughing and talking when Abir nudged me as a policeman and his female partner entered the café. They spotted us and started to make their way to our table. The conversation ceased and the coppers showed us their I.D.s. I looked at the woman detective's name it was Ella Parker. I wondered if Cornelius had noticed. I seemed to remember the name Ella was to be significant.

The male policeman appraised us and addressed Cornelius, "Cornelius Phipps?"

Cornelius looked up and nodded, "Yes, that's me."

The policeman hauled him up to cuff him. We looked on in surprise as he started to read him his rights and Mirandise him. It was then that Cornelius spotted the woman officer's ID and his eyes opened wide.

For once I didn't know what to do. I was flabbergasted and spoke up, "Wait! What is this?"

"The male officer replied, "We're arresting him for racketeering. The D.A. has a file on him ..." he made a gesture, "This thick."

I couldn't let them take him after all we had been through together and I protested, "You can't… without him we would…"

Cornelius stopped me and stood up. We looked on, stunned as he held out his hands to be cuffed. "No… It's okay. I have much to answer for."

I stood up and faced the police, "I'm his legal counsel. He's not going anywhere without me." I turned to Cornelius, "I will defend you."

"And I'll back you up," added Dante.

Cornelius' eyes filled with tears, as the police walked him away. Dante and I followed him out as Abir watched. I turned back to wave to Abir, and I could detect pride in his expression as he saw us go. We both knew it would be a tough job defending Cornelius but defend him we would, after all, he had just saved the city. "Don't say anything!" I ordered.

We followed the police car to the station and went after the cops inside and waited while they registered him at the desk. They took him to an interrogation room. Dante and I followed. I whispered to Dante, "I will have to call your father. He needs to know."

"Then you had better warn him. I don't want him suffering a heart attack."

I flipped open my cell and scrolled to Troy's home number. "Troy?"

"Sanjukta, you're back."

"Troy, please listen. There is something you have to know and you are not going to believe it. You had better sit down." There was a pause on the other end of the line.

"What is it?"

"The police have arrested Cornelius Phipps."

215

"So?"

"I am going to defend him."

"What?"

"I am going to defend him… with Dante…"

"What kind of sick joke is this?"

"Troy… Dante is alive. He is here with me now." I passed the phone to Dante.

"It's no joke, Dad. I am here. But, I wouldn't be without Sanjukta and Cornelius Phipps."

"Stop! Stop! You're not making any sense." Troy's raised voice was anguished. I could hear everything he said.

"Come to the station, Pops. Come and see for yourself," pleaded Dante.

I hear Troy catch his breath, Dante often called him Pops when he was making a point.

"Which station?"

"Thirty-sixth precinct."

"I'll be there in ten minutes."

Dante looked at me, "We had better make this good."

"We tell Troy the truth. In the meantime, we look after Cornelius."

We stood in an empty interrogation room and waited. Dante was standing facing the wall when his parents entered. Grace was with him. She smiled when she saw me, "I had to come. When he told me I had to see for myself.

Grace suddenly saw the back of her son across the room and she gasped, "Dante?"

Dante turned and Grace's hand flew to her lips and she stifled a sob, "Dante!"

The memory of Troy's face when he saw his son as he turned was something I will never ever forget. His jaw dropped in incredulity to be replaced by a look of wonder. Grace ran to her son and drew her into his arms and wept. Troy joined with her and I watched in pleasure. I had done the right thing. I may have broken the laws of nature in bringing him back for selfish reasons because he was the one I loved but, he had died for me and robbed Grace and Troy of their only child.

I felt the tears stream down my face at their reunion, "Troy, Grace, please sit. We have an amazing story to tell you, one you will find hard to believe but Dante and Cornelius Phipps will confirm that it is the truth.

They sat at the table with Dante and me. We began to talk.

In court I was in the strange position of facing my boss, Troy, regarding the arraignment of Cornelius. True to his word after Dante's return he didn't object to bail and Cornelius was allowed out to set his promises in motion. He shook my hand on the court steps. The press were eager to greet us with flash bulbs and a multitude of questions. We managed to give reasonable answers until the last one.

"Mr. Phipps, you are being heralded as a hero. How did you know what to do to get rid of that beast?"

Cornelius looked at me, "I'm no hero. Our soldiers that defend our country are the real heroes. They and my lawyer friend here."

I tried to flash him a warning look. I was afraid he would let something slip. I did not want any more media attention than I could help. Cornelius continued, "It wasn't just me. The combined efforts of the population of the city led by this respected lady here brought that demon down and returned him to hell."

I broke in, "When ordinary people combine together and make a stand anything can be accomplished." There was a muttering of assent from the assembled crowd.

"Mr. Phipps, what are your plans, now?"

"I intend to put right all the things that I have done wrong, which are many."

I whispered, "Cornelius, don't. Don't say anything that will jeopardise your case."

He took no notice, "As has been said before grief can do strange things to people and after the deaths of my son and wife … well, I am ashamed to say I became thoughtless, ruthless and greedy. I hope now to put that all behind me and start anew. Thank you gentlemen, and ladies. If you will excuse me, my work to give those I have hurt retribution, starts now."

Cornelius stepped away from the surging press pack to his waiting car. Standing at the side of the reporters was the policewoman who had arrested him, Ella Parker. She watched Cornelius and smiled. He caught her eye as he was stepping into the car and he returned her smile and gave her a small wave before the vehicle drove away.

Troy appeared on the steps and the press surged toward him. "Mr. Burgham, what do you and the DA intend to do about Cornelius Phipps. Are you going to incarcerate the hero who saved our city?"

I looked across at Troy who cleared his throat, "Cornelius Phipps is a changed man but he still has charges to answer. I have no other comment."

The newsmen still shouted out questions but Troy ignored them and he crossed to me, "Sanjukta can we return to my chambers we need to talk."

I nodded and followed Troy back into the building. We walked to his courtroom office and sat. "You and I know that Cornelius has done terrible things. For those crimes he needs to pay…"

"But…?"

"I am aware as is the whole city that we also have much to thank him for and prior to this he has done amazing charity work…"

"Get to the point, Troy," I said sounding braver than I felt.

"I believe I can broker a deal with the DA and…"

"What, let him off?"

"No. But with all the mitigating circumstances we have a good chance of a shorter custodial sentence incorporated with a heavy fine. Also, it would be good to save the city a long trial and all the expenses that would incur. What do you say? Do we have a deal?"

"You know that with everything that has happened there is not a jury in the land that would convict him after what he did."

"Yes, but do you want the truth, the whole truth to be paraded in public court? You know what that would mean?"

I nodded thoughtfully, "Yes… Let me speak to Cornelius.

I'm sure he will take my advice. It's a good offer. What fine and how much time are we talking?"

"He answers all complaints on file and recompenses those people concerned."

"He's already agreed to do that off his own back."

"A two hundred thousand dollar fine…"

"Yes?"

"Two years time, twenty four months…"

"Troy he gave you back your son…"

"Let me finish…"

"Sorry."

"But, let me also say, you, too, brought Dante back."

"But twenty-four months…"

"Twenty four months in total, to serve two and the rest suspended or in community service."

"Will the DA go for that? He's been gunning for him a very long time."

"I think I can swing it. The DA knows it will be difficult to convict him, now."

I paused before plunging in again, "Why not have the fine, the recompense etcetera, and make the whole sentence one of community service. He can do more good outside than in and get that police officer Ella Parker to oversee his work."

"Is there something you're not telling me?"

I shrugged, "They seemed to have a connection… that's all."

"I can't promise that. There's a certain protocol involved here, but I will do what I can."

"Community service and not time?"

"Sanjukta, he's not up for a misdemeanour."

"I know, but if I can convince others, those he's wronged to stand up for him, would that help?"

Troy fixed me with one of his searching looks, "And we all know how that would turn out. They would back you one hundred percent… Union."

"Well?"

There was a silence between us and I could almost hear the thoughts and arguments racing through Troy's mind. He finally spoke, "We have a deal."

"YES!" We shook hands.

"Don't go announcing it to the media, yet. Let things bubble along. The DA's office will release a statement when the timing is more appropriate."

"Agreed. I must tell Cornelius and Dante."

"Ah, Dante."

"Yes. Where is he?"

"Dante has gone away to stay with your grandfather for a few months."

"What?"

"Until we can work out a suitable story to bring him back to life and back into the firm. He tells me he is going to train with Onacoma to become an honorary warrior brave."

This news even more than the deal we had just struck for Cornelius filled me with excitement. "That's excellent news!"

"But how to explain Dante's rebirth that's the question."

"Can we not explain it as confusion over who died."

"What do you mean?"

"Well, no one identified the body as Grace was too upset. You had a closed coffin with no viewing. What if we claim Dante was so seriously ill it took him this long to recover and there was a mix up at the hospital and another patient was buried by mistake?"

Troy thought for a moment, "It may just work."

"What else can we do? We certainly can't tell the truth. No one would believe it anyway."

"Let's think about it. I'll speak to Grace and get back to you."

"And I'll phone Cornelius and tell him the good news. Then, I am ringing my grandfather."

*****

True to his word, now that Cornelius had got bail he paid his fine from company funds and set his plans in action to restore the Indian land while he worked with other offenders in Community Service work overseen by Ella Parker.

Trucks and cars left the Indian Territory taking with them

the last bits of machinery, and portakabins filled with tools. The place looked like a deserted dust bowl apart from the last three remaining Indian houses.

Across toward the perimeter one last machine was busy working. It was just a speck on the landscape and could hardly be seen as it filled in boreholes with scalpings, earth, shillet and stone.

Dante, Inola and my grandfather watched as the specialist Landscapers finished treating the land. They had planted many new shrubs, small trees and seeds. Stretches of ground were re-turfed and the ground began to look lush and green once more.

"Onacoma smiled, "It is good. I didn't think I would ever see this day. We will finally get back what was lost and maybe our community will return and grow again."

"We can but hope," added Inola.

"And now we must eat. You have worked hard, Dante, and must be hungry. Inola has prepared us a feast."

"Yes, I am. I am ravenous. What time is Union er… Sanjukta arriving?"

"She will be here soon. She should be home with us by eight tonight."

"Perfect," said Dante his face wreathed in smiles.

"And you will have much to tell her," said Onacoma. "For you are doing well."

They left the newly turfed land and made their way back into Onacoma's log cabin.

The bulldozer out on the boundary filled in the very last of the drilling shafts. There was an almighty roar and the ground trembled. The driver stopped his machine in shock and fear. He held on to the door as if to make an escape while the ground shuddered around him.

Underground Utkena roamed the labyrinth of tunnels. He howled in anger and the grotesque noise reverberated around the cavern and the earth above him shook once more.

The bulldozer became unstable in the tremor and rocked on its tracks. It was as if a sinkhole had come into view. The man cried out in terror as the machine was sucked down into the earth. It disappeared underground. The soil collapsed around it burying the machine from sight. There was nothing to show that the machine had ever been there. There was a moment of silence and then… The horrified heart-rending cry of the operator ripped through the air and mingled with the triumphant bellowing of the demon Utkena. The cries and roars became muffled and abruptly stopped.

Then all was peaceful once more.